THE GIRL IN SEAT 2A

DIANA WILKINSON

Boldwood

First published in Great Britain in 2023 by Boldwood Books Ltd.

Cover Design by 12 Orchards Ltd.

Cover Photography: Shutterstock

A CIP catalogue record for this book is available from the British Library.

Paperback ISBN 978-1-83751-019-1

Large Print ISBN 978-1-83751-018-4

Hardback ISBN 978-1-83751-017-7

Ebook ISBN 978-1-83751-020-7

Kindle ISBN 978-1-83751-021-4

Audio CD ISBN 978-1-83751-012-2

MP3 CD ISBN 978-1-83751-013-9

Digital audio download ISBN 978-1-83751-016-0

Boldwood Books Ltd
23 Bowerdean Street
London SW6 3TN
www.boldwoodbooks.com

To Lindsay, my gorgeous niece

Living like a millionaire is much more fun when you're a pauper.

PART I

JADE

PART I

JADE

1

Oh my God. This is it. We are all going to die. My eyes skitter round the cabin. Why am I the only person who knows our time is up?

Knee-jerk yelps, intakes of breath, so far are the extent of the panic. A collective woolly gasp, English, controlled, stiff upper lip. It's all there is. Even at the point of extinction, the end of the world, total decimation, embarrassed concerns float around the cabin as if a streaker has appeared at a garden party. I don't get why everyone is so relaxed.

My three-quarters-full glass of Prosecco, which swishes around in the flimsy plastic receptacle, my third since take-off, spins out of my hand. The small empty bottle rolls under the seat in front, and the bubbly liquid fizzes over my bare legs. My novel, *How to Live Like a Millionaire*, has hit the roof and bounced towards the front of the plane. I'm now bolt upright, the soporific anaesthetic of alcohol no longer weaving its calming magic.

Oh, dear God. THIS IS IT. I really am going to die.

'Help. Help. Help.' My scream gets drowned out, unable to compete with the turmoil, the crescendo of the shuddering undercarriage, the dangling end-of-life oxygen masks. A ruffled flight attendant has strapped herself in and is ignoring my pleas. No one looks my way. If I have to blow the whistle on my life jacket, fat chance anyone will respond. I'll end up sinking to the bottom of the ocean, like a broken off lump of detritus. I'm totally alone, yet surrounded by hundreds of people. They're all clinging on to something. Someone. Even if it is a stranger in the next seat. But with my seat belt firmly fastened, two empty seats alongside me, the comfort of another human being isn't possible.

I remember the Fear of Flying course I took. *Watch the faces of the cabin crew.* Their expressions. Then you'll feel relaxed, confident, and in safe hands. What the F!

The uniformed lady with the scooped-up hair, orange skin, and startled eyebrows looks much too alert. She's not even talking to her colleagues.

She-is-so-not-relaxed.

She's even closed her eyes, and although her hands are nowhere near her face, they're clasped in prayer.

A lady across the aisle, middle seat, snatches off an eye mask and pulls herself upright. Her jerky movements and edgy manner make me worse. Her knuckles are whitening as she grips both sides of the seat in front. How the hell can the man on the end be sleeping? Perhaps he's already dead. A heart attack. His fear of flying having done the job for him.

'We're going to die. We're all going to die.' My voice sounds like that of a Salvationist trying to curry support, sign up new recruits using the fear of hell as the strapline.

Help. Dear God. Save us.

The rest of the passengers seem to have woken up, as muffled prayers filter through in a group plea for mercy.

Suddenly, the plane plummets and the captain's soothing monotone is cut off. This is it. This is it. I'm certain.

I begin to mumble in a monosyllabic chant.

Connor. You prat. I do love you. (This is a lie, but sort of creeps in amongst the other eulogies.) Sorry Mum, Dad (even though you're already dead), for disappointing you. And David, I will help you out. You'll be okay. I changed my will. I so love you, big bro.

My life flashes before me as I try to scrabble for my mobile to send deathbed messages. I can't find it. It'll be in my handbag which is under the seat.

I try to stand up, and as if someone is watching me, an instant reproach screeches through the loudspeakers. It's as if they're telling me to give up, and accept my fate with dignity.

'Ladies and gentlemen. Please keep your seat belts fastened. There must be no moving around the cabin.' The message sounds automated. Perhaps the pilot has already bailed out, and there's no right-hand man.

I need to text everyone. My contact list. But my heart is racing. I can't bend down as I'm strapped in so tightly. I keep tugging at the belt, making sure if there's a slim chance of survival, I'll not be caught out. I'll be the last person sucked through the broken fuselage when the cabin doors fly off.

This is my second flight to Malaga this month, and only my third trip outside of the UK since the money landed in my bank account. If I'd chosen Perugia, Paris, Budapest, anywhere other than Marbella as a holiday destination, this wouldn't be happening. My wish list of places to visit is long. Very long. I could have gone anywhere else in the world, but I'm more comfortable with well-worn habits. And Marbella is pretty cool, with Logan waiting at the other end. We've been texting regularly since my first visit.

A child's sobbing has turned into full-blown hysteria. My feet are jittering up and down with uncontrollable spasms. I want water. Water.

No one catches my eye. No one cares if I die. If I dehydrate.

'Water. Water.' I wave my arm in the air like an eager pupil, desperate to attract the teacher's attention.

The elderly lady across the aisle is now gripping her somnolent companion. She has both her arms wrapped around his, and is weeping against his shoulder. I wonder if I was older, had lived a life, fulfilled all my dreams, whether I would still be so desperate not to pass over. But I've no one to hold. No one to comfort me in the final moments. A few hours ago, I was smug at my oneness and my new-found independence with all its possibilities. But death is my undoing. It's making me needy. Over-the-top needy. Illogical. Mortal.

I must have bitten the inside of my cheek because little blood spatters dot the back of my hand as I rub it across my mouth. The oxygen masks are still dangling but no one has put them on. We're like children awaiting instructions.

Then all of a sudden, the cabin rights itself. Calmer movement steadies the plane and there's a collective sense of relief. The lady across the aisle rather sharply unravels her tentacles from her partner, rubs her hands down her creased linen trousers and reasserts her independence. She does the sign of the cross, repositions her ear pods and closes her eyes. She's been brave. If not, she doesn't want anyone knowing. Remembering.

I slowly relax, suddenly feeling ridiculous, blushing at my own stupidity. When I notice the green vacant light sign for the toilet, I unbuckle my seat belt and am just about to slip out when a bronzed hand with manicured nails stretches my way, holding out my novel which I last saw when it catapulted through the turbulence.

'Hi. I think this is yours,' the guy says.

Jeez. He's handsome. Tall. Chiselled jaw. He's wearing a blinding white linen shirt, and Oakley shades, black rimmed with dark blue mirrored lenses, roost on his luscious wavy hair. He reaches an arm across the two empty seats.

'Oh. Thanks. Where did you find it?' My voice sounds weird. I suspect it was the near-death experience that has spiked it with an air of incredulity, and a high-pitched squeak.

'I slid on it coming out of the loo. A weird-shaped banana skin.' He beams, a wide, white, sunny, after-the-storm sort of smile. 'Anyone sitting here?'

I'm too embarrassed to own up to having booked and paid for the window spot, 2A, as well as the two adjacent seats. They're *comfort seats*. That's what the airline calls them. They're bookable, at a price. But I can afford the luxury. The extra space cushions the claustrophobia, and when it all gets too much, I lift the armrests and stretch out along all three pads. The disapproving looks I get from fellow passengers are a small price to pay for peace of mind.

'No. How lucky was I? All this space.' I'm not sure this guy is the sort to judge, but it's not the time to own up to phobias, certainly not to a fear of flying.

'Yes, you're very lucky. The rest of the plane is full. It's heaving further back.' He slips into the seat on the end, 2C, but not before I make a point of putting the book he has returned on to the seat between us. I'm not a fan of talking to strangers at the best of times, but this guy has the pull of a magnet, and now's definitely not the time to play hard to get.

'Are you okay?' His concern feels genuine as he raises a single eyebrow.

'Yes. Fine, thanks.'

I must look a mess, like a vampire, as fear has drained the blood from my body. I close my eyes against a swaying motion. When I open them, he's pointing a finger towards my lips, getting very close, too close for healthy social distancing, until I realise he's indicating a red deposit.

'Your lip's bleeding. Right a little. Left a bit. There, spot on. Let me get you a drink. I'm Isaac, by the way.' As he talks, he pops his head into the aisle and clicks his fingers for attention.

'I'm Jade, and yes, a drink would be great.' I bend over, retrieve the Prosecco bottle which has settled back by my feet, and wiggle it in front of him.

'Bubbles. I'll join you and we can celebrate still being alive,' he says.

It's hard to tell if he's laughing at me, making light of my apparent distress, or if he's flirting. Whatever, I'm glad of the company, and desperate for another drink.

Flight 2904 to Malaga; 14.30 hours. I have a feeling I'll not forget this flight. This guy is drop-dead gorgeous.

2

I have trouble getting out of my seat when we land at Malaga airport. Isaac went back to his seat when the seat belt signs went on, and I'm feeling really disorientated.

As soon as the plane doors are thrown open, the Spanish heat, worse than a sauna, smacks me in the face. I have to grip the handrail as I stagger down the rickety metal steps which seem to be moving.

Suddenly, I lose grip of my cabin bag. It careers past the passengers in front of me, and somersaults on to the tarmac. WTF. Withering looks, and a load of tutting, are pretty targeted. A guy in a navy business suit shoves past me, muttering under his breath. I can't work out where I am. That's how fuzzy my head feels, as if it's engulfed in fog.

Passengers flock past me. So much for being in seat 2A and getting to passport control before the crowds. It is so hot outside that the ground is bubbling. Well, it looks as if it's bubbling, but it could be my vision. I bend to retrieve my bag which Mr City Slicker has kicked under the flimsy set of stairs.

I pick it up, but when I try to straighten up again, I list from side to side. The ground is definitely moving, and I can't stay upright. To make it worse, my vision is blurring. Zigzag lines are zapping round the edges.

'Jade? Are you okay?'

I hear the voice before I see the person. It's the Brad Pitt lookalike from the plane. How did he get here? I thought he had disembarked first. He's hovering over me, a good six inches up. It could be 2 feet up he looks that tall. What did he say his name was? I can't remember anything other than the dangling oxygen masks. Did we really all nearly die? Plummet into the ocean?

My legs suddenly buckle, as the hunk's image comes in and out of focus.

I can't be that drunk, can I? It's as if I'm on another planet.

'Pardon?' I think it's me speaking, but I can't be sure. What is this guy's name again, and what has he just asked me? It's all a blank.

'Here. Let me help. Take my arm.' He hoists me up, as if I'm old Mrs Cunningham from the nursing home. She can no longer feed herself or make it to the toilet on her own.

I smile up at Isaac. Yes. Isaac. That's his name. It's from the Bible, I remember now. He handed me back my book, *How to Live Like a Millionaire*, when it catapulted to the front of the plane.

He really does look like Brad Pitt. Well, Brad Pitt before he got married and divorced a couple of times. Blond-haired, and chiseljawed. He grips my arm very tightly and propels me towards the terminal.

When we reach the passport queue, he attaches my hands to a metal rail, and instructs me not to move. As I try to stay upright, he opens his passport, and asks me where mine is. I whisper that it's in my bag, worried that I might look like an illegal immigrant.

'I must be very drunk. Oops.' A giggle pops out, although I think I'm the only one who heard it. Everyone is avoiding eye contact.

'You could say that.' Isaac winks, but gives me a stern look. A warning that I need to sober up. 'Let me have your passport, and we'll go through together.'

'Is this what you're looking for?' I dip my hand into the zipped end of my bag and wave my passport in the air.

He takes it off me, and says, 'Let's go, but try not to say too much.'

He's treating me like a child, but in the state I'm in, it feels good to have him take control.

As he nudges my waving arm down by my side, his fingers brush mine. Despite the wooziness, I have the most dreadful urge to grab them.

The passport official behind the glass panel looks from Isaac to me and back again. He smiles at Isaac, asks how he's keeping. I can't hear anything, but I assume that's what he's asking, because his smile is broad and he's much more friendly with Isaac than with the other passengers.

My ears are blocked from the cabin pressure. I pinch my nose, keep my mouth closed, and heave through my nostrils until something pops.

I wonder why I'm shaking. Jeez, if I'm not careful the police will take me away.

Isaac seems to be talking in a foreign language now. I know *gracias* means thank you, but that's about it. I think he's trying to explain we're together.

'Yes, we're together,' I announce, and push in beside him. I grab his arm before linking our fingers. Isaac smiles, and raises his eyes heavenward. He's got the most perfect teeth. Even in the state I'm in, I can see he's movie-star handsome.

Once we get through to the arrivals hall, everything is even more of a blur. How much did I drink?

Holy shit. I suddenly remember the emergency diazepam tablets. The sedatives that would knock me out in an emergency. Did I take a couple when we were having the near-death experience? I need to check the strip and see how many are missing. Alcohol and tranquillisers *so-do-not* mix.

Isaac is dragging me along like a petulant child.

'I think we need to go and get you a coffee. Or perhaps two or three,' he says.

I manage to unravel myself from his grip, and tell him I've got a case in the hold.

'You don't need to worry about me. I'll be fine now. But thanks...' I've forgotten his name again. Ishmael? Isiah? I know it starts with the letter I, and it's something biblical. Shit. Shit. Why can't I remember?

I leave him standing as I swagger off to find my suitcase. Before I realise what's happening, he has sped up and grabbed me from behind.

'You're in no fit state to go anywhere.' His voice is so sexy. Masterful. 'Do you want to pass out on the carousel?'

'Isaac. Isaac, that's it,' I whoop, thrilled that I've remembered.

I pick up an edge of laughter in his voice. Even though I'm in a state of delirium, I visualise him ripping off my clothes and jumping on top of me. And even though he's making fun, he's definitely flirting.

'I'll take you to wherever you're going. I've got a driver outside. If I leave you, you'll probably end up in hospital. Worse still, a police cell.'

He definitely fancies me. Only my second trip to Marbella, and I could have met my Mr Right. Logan is best-friend nice, but this guy is bloody hot.

This is when I pass out.

3

It's dark outside when I wake up. Drowsy intrigue soon gives way to panic.

Shit. Shit. Shit. Where am I? Where the f— am I? I haul myself up from an enormous bed, which could easily sleep six. My head is so heavy that I'm tempted to turn over and go back to sleep.

There's not a sound anywhere. The only light comes from a couple of dimmed wall sconces. Porcelain white. Actually, everything I can see through dry eyes appears to be white. Through a door at the end of the bed, I can see into what must be an en-suite bathroom. A free-standing bath on gold-clawed feet is lit from above like a stage prop.

I feel like Sleeping Beauty coming round after a hundred years. I rub my eyes. They're so dry I can't focus. Pillows are plumped up on either side of me, presumably to stop me slithering to the floor. Beside the bed, on a white marble-topped cabinet, I spot my phone. I make a grab for it, and luckily it still has battery. It lights up when I lift it.

Holy shit. It's midnight. How long have I been here? I wrack my brain to remember exactly what happened. My mind is a total blank. I need to get up, move around, and shake myself alert.

No idea why, but it seems important that I don't make a noise. Call it gut instinct.

At least I'm not naked. In fact, I'm pretty much fully clothed, apart from my new silver-studded trainers which are neatly placed by the floor-to-ceiling window. The window runs the whole length of the room.

I fling aside the light cotton bedding. My skirt is riding up round my thighs, but at least I'm wearing knickers. My blouse is crinkled, scrunched up as if it's been in the laundry basket, but the buttons are still done up.

I listen for sound. Noises. Anything to give me a clue as to where I am, and to let me know I'm not a prisoner.

Suddenly, I remember Isaac. Isaac. The tall handsome guy from the plane who got me through passport control.

What happened next? I'm now starting to panic. He could be some kind of weirdo. Perhaps he's kidnapped me. At least I haven't been raped.

I slide out of bed and let out a yelp as my feet hit the icy floor. The room must be air-conditioned because I can hear a humming noise, but I'm still coated in sweat and my hands are shaking. It's likely the alcohol, but the worry isn't helping.

I tiptoe towards the door. It's slightly cracked, and I can see out on to the landing. As far as the eye can see, everything is white except for a grey wrought-iron railing that breaks the monotony. I take a tentative step out, and push my back against a wall.

There are muffled voices down below. Well, one muffled voice, but I can't hear very well. It's most likely Isaac. Who else could it be?

He's talking into a phone. 'I'm sorry. I need more time.'

I crane my neck round the end of the wall and peer through the railing. Isaac is strolling up and down an enormous room. It's like a room from *Grand Designs*. The decor screams expense. Think white and gold. Marble and glass, and a random fountain sculpture at one end is gushing water. At least I'm not locked in a dank dark cellar.

'I've got to go. I'll call you tomorrow. I've told you already. I'll sort it.' He sounds quite snappy, and seems to cut the caller off. He certainly doesn't waste time on goodbye pleasantries.

My pulse races as I duck back into the bedroom, but before I reach the bed, I hear firm footsteps on the winding staircase. A light rap, and the door creaks open. It doesn't strike me as a creepy place, but the creak isn't selling it to me.

'You're up.' Isaac appears, hands in his pockets, and wanders in. 'How are you now? Do you feel any better?'

He's grinning from ear to ear.

'Where am I?' I sit on the edge of the bed, keeping a distance from my possible captor. 'I can't remember what happened.'

'I'm Isaac. I saved you a trip to the hospital when you crashed out at the airport. I had to convince airport medics that it's happened before, that you suffer from a rare condition.'

'What sort of rare condition?'

The bastard is laughing at me. Perhaps he's a mad, deranged, hysterical captor, but he's so goddam magnetic that I'm not sure I care.

A flashback of collapsing on the floor by the carousel comes back to me. My suitcase.

Where's my suitcase?

'My suitcase. Where's my suitcase?'

'Don't worry. It's under the bed.'

Isaac bends down and yanks out my case. Since we got off the plane, he's changed into shorts and a light-coloured cotton shirt. I can't keep my eyes off his tanned muscled legs and work-out biceps. He can't be a kidnapper, surely.

'Voila!' He stands the pink case upright. The familiar sight is comforting, if weirdly embarrassing with its White Star Line sticky label. 'Why don't you have a shower and come down and I'll get you a drink. I can fill you in on what happened next.'

'Okay.'

I don't move until I hear his footsteps retreat, and know for certain that he's gone. Then I take my phone, text Mum, and tell her I've arrived safely.

Plane delayed. Battery flat. But all's well. Reached my B&B safely. xx

At least they'll be able to trace the text message should I mysteriously disappear. Never to be seen again. I haven't told Mum I'm staying at Marbella's most expensive five-star hotel. She thinks I should invest my winnings wisely.

But it might be too late to sign in at my hotel tonight. Looks as if I'm here until the morning.

mortified this morning,

4

Although I've hardly slept a wink, no more than three hours, I'm up with
the lark. I'm far too excited to lie in, and today is the start of my holiday
proper. I can't wait to get to my hotel, but first, I'll be having a serious
mooch around this villa.

Last night, when I joined Isaac for midnight drinks, he told me he has
a chauffeur. Pablo, his driver, drove us back from the airport, but I was so
far gone that I don't remember anything after I passed out. Isaac had to
fill me in.

I am so living the millionaire lifestyle, because this morning Pablo
will be chauffeuring me to Los Molinos, the five-star hotel on the beach-
front where I'm staying for the week. It's my second visit to the hotel since
my windfall, and already feels scarily like home. I dream one day of
moving in.

Pablo will drive me when I'm ready. Apparently, he doubles up as
gardener, pool maintenance man and general dogsbody.

'Pablo is a great multitasker.' Isaac laughed in the telling, his eyes
crinkling at the corners.

'A bit like a woman,' I said, and Isaac laughed even louder.

We talked till three in the morning. Isaac is not married, and there's
no sign of a wedding band. I'm not sure who he was talking to on the

phone, it could have been his mother, but worrying about the possibility of a significant other would certainly be jumping the gun.

And can you believe it? He owns a penthouse in London, south of the river. He's originally from Peckham, and works out of both London and Marbella. Perhaps I shouldn't have told him I live in a penthouse north of the river, but it certainly wasn't the time to tell him about the one-bed flat with the spider infestation.

He had the cheek to ask how old I was. I told him a gentleman should never ask a lady's age, but when he owned up to being thirty-eight, I admitted to being marginally on the wrong side of thirty. Whatever, he more than fits the perfect profile.

We got on so well, I'd probably have hopped into bed with him if he'd asked. Not only is he hot, but he's also funny, interesting (okay, his millions do help here), and we really hit it off. If I'd met him in my Crouch End local, I'd be planning the wedding.

This morning, I rifle through my suitcase for an alluring outfit. Casual but sexy, and a tad see-through up top. I'm a bundle of nerves thinking about seeing Isaac again, but when I get down to the open-plan expanse of lounge, kitchen and indoor dip pool (yes, really), there's no sign of him. Instead, there's a small, tanned lady in a blue apron with frizzy jet-black hair sniffing the dregs in the bottom of a glass. She won't need to be a connoisseur of fine wines to know that we were drinking champagne. Moët & Chandon no less. The empty bottle is upside down in a silver bucket.

'Hi,' I say.

She nods, with the merest upturn of lips, before disappearing through another door. I assume she's a housekeeper, or a villa keeper, more like. She's certainly not bursting with enthusiasm at seeing me. Maybe she got out of the wrong side of bed, but she's uncomfortably icy.

Five minutes later, she reappears with a couple of croissants and a cup of coffee. She sets them down in front of me with such force, coffee spills over.

She ignores the mess and carries on working round me in total silence. She creeps about, with a definite lack of eye contact. I wonder if she's not allowed to talk to guests. Or perhaps she doesn't speak

English. Anyway, I drink up what coffee is left, and go to collect my things.

It doesn't take long, and when I get back down, the maid is nowhere to be seen. Isaac told me Pablo should be working outside somewhere, so I dump my case and head out through the wall-to-wall expanse of glass facing onto the garden. I have to squeeze through a small open panel at one end, as there doesn't seem to be any other way out.

Wow. Wow. Wow. From the upstairs window, I could see the sea in the distance, through tall pine trees, but it was too high up to appreciate the grounds. The marbled patio has about the same floor space as my dingy bedsit multiplied by ten. The tiles have been recently cleaned, and I skate across them. Landscaping work seems to be ongoing, as tools, and new tiles, are neatly laid out to one side.

The whole property is surrounded by towering white walls, and fancy iron spikes sit atop the side perimeters. I head towards a set of steps at the far end of the patio, and gasp. An enormous infinity pool, just a few feet lower down, is as wide as the patio. In the silence, I listen to the water cascading over the edge.

I glance over my shoulder, thinking I heard a rustle from behind a cluster of enormous olive trees. A rabbit shoots past, and I remember Isaac telling me wild rabbit stew is one of his favourite Spanish dishes.

'You can get a whole rabbit carcass in the Mercadona,' he'd announced.

'Mercadona?'

'Spanish equivalent to Tesco,' he laughed.

I look up, and see a face at an upstairs window. Although it's already sweltering in the morning sun, I shiver. The maid is staring out. She could be looking out to sea, but I've an uncomfortable feeling she's watching me.

At the top of the villa is a large, enclosed roof terrace. Isaac said I should have a look, as the views from there are even more stunning. But with the dark eyes of the maid boring into me, I think I'll give it a miss this time.

I mosey along the length of the infinity pool and on through a small, landscaped area, until I come to the boundary of the property. There is no wall as such, just an enormous drop down to a small, secluded beach. I'm so high up, the sunbathers nestled on rows of sun-loungers, under yellow and white-striped umbrellas, are the size of ants. If I wasn't anxious to check in to the hotel, I might see if there's a way to clamber down.

Although there's no fencing this far up, at the bottom of the sheer drop are gunmetal railings, through which there doesn't seem to be a way out.

'*Hola! Hola!*'

I nearly jump out of my skin when someone creeps up behind.

'Shit. You scared me to death.'

'*Buenos dias.* I'm Pablo. Pleased to meet you.' A leathery-skinned guy offers a thick calloused hand.

'Hi. I'm Jade.' My white skin gets swallowed up in his enormous grasp.

'You would like a lift to Los Molinos?' The question reveals very white teeth, with a couple chipped on one side.

'Please. That would be great.'

'Come. You wait by the front gates, and I'll get the car.'

I follow him back up to the villa, the steep incline getting my heart racing. I'm not sure the Peloton classes have done their job yet, but it's early days. Going down was easy, but it's like mountain climbing getting to the top.

Pablo disappears when I go inside to collect my case. I wheel it to the front door, which is made up of three large wooden panels with frosted glass either side. I try to turn the door handle, but it won't budge. I jiggle it, but still nothing. Shit.

Pablo might have the stealth of a tiger, but the maid is even worse. She appears out of nowhere, like a floating ghost, and without a word, slips a bunch of keys from her pocket, jangles them, and puts one in a lock. Then she keys in numbers on a keypad to the left of the door, covering the pad with a spare hand as she does so, and hey presto, it opens.

'Thank you.'

'*De nada,*' she says, not a hint of Pablo's smile, and not a glimpse of teeth. She looks at the ground, rather than at me, as I wheel my case away.

A large Mercedes saloon purrs up to the front of the villa, and when Pablo gets out to open the passenger door, I hear the key turn in the lock behind me.

If I thought it was difficult getting out of the villa, getting out of the grounds looks impossible. Think Colditz. Pablo uses a remote-control gadget to slide back solid dark-green metal gates which are slotted into the towering, whitewashed walls. Security cameras are placed all along the tops.

As we drive away, I notice a blue ceramic nameplate on the outside wall.

Casa De Astrid.

5

Pablo speeds up as soon as we're out of the villa grounds. He drives like a maniac, and I hold my breath the whole way to the hotel.

I breathe more easily when the car slows down by the front entrance. Pablo pulls up, climbs out, and comes round to open the door for me. When I try to get out, my legs are seriously wobbly. I'm not sure if it's all down to Pablo's maniacal driving or the freakishness of the last twenty-four hours. Whatever, it's a relief to have got here.

I unzip my handbag to dig out a ten-euro tip, but I'm much too slow. He quickly unloads my case, hops back into the car, and in a couple of seconds the tail end of the Merc is disappearing through the gates.

In the foyer, I pull along my pink tortoise-shell suitcase. It suddenly seems tatty, although it was the first thing I bought after THE Saturday night, and it's only the third time of using. It might not be Gucci, or Christian Dior, but it was the most expensive TK Maxx had on offer. The pink Polycarbonate ABS exterior (I googled hardwearing, top-of-the range) now seems gaudy rather than extravagant. I've certainly got a lot of work to do in living like a proper millionaire, but at least I've money to spend.

Ahead of me, a uniformed concierge is in charge of a gold trolley stacked high with a set of Louis Vuitton canvas and leather-trimmed luggage, gold and black. The guy is carefully negotiating past milling guests. I push down the retractable handle on my bomb-proof shiny case and use my hand to gently wheel it towards the reception desk.

Even my outfit of Ted Baker silver spangled trainers, canary yellow M & S capri pants and Mint Velvet blouse, floaty and provocatively suggestive through the see-through lemony cotton, suddenly seems less than impressive. Despite the fact the total bill came to more than I was earning in a month at the retirement home.

'Wiltshire. Jade Wiltshire,' I say, announcing my arrival. My voice trembles, as if I'm applying for a job which I don't hold out much hope of getting. Pale beads of sweat bobble round my neck and hairline, and my cheeks flush as I run a palm across my throat. Millionaire status doesn't come easily. The dreams aren't yet matching reality.

'Good afternoon, madam. Welcome to Los Molinos.' A pretty girl in a tight-fitting navy A-line skirt, an even closer-fitting red blouse, and with a strange exotic accent, swipes her long, red-varnished nails across a screen. Thick dark tattooed eyebrows have a natural questioning look, and she reminds me of the air hostess who ignored my pleas for mercy as the plane shuddered. Her lips are so filled out that she seems to have trouble speaking, and a long pink tongue circles constantly to provide moisture.

'Love the suitcase. A pink tortoise.' A deep-throated laugh accompanies the words. It takes a couple of seconds to twig the stranger behind is talking to me. I crane my neck, unwilling to turn right round. The man is very dark-skinned – not suntanned, rather swarthy through ethnicity. I can't help staring at the black swirling hairs which seem to cover his body. They rampage along his arms and up his throat as if they're strangling him. His wide smile dazzles like a tooth advert.

'Thanks. At least I won't lose it,' I say.

I concentrate my gaze on the receptionist, willing him to go away. Fat chance.

'Carlos,' he says by way of introduction. 'I think you might be English? Or American perhaps?'

He nudges in alongside me at the counter, too close to easily ignore.

'English.' I'm not sure it's the best idea to give this random guy dressed in an orange and blue shirt plastered over with exotic birds that look like toucans my name, but he's hard to ignore.

'Are you on holiday?'

'Madam, can you sign here please?' The girl with the plumped-up lips swivels a form around so it's facing me, requesting a couple of signatures before I hand across my NatWest credit card. The lack of a platinum or gold card mocks my healthy bank balance. But I can't think of that. I need to get to my room, close the door and breathe. I'm here to enjoy myself, but it's hard to get the party started.

Carlos taps me on the shoulder and thrusts a business card my way.

'Property adviser if you're in need,' he says. 'I hope you enjoy your stay.'

'Thanks.'

When I finally get my room key card, I notice Carlos hovering by the lifts. I motion to a porter and ask if he'll take my case up to my room on the fifth floor while I head off in the direction of the stairs.

* * *

I'm puffing heavily by the time I reach my room, and slip the card into the slot. A few seconds later, and I'm in.

It's hard to tone down the excitement when I look round the room. I'd forgotten how huge the bed is, and the view across the Med is picture-postcard stunning. The tasteful balcony tries to mock my oneness with its furniture for two – two chairs either side of a tile-topped table and a cosy sofa for two nestled under a butcher-style awning in green and white – but I couldn't be happier. Two for the price of one is my half-full approach. It's luxury with a capital L.

I might even stay in my room on my own for the whole week, it's that palatial, and utterly perfect. After what I've been through in the last twenty-four hours, it's tempting not to go anywhere.

'On your own?' my mother had screeched in horror when I told her I was setting off.

'Why not?'

'Where will you stay? On your own? Oh my God. What is the world coming to?'

Her hissing repetitiveness sent me further down the road of lies, and rebellion.

'A small B&B slightly inland. Cheap and cheerful. Near enough to Malaga airport. Budget flights.'

'I should hope so. Get a deposit down on a flat, settle down. Use the money wisely.'

I wonder why my mother is so keen for me to follow in her dull footsteps. The two-up, two-down maisonette, a canny purchase when my parents first married, has imprisoned her in Milton Keynes' mediocrity ever since Dad died. I was only ten at the time. Now I think Mum wants assurances that she made wise life choices, and that she hasn't completely wasted her life.

I slide open the glass doors to the balcony and luxuriate in the Mediterranean heat which blankets my skin. In the distance, the sea shimmers, a vast sheet of azure blue, sparks of sunlight zapping off the glass surface. Boats bob up and down in the distance, and if I stand right in the corner of the balcony, up against the railing, I have a clear view on to the hotel's stretch of private sand. Yellow parasols, buckets and spades are waving at me to get a move on.

A gentle rap on the door makes me jump. I hurry across the carpet, and open the door to the tall skinny porter who presents me with my case.

'Just a moment.' I scoot back into the bedroom and dig out a twenty-euro note. I'm not sure if it's enough, or too much, but his cheeks redden. He bends his head, nods his thanks and shuffles backwards into the corridor.

I slam the door shut, fling the case on the bed, throw myself alongside it, and kick my legs in the air, whooping like a mad person who has been let out of prison after thirty years. I sit back up, tear open the zip, upend the contents and pluck out my bikini top and bottoms. Yellow polka dots. They were too irresistible.

I slip off my clothes, pull on my bikini and throw over my head a matching white and yellow oversize shirt. I swivel in front of the mirror that runs from floor to ceiling on the outside of the walk-in wardrobe. The shirt's deep neckline, its side vents, and rolled up sleeves certainly suit my shape, but I gasp in horror at the white flesh on view.

Last but not least, I pop open the straw hat, tug off the price tag, and set it squarely on my tangled hair. As I don't know anyone, and have no intention of getting into random conversations, the sight of my unmanageable tangles of blonde curls are easy to ignore. I'm here to enjoy myself.

Never go out without your make up on. Always be prepared. You never know when Mr Right will come along. My mother's mantras. But at this particular moment, I'm so not worried about meeting Mr Right. I'm after sun, sand and a few sangrias.

As I rifle through my case for my book, *How to Live Like a Millionaire*, I realise I'm only halfway through. Although it reads like fiction, it's deadly serious. The author is a wannabe-millionaire who has researched the rich and famous. There's been no mention of Mr Right, setting up home or how to cook.

Money. That's what the random charity-shop book is all about, and the wisest way to use it. Spend it. And attract attention. I've some way to go, but as I slip the key card out of its slot, beach bag slung over one shoulder, I make a rash decision to live dangerously and take the lift down to the basement, where it's quicker to reach the beach.

I'm soon sweaty, panicky, as the less than smooth short ride downwards makes me regret my decision. The lift picks up an elderly lady on the second floor, and as it starts up again the movement inside the shiny silver metal box is juddery, hesitant, and slow. For a few awful seconds, it's as if I'm back in the cabin of the aeroplane. Waiting for the seat belt signs to appear, and the turbulence to send us plummeting into the ocean. I close my eyes tight, until the doors scrape open again. As I step out, I finally manage a broad smile for my fellow passenger.

I stride off in the direction of the beach, and as I near the golden stretch of sand, I have a quick check of my mobile, and see there's a new message from Logan.

Hope you've arrived safely. Meet in reception 8 o'clock? Have booked the fish restaurant as promised. Can't wait to see you. L xx

I start to sing. Who needs Tinder or Hinge? Boyfriend possibilities are coming at me from all angles. Logan is a great guy. But Isaac? The millionaire with the to-die-for villa. He's on another level. Let the holiday begin.

6

Millionaires like to be late. Actually, millionaires are always late. It's an entitlement thing, so my book says.

> Be late for every date. Millionaires keep people waiting, and when you're that wealthy, people will wait all day. And all night.

I fell asleep on the sunbed, and am now back in my room, desperately trying to cool down. I flick through the pages of my book, skimming through all the tips on how to live as if I'm loaded. I stretch out on the bed and count down to eight o'clock. The cool of the sheets is helping to calm down the heat from the sunburn, but falling asleep on the beach was *so not* on the agenda.

When I got back from the beach I'd already started to look like a lobster. Luckily, in amongst the free array of bathroom toiletries (toothbrush, shower gel, bubble bath, shower cap, sewing kit (!), sponge, comb, soap) there was a small bottle of after-sun lotion. I've slathered it over my shoulders, nose, and feet, but it stings like hell. The rest of the chemist shop items are already tucked into the bottom of my case. By the end of the week, I might need an extra case. I've also zipped up the free Nespresso capsules, and herbal tea bags. I'm not used to such luxury, and assume all the items are gratis. Included in the price. I squirrelled them away on my first visit, and won't be leaving anything behind this time either.

At two minutes to eight, it's time to get dressed. I'm not sure wearing white linen trousers and a white T-shirt is the best idea, as the colour isn't showcasing a healthy tan, so much as giving me the appearance of a red berry Viennetta. There's a small chance Logan won't recognise me, as I'm having trouble recognising myself.

Ten past eight, and I saunter down the stairs. I'll not need the Peloton classes this week, as walking up and down five flights of stairs should get the heart working. I definitely won't be risking the lift a second time.

Logan, from a distance, reminds me of my brother, David. They're similar in height (six feet, give or take), and in their muscular builds. Upper body workouts have given them bulk on top, but too-tight jeans can't disguise the skinny leg thing. They've both got straight brown hair, a floppy fringe, and soulful grey eyes.

Logan is fidgeting, jiggling one foot up and down, and is standing by the exit doors as if for a speedy getaway. His face lights up when I appear.

'Jade?' He covers his eyes against the glare of my sunburn.

'Yep. It's me.' I roll my eyes. 'Fell asleep on the sunbed. How are you?'

I let out a childish squeal when he grabs me, kisses me on the cheek and lets his lips linger.

'All the better for seeing you. You look... erm.'

'Go on. Say it. Like a lobster?'

'Lovely.' He blushes until his cheeks match my nose.

We stroll outside, where the cool of the air-con gives way to suffocating temperatures. Even this late in the day, the heat is relentless, and my armpits squelch like sodden sponges.

Five minutes from the hotel, we reach the beach, and my trainers fill with crunchy sand. Closer to the water's edge we reach firmer ground, where the sand is saturated and it's easier to walk. I jog along, while Logan strolls with his hands stuffed inside his khaki shorts.

La Plancha beach bar and restaurant sits on a promontory. Logan tells me he's booked the best table inside, by the window, where we have a stunning view of the Med.

'Jeez. I'd forgotten how amazing it is,' I lie. I haven't forgotten at all, and have been counting down the days.

'Seafood casserole again?' he asks as we sit down.

'What else?'

I've been dreaming of the fresh meaty fish with prawns, calamari, and octopus in the white wine sauce since my first visit. Logan suggests we share a baked potato again, and mush it round in the jus once the fish has been devoured. Heaven with a capital H.

Once inside, and settled at our table, Logan asks me how I've been. He stretches his legs off to the side, and trills his fingers on the table.

'You'll never believe what happened yesterday,' I say.

'What? After you arrived?' He sits up straighter, slides his legs back under the table.

'On the aeroplane. It was an absolute nightmare.' I lean over, and between healthy slugs of a ridiculously expensive bottle of Marqués de Riscal (Logan suggested the Viña Sol, and quipped 'why not?' to the more expensive bottle when I said tonight was my treat), I tell him what happened. And about Isaac, and my crashing at his villa.

'Oh. Where was this Isaac's villa?' Logan shields his eyes against an imaginary glare of the sun, the way he did against my sunburn, and moves his chair back a bit.

'No idea. Along the beach, back towards Malaga, I think. Everywhere looks the same around here. But you should have seen the villa. Wow. It was something else.'

'And Isaac? Was he a gold-jewellery-toting sugar daddy?'

Something tells me to tone down the excitement in my voice, so I lie, and curb the enthusiasm.

'He was okay. A bit of a bore, but he looked after me. I don't know what would have happened if he hadn't been around.'

'Scary,' he says, tucking a serviette into the top of his brightly coloured shirt. I think of the patients in the nursing home. I've tucked plenty of serviettes into scrawny necks, and wonder at Logan's covering up against spillages. I'll not be covering up, as the hotel has a great laundry service.

When the stew arrives, we get stuck in, and the conversation veers away from Isaac, and my adventures. Instead, Logan reminds me he went to university in Exeter, worked in banking for a few years, and is taking a late-in-the-day gap year (or two). He enjoys working at Los Molinos, and he laughs when he tells me he's been promoted to run the tapas bar by the pool.

When the bill comes, I open my fake gold-clasped Gucci bag with a flourish. The bag is as authentic as the real thing. I just can't bring myself to spend £1,000 on the genuine article. My millionaire's book bible has a footnote, owning up that fakes can do the trick. But, it also says to:

Check out current trends in designer labels. Accessorise like you mean it, and keep up-to-date.

Logan pulls out a ten-euro note to tip the waiter, but I slap a hand on top of his, command he puts it away.

'No. This is *my* treat.'

The waiter stands to attention when I fling a fifty-euro note his way, and bows. Bowing seems to follow on from healthy tips. But you know what? It feels so good to give. Almost better than spending on myself.

We walk back towards the hotel in silence. Logan declines the suggestion of a nightcap, uncomfortable drinking where he works, and also he has an early start in the morning. Preparing for his new role as tapas king.

'Thanks for a great evening,' he says. 'Next time, my treat.'

'Listen. I can afford it, so no sweat.' I'm definitely very drunk as we shared two bottles of white wine.

I have to remind myself that Logan drank gallons of water in between, but that is so not my way. Not since the win. No more counting pennies, or diluting the fun.

'See you tomorrow then,' he says. 'Pop by the bar, and I'll slip you some garlic prawns.'

'Sounds like a plan.'

He leans in, gives me a tentative kiss on one cheek, and pops a strand of fly-away hair behind my ear.

'Till tomorrow then,' he says, and turns to head off, but hesitates, as if he's just remembered something. 'Will you be seeing that Isaac again?' He looks at me with a droopy expression.

Can he really be jealous of a random guy who came to my rescue?

What can I say? I'd love to see Isaac again, although I doubt I'll be that lucky.

'Unlikely,' I say, and wave him off.

7

When I get up to my room, I yank open the door of the minibar. It's stacked with beer, soft drinks, wine, and even quarter bottles of Moët & Chandon champagne. One can't hurt, surely.

Habit makes me check the prices, and I gasp when I see the quarter bottle of fizz is twenty-five euros. Surely that would buy a whole bottle? Who cares? I unscrew the cap, wondering, at that price, why it hasn't a celebratory popping cork.

I settle back on the bed and start to scratch my lobster-coloured arms. I'd probably be less gung-ho with the scratching if I was sober, but for now it feels so good as my nail gels rake up and down. I try to turn on the TV, but soon lose the will, when the screen keeps coming back to pictures of the hotel facilities.

The bed is so comfortable, luxurious, and I am so relaxed (and drunk) that I snuggle down under the duvet and start to doze off. My mind wanders back to my first trip to Marbella. Only four weeks ago. At least the plane journey was less traumatic that time, but as my dreams take over, the fear of flying comes back. I remember the trip, in the aftermath of my win, and how my life began to change forever.

The plane banked, tipped to the side, as it curled away from Luton airport. I gripped the Evian bottle, took greedy gulps, grateful to be a white wine drinker. Although the contents had a hint of yellowing urine, rather than the glassy crispness of bottled water, no one bothered to check that I was drinking anything other than water. They'll have seen it all before, and it's not worth the hassle to tackle passengers about bringing their own booze on board. It ran down my throat like Nectar. It wasn't that I didn't want to spend on airplane wine, the trolley just doesn't come round soon enough for nervous passengers.

Through the porthole of the Boeing 737, the homes got smaller, until they were like dolls' houses. Miniature. Unreal. Cars crawled like ants along the arteries that snaked in radials away from the terminal. Even after two large glasses of wine before take-off, and humongous gulps from my Evian bottle, my teeth still ground.

My body automatically goes into rigor mortis when we race along the runway, and the plane slowly levers off the ground. It's the noise I hate most. Christ. Can't they turn it down? I stuffed my fingers in my ears, jamming the tips right in to muffle the sounds. Although I managed to silence the worst of it, there's always the need to stay alert. That need never goes away, and I have to hum constantly to distract myself.

'Why are you going to Spain? You hate flying.' Connor had spat, in between softer cajoling tones telling me he loved me more than life itself. Funny, his full-on declarations of love only came after the Saturday night, which was a little over a month ago, but a lifetime in terms of events.

Before *the* night, I'd already moved out of the flat I shared with him into a dingy bedsit in a Z-lister part of Crouch End. It was infested with spiders – still is – with mould stuck to the ceiling like black Rorschach ink blots. I had spent the month before my windfall alone in the cramped space, crying, large, uncontrollable sobs watching reruns of romantic comedies in a masochistic ritual. *Pretty Woman. Love Happens. The Girl Next Door. Mamma Mia!* I should have concentrated on crime thrillers. Dark tales of death, and grisly dismemberment. It would have helped shelve the tears, disappointment, loneliness. Weird how my isolation made me think I missed Connor. It painted him in romantic hues, pulling the early happy memories to the fore, and burying all the doubts and disgust under the floorboards.

As the thin, broken, wispy clouds welcomed us into the stratosphere, swirling like candy floss round the plane, I sank back into my seat. I rested my head against the window of seat 2A, and tried to let the warmth of the sun against the glass weave a soothing magic. I never unbuckle my belt, only loosen it ever so slightly if I feel brave enough. I'm like a wife waiting for her abusive spouse to return home after a drinking bout. That's how alert I am. Always prepared.

On my first trip, I avoided the diazepam tablets which I keep secreted in my purse. Emergencies only. They don't mix with alcohol, and I prefer the buzz from the latter, rather than the comatose state induced by the former. But it's good to have options. Just in case.

I know the noises the plane makes. I'm learning. I talked myself through the various jerks and judders, a list of which I keep on my phone.

As I tried to relax, I smiled at an anxious guy in seat number 2D, on the other side of the aisle. He probably didn't recognise the noises like I did. He was young, I reckon late teens, early twenties, and his left foot tapped up and down, no doubt keeping rhythm to music from his ear pods. I caught his eye. Smiled. Tried to pass across my own relief at winding down from the heights of anxiety and panic. I wanted to share.

Even now, in my comatose state, between sleeping and waking, I giggle. I remember the guy blushed and ran a white hand through lanky locks as he looked down at the floor. I'd have been an older woman to him, and likely gave him a good ten years.

The world slowly disappeared from view, along with about 50 per cent of the angst. The spare 50 per cent of mind space relived the turmoil of what happened after my lottery win.

The upheaval, begging phone calls from strangers and incessant knocks on the door from random people claiming to be friends. Matthew Harvey, *whoever-the-f* he was, called round half a dozen times to say how sorry he was for not contacting me after our date. He's the sort of guy I might have dated, but hey, I don't have dementia.

News certainly travels fast when people are after something. My windfall swept through the grapevine at the speed of a bush fire. People I'd never met started sending friend requests on Facebook and triple the number of strange men in doctor's scrubs and military uniforms began following me on Instagram. Messaging me with proposals, and even a couple of marriage requests. I should have been more social media savvy, and deleted my accounts, but I'm good at hindsight.

number of things then and came inside and mingled, pinching fingers follows me like freeze-frame. Here, pop me with a prosecco and even a couple of marriage requests. I should have been more social, more chatty and...

8

Anyway, up in the air, I became excited about my first trip to Marbella. Millionaires' playground. And so much more fun than a dating app. No more swiping right or left. I've now got bargaining tools. I stared out the window until my eyelids grew heavy. Ha, ha. I nearly fell for that one, but not quite.

I do not sleep on planes.

I pulled myself up, checked the seat was in the upright position and stretched out my neck.

The cabin crew rattled a wonky trolley through the cabin. Well, a skinny man pushed, and a fierce-looking woman pulled. Nuts, snacks, Pringles, cheese and biscuits, and paninis. Synthetic smiles, bleached white, could be offering up caviar and champagne but what was on offer was luxury for me. I'm a snack-food junkie. Worse after a few glasses.

For the first time in my life, I pulled out a twenty-pound note and told the young steward to keep the change. Sharing my good fortune felt so good, attracting smiles, and thank-yous. I wonder how great Jeff Bezos or Elon Musk must feel all the time. For me, the largesse makes me feel more appealing, more attractive, as if my magnanimity is somehow linked to intelligence, and beauty. Since we'd been together, as a couple,

Connor had chipped away at an already flagging natural belief in myself, my abilities, until I was a shell without a centre.

But now I'm going back to the beginning. Back to before Connor, and reassessing myself with fresh eyes. After a facial, a new haircut, gel nails, and an all-over body tan, I saw myself in the mirror with fresh eyes.

Connor had just shrugged when I eventually moved out. He even offered to help me pack. Big mistake on his part. He assumed I'd be back begging for crumbs. We'd been living together in a small flat in Wood Green for only a few months. Early declarations of undying love, generally offered up immediately before climax, soon petered out and post-coital conversations consisted of throwaway suggestions on how to spend the next few hours.

Fancy a takeaway? What say we pop down the pub? Join the lads. I can play some darts. Life was all about Connor and what Connor wanted. Grown-up compromise was something he didn't really get.

I'd met Connor at school when we were only fifteen, and soon, plans to buy a flat together, and make a firm commitment had left the party, and Connor had reverted to bachelor days of sex, drugs and rock 'n' roll. He wasn't overly concerned when I started packing, assuming a click of his fingers was all it would take. Okay, maybe so. But we'll never know.

The Saturday night followed soon after.

It was midnight. I'd overdone the wine, overdone the tears, the self-pity, and was about to flop into bed, when I remembered I'd bought a scratch card. No idea why, but it had been an impulse thing when I discovered a couple of loose coins jangling in my pocket.

Bleary-eyed, I dug out the scrunched-up card from the bottom of my sisal shoulder bag, and began scratching with a rough-edged nail. There were loads of boxes with pound signs. I was half asleep, slumped on the end of my mattress, and I only sat up when I'd peeled open the last box. I had three gold matching chests of the winning jackpot amount. My slouch soon turned into an upright position. A bit like my rigid fear-of-flying pose.

I checked it several times. I was so drunk, it was hard to focus. I read the rules on the back of the card, and kept blinking to clear my vision. I must have missed something because I couldn't possibly have won. I never buy lottery tickets, or scratch cards, and I certainly don't win things. Jeez, I couldn't work it out. But funny how quickly I sobered up.

I turned on the centre light in my bedsit, whacked a magazine at a two-inch spider scuttling along the skirting board, and tried to calm my heart. It was banging like a drum. One scratch card. What were the chances?

That same Saturday night, there were three winners of the main Lotto jackpot, sharing a rollover pot of £60 million. Can you believe it? All the winners remained anonymous. That was the advice, and I can certainly see why.

By the time Connor heard the rumours, I was like a pig in shit, relishing the opportunity to rub his nose in it. I never let on I'd won only on a scratch card; rubbing his nose in a £20 million jackpot was much more satisfying.

It wasn't long till he came begging. A couple of days was all it took. He certainly didn't wait around. With a hangdog look of remorse, and a small tatty green and gold-embossed box in his hand, he was always going to give it his best shot. I'd suddenly become really attractive. And Connor? Jeez, what a creep.

'I'm really sorry, Jade. I've been such a prat.' He was by this stage down on one knee, neck thrown back like a turtle, proffering up a miniscule solitaire engagement ring.

I stared at him. Funny how perceptions can alter in a second. I never realised how pasty a complexion my ex-boyfriend had, and as his outstretched hand shook, it was as if I was seeing him properly for the first time. Standing over him, I noticed the thinning patch of hair across his crown.

'You're too late.'

What else could I say?

'I'll try harder. I promise. I love you. Please give me another chance.'

I've no idea how he squeezed a tear from his eye. But I laughed, which was probably not such a wise idea. Anyway, he chucked the box against the wall and stormed out, muttering that he'd be back. The threatening tone was hard to miss.

My first flight to Malaga was uneventful, and pretty smooth, all things considered. When the seat-belt sign pinged on, I woke up, no idea how I'd managed to fall asleep.

Cabin crew. Ten minutes to landing.

I yanked myself upright when I heard the captain's announcement. The one I wait for every time I fly. Soon my feet would be on dry land. For me, flying feels like climbing Everest, it takes such an effort.

I looked out over the sea as the plane banked steeply and noisily over the water. I stuck my fingers back in my ears to block out the heavy clunking sounds. As soon as I had heard the captain's announcement, I set the stopwatch on my phone. I knew that in ten minutes exactly, the plane would hit the runway and I'd have survived my first flight in over five years.

Nine minutes. Eight minutes. Seven minutes. I could have been counting down in hours. But soon I was counting down in seconds. Five, four, three, two, one... The wheels crashed on to the tarmac, and my stomach whooped as the plane bumped from side to side, rolling along the runway until it ground to a standstill.

I exhaled the bottled-up air, puffed out my lips, and smiled across the aisle. It was a smug victory smile, but no one was looking. The young man was already packing up his rucksack.

A minor achievement for some. But a world war victory for me.

I still haven't owned up to anyone that I only won £50,000 on a scratch card. Connor told everyone, even my mother, that I'd won the lottery, and that I was a multi-millionaire. I didn't let on otherwise, and don't intend to. My mother will probably soon work it out, but I suspect she'll enjoy being linked to a millionaire daughter, and I'm banking on her keeping schtum.

I certainly prefer the way I'm being treated when people think I have £20 million in the bank. I doubt I'd be such a celebrity if they knew I only had a meagre £50k to my name.

9

I wake with a start, no idea where I am, and think I'm still dreaming. Until the pain hits.

Ouch. I must have smacked my head against the headboard because the pain in my temple is fierce. I flick open an eyelid and spot the titchy champagne bottle on the bedside table. It looks like a taster sample. The TV is flickering on and off, and the minibar door is wide open.

Burglars? It's my first thought as I start to come round. Surely a five-star hotel doesn't suffer break-ins with all the CCTV footage around. When I scan the room, there's no sign of a break-in, and the chain is still fastened across the bedroom door. I haul myself up, and have the strongest urge to lie down again, and go back to sleep. I reach for my mobile, and holy shit. It's 10 a.m. The blackout curtains are so efficient, it could be two in the morning.

There are three messages on WhatsApp, but I ignore them, desperate to get down to breakfast which ends at eleven. There's no way I'll miss out on the all-inclusive gluttony. I tumble into the bathroom, brush my teeth, and think I'm hallucinating because I'm not just lobster coloured, but I've got huge white rings round my eyes from the obscenely large sunglasses I was wearing. The white circles look as if they've been painted on. So much for millionaire perfection.

I haul out a pair of navy shorts, and a red and white striped top, and frantically try to locate the offending sunglasses to camouflage the white shapes. It's nearly 10.30 by the time I look half decent.

As I career down the five flights of stairs, I get strange looks from random guests, but even in an emergency, I'll not be tempted by the sardine can of a lift.

Although I've been before, the sight of the dining room takes my breath away. It's like a very exclusive canteen, tables and chairs arranged in neat lines, pristine white starched runners, and gleaming Villeroy & Boch china on each table.

I reserve a table for two by setting my key card on top, and head straight for the Nespresso machine where I slip in a flying-saucer-shaped capsule. *Intenso*. Full strength. I'll be back at least four times before I'm pumped for action.

When no one is looking, I slip a couple of fancy wrapped tea bags into my pocket. I always bring my handbag to breakfast, and pop in tea bags, sugar sachets, and anything else I can lay my hands on when no one is looking. My handbag is extra-large, the one for under my seat in the plane, and by the time I leave the restaurant, it'll be full to the brim with ham and cheese rolls, fruit, and pastries for day-time snacking.

If I was hoping for *Love Island* type of guests, I'm definitely in the wrong place. The more mature guests are about the same age as the nursing home patients I used to work with, only slightly more mobile, and presumably with all their marbles – and extremely bulging wallets. All of a sudden, a couple of families appear with noisy children, and bring the mean age down a few decades, their violent activity grating against my headache.

I decide an omelette is the way to go, hoping all the protein will help temper the hangover, and I join the queue for the healthy options. As I point at various ingredients to a guy with long hair in a ponytail and white cap perched on top, my stomach does a sudden flip. A tall handsome guy, totally gorgeous, appears by the entrance to the dining room. He hands something to the waitress who is checking guests against room numbers, and strolls across the room. He's weirdly familiar, but out of context, it takes a moment to click.

Oh my F! It's bloody Isaac. I flick my sunglasses down from the top of my head, and turn and face the chef who is cracking eggs onto the hot plate. Shit. Shit. Shit. The chef now has an irritating grin in place, but continues to point at the choice of tempting ingredients: onions, peppers, green beans, mushrooms, tomatoes. You name it. The list is endless. He's keen for me to try everything on offer. And now he can no longer see my eyes through the sunglasses, he becomes more persistent with the pointing.

'Jade?'

It's Isaac. He's directly behind me. His schmoozing tones are etched in my memory. Perhaps, if I don't turn, he might go away.

Fat chance.

'Jade. I know it's you.'

He's going nowhere.

'Isaac? What a surprise.' I don't dare take my sunglasses off, but the bastard does it for me. His tanned fingers gently lift away the white frames, and hands them to me.

'Goodness. What's happened to your eyes?'

'I got a bit burnt yesterday. That's all.'

The chef is now holding out my omelette which is laden with the full list of possible ingredients. I want to deny it's mine, and to ask for a single boiled egg instead.

'Hm. That looks good. Perhaps I can join you.' His voice is full of smirk.

I'm having trouble holding the plate. I'm not sure if my hands are shaking through the most horrendous hangover, or from the turmoil of Isaac standing so close. What the hell is he doing here, at this hour?

He follows me and – the cheek of it – sits down opposite and upturns one of the fancy teacups.

'Can I get you a tea? Or another coffee?' He nods towards my two used espresso cups, which a waitress suddenly whisks away. Why did she smile at Isaac when they're my cups?

'Another coffee would be good. Are you staying here?'

'No. But I know the restaurant manager. She's by the door. See over there?'

Yep. I see her. Long black silky hair, tight black skirt, shapely calves, and a very snug-fitting white blouse.

I cut the omelette into miniscule pieces and move them round the plate like travel-set chess pieces. Isaac has the cheek to spear a piece with a fork.

'Good. Very good.' He's laughing at me, and I have the most violent urge to smack him.

'What are you doing here?' I ask.

'I'm here to find you. Don't look so surprised.'

'What for?'

'I thought you might fancy a trip around the bay in my yacht.'

I want to say, *Why me?* Instead, I nod, and say, 'That sounds fun.'

It sounds bloody awful, but what choice do I have?

'Great. I'll pick you up at, say, midday?'

He's already on his feet, and puts a hand on my shoulder.

'And don't forget to bring your suncream.'

Two minutes later, he's gone.

WTF. WTF. I might be *scared* of flying, but I'm absolutely petrified of water. I knock back my third espresso, fearful it might come straight back up. But I now need to sober up, and fast.

I dare swivel my head, just an inch, towards the door as Isaac leaves, and when I turn back, I see Logan. He's at the other side of the dining room, staring at me.

He looks far from happy.

10

Reception calls up to my room at 11.50 exactly to tell me there is a gentleman waiting for me in the foyer.

I grab my bag, suncream, and huge straw sun hat, and hurry down the stairs. Instead of being fashionably late, as befits the behaviour of an entitled millionaire, I do the five flights in record time. It's one minute to midday when I spot Isaac standing by the entrance. You couldn't miss him.

My heart is pounding from both the exercise and the sight of my date. Drop-dead gorgeous doesn't do him justice. He's photo-shoot perfection.

'Hi. Are you ready?' he asks. He takes his hands out of his linen shorts and gently propels me out the door. I shiver when his hand makes contact with my lower back.

'As ready as I'll ever be.'

Isaac leads me to the car, where Pablo is waiting at the wheel, and before we get in, Isaac leans across and taps the brim of my enormous sun hat.

'You'll not need this,' he says, telling me his supercharged motor yacht has an awning that covers the whole seated section. 'Sunburn shouldn't be a problem.'

He grins, displaying dazzling big white wolf teeth. He's definitely flirting, but why do I sense he's also making fun of me?

'Well, that's a blessing,' I say.

Isaac and I slip into the back seat, and as Pablo drives carefully away from the hotel entrance, I'm hopeful, with his boss in the car, he might drive more slowly than before. No such luck. He speeds along the motorway as if we're in a getaway car, his driving worse than ever. He's mastered the art of weaving and switching lanes as if we're on fairground dodgems.

By the time we get to Puerto Banus, my head is spinning, and the headache is ten times worse than it was at breakfast. I'm already craving another drink to calm me down.

When Pablo pulls up the Merc, Isaac gets out, opens my door, and takes my hand. He whispers something to Pablo, who nods, and drives off.

Isaac leads me round the port, and is soon pointing to a very slick motor yacht at one end. It's not huge, a quarter the size of the serious players, but it's totally amazing. It's a Rinker 270 Fiesta Vee apparently. No idea what that is, probably the Rolls-Royce of motor cruisers, but it's luxury with a capital L.

As we step aboard, Isaac reads my mind, and suggests we share a bottle of Cava. Okay, it's early, but I'm seriously in need of something, and it is nearly lunchtime.

'Do you like boats?' he asks.

I want to ask if he means the sort I play with in the bathtub, but being a very wealthy millionairess (heiress for all he knows), I think he's guessing I'm a dab hand at yachting.

'The truth?' There's only so much playing at being a millionaire that I can muster. 'Never been on one before.'

'You've never been on a boat?' He widens his eyes, before settling a hand on my lower back (again), and propelling me towards the front of the craft. He's good at propelling, that's for sure, as his fingers don't invite argument.

'Unless a ferry to Larne in Northern Ireland counts, but nothing like this. Also...' My legs are very shaky. 'I'm not a fan of choppy waters.'

I nearly jump out of my skin when a tall athletic guy, dressed all in white, suddenly appears from behind a large wooden wheel. He must have been sitting down when we came on board, but I do breathe slightly easier when I realise we've got company.

'Jade. Meet Mario, the skipper.'

'Hi.' I do the most embarrassing wave thing, and Mario nods. When he doesn't answer, I suspect he's not English. He looks like the perfect sea captain, with his healthy suntan and upright posture.

While we watch on, Mario slips on a red and yellow cap which blends in with a small matching flag sticking out from the brow of the boat. I try to ignore the fluttering of the flag, petrified that the quivering might be an indicator of choppy waters. From the clues, I guess Mario is Spanish, but I'm far too nervy to start asking questions, or making small talk. I slip under the awning and grip the top of one of the leather benches.

'How fast does this thing go?' I ask, shielding my eyes against the brightness.

'Top speed? Thirty knots,' Isaac says.

'In miles per hour?'

'Thirty-four. Like driving slightly too fast in a built-up area. Now sit down and relax.'

It's an order.

Mario revs up, and without comment, we set off. He reminds me of Pablo, and Marta, with the lack of conversation. It must be something to do with working for Isaac, as they all seem overly subservient. And quiet.

Wow. I'm soon loving it. The Cava is definitely helping the sea legs, and Isaac is hilarious. Twenty minutes round the coast, and he takes me on a guided tour of the yacht, gripping my hand tightly, perhaps in deference to my wobbling, but it feels really good.

The upper deck area is so plush. Leather seats, eating area, the ultimate in comfy. It's only when he takes me down a few steps that my heart rate speeds up. There's a whole bedsit below deck. I could live in it. Two double beds, FFS. A toilet, shower, kitchen area. Isaac is now so close as there's little space to move around. When he bumps into me, he holds on for several seconds.

If I was lobster coloured when I arrived, the colour of my cheeks must now be off the charts.

'Oops.' I fall down as the boat rears up and speeds off. 'Thirty-four miles per hour? You've got to be kidding me.'

'Yep. Come on. Let's go back up on deck. Unless you want to change into your swimming costume?'

'Ha, ha. Hilarious.' He knows I don't have swimming gear, but I'm scared he means it, and that he might have a spare bikini lying around.

'Deadly serious.' Isaac produces a snorkel from a bedside cupboard, and pulls it on. His eyes are scarily distorted behind the glass. He's hard to recognise, but from where I'm standing, he's still drop-dead gorgeous.

Have I really managed to hook a millionaire?

* * *

Two hours later, we stagger off the boat. Well, I stagger, Isaac strolls. He slips something into Mario's hand. Isaac is good at slipping people things, I note, as I remember the waitress at the hotel.

Mario looks at me, his lips tightly pursed, his eyes cold. Perhaps it's because he's looking into the sun that he's not smiling. He's not even making an effort at pleasantries, but no doubt he's seen it all before. Maybe he's jealous, having to skipper for such a cool dude. Must say, I don't feel like a cool chick, as my hair is a swirling, matted tangle as if it's been rinsed in salt water without shampoo. It's soaking because, halfway round, Isaac rolled back the awning so that we could enjoy the full force of the wind. I'm not sure *enjoy* is the word I'd have used. The assault from sea spray felt like having a cold shower with your clothes on.

'What are you doing for dinner this evening?' Isaac asks as we head back to the car. I don't remember him texting, or using his phone since we've been out, but up ahead I see Pablo leaning against the Mercedes with a cigarette end hanging out one side of his mouth. When he spots us, he whisks out the butt and grinds it with his foot.

'What did you have in mind?'

'I know this great little seafood place round the corner from your hotel. What say I pick you up around nine?'

Jeez. It's more than okay.

Now isn't the time to wonder why he's asking.

Isaac pats Pablo on the back, thanks him for being there. I wonder how long the guy's been hanging around, or if the boat trip always takes two hours exactly. But my misgivings at things being slightly too regimented are pretty easy to ignore. I'm living the dream.

This guy is so magnetic, I wouldn't care if he has done this fifty times before. This is my time, and I'm going to make the most of it.

'Nine it is then,' I say. And with that we climb into the back seat, and without a word, Pablo screeches out onto the motorway, and with one finger on the wheel, drives like a lunatic back to Los Molinos.

11

After getting back from the boat trip, I laze around, and after a thirty-minute nap, I wake much more refreshed.

I lounge in the bath, wash my hair and repaint my toenails, and finally give into temptation, unscrewing the top of another quarter bottle of Moët from the minibar. It gets stocked up quickly, that's for sure. There seems to be an extra two bottles this time. But, hey ho, I'm here to enjoy myself.

I spend a couple of hours dancing round my bedroom with my Spotify playlist turned up full volume. This is the life. I haven't even bothered checking my phone, and suddenly remember the three WhatsApp messages from earlier. I've been in a fantasy world since Isaac turned up this morning, and forgot all about them.

I suddenly panic, not knowing where my phone is, until I locate it in the minibar.

> How is Spain? Hope you're having fun, but don't waste your money. I'm attaching details of a nice little flat in Muswell Hill. What do you think? Mum xx

Mum doesn't seem to realise how far £20 million would go, as the flat in Muswell Hill has been reduced in price from £750,000 to £695,000. A snip if I really was a multi-millionaire. Does she seriously think I'm going to splash £20 million in one go? She can't possibly know I only won £50k, no one does. But typical Mum, she's got me worried, and her text reminds me to keep an eye on my bank account. Mum can read me like a book, and it's more than likely she's worked out I haven't won the jackpot. The fact that I haven't even bought her a new car is a big giveaway. But good old Mum. She'll never let on.

I keep my answer short and sweet, enough to put her mind at rest.

All great. B&B very cosy. Will look through the flat details when I get back. Love you. xx

The next text is from Connor.

I MISS YOU. I LOVE YOU. C. XXXX

He's certainly running out of novel ways to suck me back in, and I instantly press *delete*. I'm guessing he's already spent his weekly benefits on booze and betting.

The final text is from Logan.

Hope you're feeling okay this morning. Was great fun last night. Are you around this evening? At the tapas bar until 9. Pop down. Logan X

Shit. In all the excitement with Isaac, I'd forgotten about Logan. He saw me at breakfast talking to Isaac and didn't look so happy. If I hurry, I can pop down to the tapas bar, and tell him I've other plans this evening but maybe we can catch up tomorrow. Hopefully, Isaac will wait in reception and not come looking for me. Something tells me Logan might be the jealous sort. Call it intuition.

But what fun having two men after me.

* * *

There's no sign of Logan when I get to the tapas bar. It's only 8.30, but he seems to have already clocked off. A young guy, who looks a bit like Connor when we first met (all of fifteen years of age with erupting skin and shaky hands) is mixing cocktails and chopping lime slices.

'Logan?' I ask, looking all around.

'*Hola*,' he says as if Logan is a strange foreign word he's never heard before.

'*Nada. Gracias.*' I use my default Google words.

A tap on my bare shoulder and I swing round.

'Hi, gorgeous.' It's Isaac. All smiles and teeth, and *Love Island* looks.

'Hi.' If I was tongue-tied with the barman, I'm now having trouble breathing, let alone speaking. I was expecting to meet Isaac in reception. No idea why he's turned up at the tapas bar.

'Are you ready?' he asks.

I nod. 'Yep.'

'Let's go then.' He takes my hand, links our fingers, and as we head out, I spot the waitress from this morning scowl from behind the reception desk. She's really pretty. Think Penelope Cruz. All exotic skin and features. As I flick back my wayward curls, and straighten my shoulders, I wonder for the millionth time, *why me?* This guy could have any woman he wanted. Perhaps he's heard I'm a millionaire, but who cares? He's a millionaire too, so what's the difference?

That's the thing about drinking champagne, it makes the world seem a lighter place, and things not so dramatic. 'Make hay while the sun shines' is my new go-to motto.

Before we exit the hotel, I hesitate by reception, and make an excuse to pop to the ladies' room.

'Don't be long,' he says.

'Just a tick.'

I've no idea why I feel the need to text Logan away from Isaac's prying eyes, but as soon as I'm in the cloakroom, I send a message.

Couldn't find you at the tapas bar. Catch up tomorrow. Jade

I may as well keep my options open, as underneath all Isaac's eagerness, I doubt he'll hang around too long. Also, I do feel pretty mean about dumping Logan as soon as Isaac appeared.

Isaac stretches out his hand when I return, and he walks me round the back of the hotel, down a steep ramp until we come to the small roundabout very close to the AP-7 motorway, the one Pablo uses as a racetrack.

He pulls me right, and left, then right again, as we weave in and out through black bollards that line the pavement.

'Hurry up. You're like a tortoise.'

'What's the rush?'

'Aren't you hungry? I'm starving. And wait till you taste the food.'

Five minutes later, Isaac slows up outside a place that looks like Joe's Café in the centre of Crouch End. All greasy spoon, and ketchup containers. There are rows and rows of empty chairs and tables outside, but he leads me through a wooden door with frosted glass panels.

Inside Casa Celeste, the place is packed. Wall to wall. The smell of seafood makes my stomach lurch, and I wonder where we're going to sit. I needn't have worried, because Celeste, another smooth-skinned beauty (they're everywhere) appears, squealing with excitement when she sees Isaac.

'Isaac. Your table is ready.' She points to the far corner, glances briefly my way, and leads us over.

'Perfect.' Isaac beams at me, and I can't help wondering at the red candle flickering inside a holder in the centre of the table. It's the only lit candle in the place.

'What would you like to drink? Your usual?' Celeste asks.

'Please. A carafe of house red. Jade? Are you happy with red?'

I'd be happy with tap water, but red wine should more than hit the spot.

Isaac doesn't linger over the menu, but suggests I follow his recommendations.

'The hake casserole is to die for.'

From where I'm sitting, Isaac is the one that's to die for, but for now I need to get my stomach geared up for effort. Seafood casseroles seem to be the thing, as Isaac's description of the speciality at Casa Celeste sounds weirdly familiar to the meal I had with Logan at the beach restaurant.

When Celeste has taken our order and disappeared, hopefully for the next couple of hours at least, I notice a middle-aged woman in gold diamanté sandals and a grey floaty kaftan thing standing in the doorway. She's staring in our direction. Staring at Isaac to be more precise. Her straggly mousy hair is scraped to one side in the manner of a lopsided ponytail, and her fair skin has patches of sun spots which are hard to miss, even from a distance.

Isaac stiffens when he sees her, takes his hand off the top of mine, and tries to push his chair back so he can stand. We're so tight to the corner that he has to squirm uncomfortably to extricate himself.

'Emmeline,' he says, when the apparition appears alongside us. 'Can you excuse me for a moment, Jade?'

He's not expecting an answer as he takes Emmeline's hand, in rather a tight grip, and leads her back towards the entrance. The steady hum of conversation in the restaurant quietens, as several sets of eyes follow the pair out. I stare down at the red and white checked tablecloth, until Celeste returns with the carafe. I let her fill my glass. When she's done, like the other guests, she turns and watches through the opaque glass.

Even from where I'm sitting, and through the closed door, there's no mistaking the sound. Emmeline is bawling, howling like a baby, and Isaac's hand is nestled loosely on her shoulder.

12

When Emmeline has finally gone, Isaac hovers outside for a few moments, before he returns to the table.

To give Isaac his due, he tells me all about Emmeline without me having to ask. Which is good, because although I'm curious, it's much too soon to appear neurotic by asking loaded questions.

'I also met her at Los Molinos,' he says. I don't remind him that actually we met on the Boeing 737 when we were plummeting to certain death, and not at the hotel. But he's more than happy to tell me all about Emmeline, and I'm more than happy to listen.

'We sort of hit it off, liked the same sort of things. Eating out. Playing golf, sightseeing. And, I hate to admit it, but she was a great cook.' He makes a phoney guilty expression, pursed lips, rolling eyes. 'And expect she still is a great cook.' He laughs at this.

I must say, he's certainly not giving off any guilty or regretful vibes. But then I suppose he's dumped quite a few ladies in his time.

'Did you take her out on the yacht?' The question sort of pops out. Isaac is holding his wine glass with both hands wrapped round the bulb. His lips are already slightly stained from the tannins, but I resist the urge to tell him.

'Yes. As a matter of fact, I did.' He manages to look surprised, as if it was an interesting coincidence. He's good at expressions, like he's had acting lessons.

'Were you dating?' It sounds the sort of question Mum asks me whenever I mention random boys' names. Mum is savvy enough not to ask if I've slept with them, but that's the angle I'm now coming from. Not sure why I need to know, but Isaac looks so hot under the glow of the flickering candle that it suddenly seems an important question.

'Yes. You could say that.' He smiles. 'But it's over, so no need to worry.' He slides a hand from around his glass, and nudges his fingertips towards mine.

'I wasn't worried,' I say, laughing wildly. Of course, I'm worried. I already want Isaac all to myself, especially as the longing butterflies are battering my insides.

'She keeps coming round to the villa, and phoning me. I told her it was over but she's not going quietly.' He rolls his eyes.

He's likely ghosted her. Not unlike me with Connor.

'Oh. Where's she staying?' No idea where this question has come from, but I'm curious.

'Not at Los Molinos, that I do know. I asked at the hotel to see if she was staying there again. But she's not.'

Celeste suddenly appears, accompanied by an ageing waiter who has white serviettes thrown across both arms and is carrying a hot sizzling dish. He sets it down in front of me, and a few seconds later, reappears with a second dish for Isaac.

'Enjoy,' Celeste says, thrusting a hand towards each of our plates, as if we're about to take in a West End show.

Isaac bends his head, and sniffs. No idea why because the smell is overpowering. Rich and fishy. Even if I couldn't see the food, I'd know something good was on offer. Mum used to accuse me of eating with my eyes, rather than my taste buds, but the sight of the bubbling white wine jus, prawns, clams, calamari and hake is certainly doing its pitch. I'm suddenly feeling hungry, and my appetite has definitely been fired up by hearing that Emmeline is ancient history.

'Calahonda,' Isaac suddenly says, as if he's just remembered something.

I stir the casserole to cool it down, and wonder if Calahonda is a type of fish.

'Emmeline has a friend with a little flat in Calahonda. I think that's where she's likely to be. Funny, I've just remembered,' he says, spearing a prawn with a fork and offering it my way. 'Nothing like fresh seafood. My absolute favourite.'

Isaac is right. It's the best fish stew I've ever tasted, although I know better than to own up that the only other fish stew I've tasted has been with Logan.

* * *

After a carafe of wine, fish stew, Catalan tart and Manchego cheese with almonds, I feel ready to burst. I've never been on a date where I've eaten so heartily. Though, apart from Connor and a couple of Hinge hook-ups, I haven't been on many dates. Certainly, never with anyone so absolutely hot.

We stroll back, arm in arm, and when we get to the hotel entrance, Pablo is leaning up against the Merc with another fag hanging out of his mouth. How did he know what time we'd get back? It's like when we got off the yacht, and he was already there waiting. Tonight, Isaac hasn't checked his phone once. He could have when he went to the toilet, I suppose, but that was on the way out.

Perhaps after Pablo dropped him off earlier at the hotel, he's been hanging around ever since. The thought spooks me, but it's been such a great night, I don't want to spoil the moment by being downright nosy. Maybe this is the way millionaires live, though in my *How to Live Like a Millionaire* book, there's no mention of staff hanging around 24/7. I wonder how much it costs to keep Pablo on his toes.

I feel really woozy, and the sight of Pablo has knocked back any suggestion of sharing the contents of the minibar, or a nightcap by the pool. It looks as if Isaac planned in advance to go straight home.

When Isaac spots Pablo, he holds up five fingers, twice, presumably to let him know he'll be there in ten minutes.

Isaac walks me inside to the foyer, and pulls me down to sit beside him on a long Moroccan bench, exquisitely carved and slatted.

My insides are gurgling, and I'm starting to feel decidedly queasy.

He turns to face me, and looks really intense, scary actually. I get the most dreadful premonition he's going to tell me it's been fun, but he's not up for anything serious. Perhaps he's leaving the country, going away on business. Whatever, I'm more concerned that I'm about to throw up.

'When do you leave?' he asks.

'I check out on Saturday. Why?' My heartbeat is now competing with the gurgling.

'What say you stay on for a few days, and come and keep me company at the villa?'

Holy Shit. WTF!

I'm never speechless, but I can't get the words out.

'Is that a yes?' Isaac is now laughing at me.

Out of the corner of my eye, I see Logan lurking by reception. He's staring straight at me, and shaking his head. He's either totally pissed off, or he's telling me not to agree to whatever Isaac is suggesting.

'Yes. Why not? Hopefully your rates won't be as steep as at the hotel.'

'For you? No charge.'

'I'll be back in a mo. Sorry.'

With that, I spring up, and make a dash for the ladies' loo again. In a couple of minutes, all the wonderful fish stew has come back up, but I can't help grinning from ear to ear.

Bloody hell. I really am living the dream. I mustn't forget to change the dates for my return flight. I don't linger on the worry that seats 2A, B and C might not be available.

You know what? Tonight, it's hard to care.

13

I spend the next few days on the beach, topping up my all-over tan, with very dedicated application of factor 30 suncream. I won't be risking the lobster look again, rather aiming for St Tropez golden.

Logan, for some reason, seems to be avoiding me. He hasn't responded to my text about catching up, but has likely added two and two, having spotted me and Isaac together.

It's my last night at the hotel before I move into Isaac's villa, so I get down to the tapas bar early hoping Logan will be on duty, and at least I'll get a chance to say goodbye.

He's there all right, chatting to a couple of pretty girls draped over the bar stools. They look like teenagers, and suddenly I don't feel so guilty.

I sit on one of the tables outside, and stare out across the huge pool towards the ocean. Even from this far back, I get a warm feeling when I notice boats bobbing around. Likely more millionaire yachts.

'Jade.' Logan suddenly appears, and in an efficient-waiter voice, interrupts my thoughts. 'What can I get you?'

Logan has the serviette thing going on over one arm, while clutching a wooden tray. The other arm is bent, the back of his hand into his back. Jeez, he's so pissed off he's playing the professional I'm-so-not-bothered card. That's certainly the way it looks.

'Logan. Listen. I'm really sorry I haven't been around much—'

He's pretty quick to interrupt.

'Not a problem. Anyway, you seem to have been enjoying yourself?'

I'm not sure if he's really pissed off, or curious. Either way, he seems to have accepted that the best he can hope for is a passing acquaintance scenario.

'Yes. I've been having fun.'

'Watch that Isaac. He's not all he seems.' He whispers these words, as he sets down a drinks coaster, and avoids eye contact. 'Anyway. What would you like to drink, madam?' He straightens, and speaks more loudly.

'Enough of the "madam", please. A gin and tonic would be good.'

'Coming up.'

With that he's gone, and over my shoulder I see him laughing, rather too loudly as he chats with the teenagers. At least he doesn't seem too upset, which is a relief. But what does he mean about Isaac? Not all he seems? Maybe he's just plain jealous, but I can't really blame him. What man wouldn't be jealous of Isaac?

I sip my drink for the next half-hour, skipping through the last section of my book. Maybe Isaac isn't all that he seems, but does it matter? I'm certainly not all I seem. I checked my bank balance earlier, and I'm already £20,000 down. So much for £20 million. It would be nice, but I need to spend my last £30k wisely. Especially if I want to live like a millionaire a while longer.

* * *

When I get down to breakfast for the last time at the hotel, it's a full house, and the dining room is packed. I'm not so self-conscious when I stuff loads of extra food in my large bag. I feel like a very slick shoplifter, but remind myself that I've paid good money, and it all looks delicious. By lunchtime, I'll be starving, and it seems as good a way to start economising by stocking up on what I've already paid for. Isaac texted to say he might not be back until suppertime, although he'll try to get back earlier, so my stockpile should be more than enough to keep me going until then.

I can see the waitress-cum-room-number-checker by the desk watching. Her eyes follow me like a hawk from the cold meats to the cereals, to the fresh juices, and all the way round the room to the cooked breakfast section.

A final omelette should sop up last night's three G and Ts. This morning, I get the chef to include onion, tomatoes, peppers, bacon and everything else that he's got on offer. He gives me his trademark grin, his eyes twinkling under an increasingly wayward fringe.

I'll really miss the hotel, the luxuries, and anonymity. Here, I can be anyone. Nobody knows me, and it's been fun playing out my new role of millionaire.

When I'm full, I skip up the stairs to my room to pack. I'm already fitter than when I arrived. First thing I do is shovel all the remaining gratis toiletries from the bathroom into my suitcase, and for a second wonder if my bag will still meet the airline weight restrictions going home. I doubt I'll ever use the sewing kit, the comb, the shaving gel, but it's hard to leave free stuff behind.

I then upend the tea bags, the half dozen Nespresso capsules, sugar and long-life milk cartons into a Mercadona carrier bag, and somehow cram the lot into my case.

After one last lingering look out over the grounds and pool below, I make a final visit to the bathroom. I wonder if I'll be back. If I am to return, I need to start tightening my belt, that's for sure. Anyway, all in good time.

A final check of the room, and I lug my suitcase down the stairs, preparing to settle my bill. I'm to wait for Pablo out front by the taxi rank.

This might be the end of one chapter, but I'm beyond excited for the next. A whole week with Isaac all to myself. I'm feeling so happy that I pull out a fifty-euro note, and ask the receptionist for an envelope. I scribble Logan's name on the front, and include a short note.

Hope to see you again. Keep in touch, and thanks.
    Jade

No idea what I'm thanking him for, but he was a pretty cool waiter. And I'm feeling ridiculously magnanimous, and weirdly, still a little guilty.

After today, I'll cut the tips. Who knows, if things work out with Isaac, I can start them up again.

14

_____

Isaac isn't at the villa when I arrive. I reread his latest text.

> I'm at work. Make yourself at home, and I'll see you for supper around 7. If there's anything you need in the meanwhile, speak to Marta.
> Isaac X

I'd almost forgotten about Marta.

Pablo drops me off by the front door, and before he drives away, presumably to garage the car somewhere, he tells me to ring the bell. Marta will let me in.

Marta seems as indispensable as Pablo, but even less communicative. When she opens the front door, having taken at least five minutes from my first stab at the bell, her expression has the set of a snarly bulldog.

'Hi. I'm Jade,' I say, extending a hand. Of course we've met before, and she must know my name, but anything to break the ice. She's so not the sort of person you'd voluntarily kiss, and she seems determined not to connect. She keeps her eyes averted, as if my stare might turn her to stone.

'Come,' she says, nodding with a tic of her head for me to follow.

Without preamble, she heads up the central winding staircase towards the bedroom I stayed in the night Isaac rescued me at Malaga airport.

It's hard not to cringe when I think back to what happened, but it seems so long ago. I manage to lug my case up the stairwell, and breathe more easily when I can wheel it the last few yards. Marta flings open the door, points to the bed, and disappears pretty sharpish.

I'm not sure whether to unpack, or wait for Isaac. If he asks me to share his room, I doubt I'll hesitate, but I mustn't jump the gun. There's always the chance that he feels sorry for me and is offering a charitable bed for the week. Who am I kidding? Sex is likely much higher up his priority list than charity work. The thought makes me blush.

It's really cold in the room, the air-conditioning up full blast. I can't work out how to open the glass doors that lead on to a balcony, as there doesn't seem to be a latch top or bottom, and the single windows either end are too high up to reach, and look to have integrated locks.

I get out my phone and check the weather, noting that there are amber alerts all over southern Spain, with daytime temperatures expected to climb to forty degrees in the next forty-eight hours. At least the air-con is working, but I can't face getting my swimming costume on until I'm outside. It's so cold, I could be in a butcher's walk-in freezer.

The en-suite bathroom is laid out with new soft white fluffy towels and a bathrobe wrapped up with towelling slippers inside, as if it's a hotel. There's even an array of mini toiletries. Shampoo, shower gel and scented soap bars. It would certainly make a great Airbnb destination. I unravel the gown, slide my frozen feet into the slippers and start to unpack essentials from my case. I plug in my electric toothbrush and pull a brush through my hair. Isaac isn't due back until around seven, so there'll be plenty of time for a shower and beauty session after some serious looking around.

I creep out of the bedroom and notice a little trail of dirt leading along the landing to my room. I don't remember walking over sand, or rough ground, so suspect it must be down to Marta. Or Pablo, perhaps. I tiptoe round, and head back downstairs.

The doors to outside are all also closed, and it's even colder than upstairs. I shiver as I wander around, looking for a way out. There must be a door somewhere that opens. It's so quiet that a faint scuffle of feet is hard to miss.

Marta appears from what I assume must be the kitchen, and stands in the doorway, blocking my way.

'Hi. How do I get out?' I ask. Even if she's not fluent in English, I doubt Isaac would employ staff with whom communication is impossible.

Marta leads the way down a corridor that seems to connect two separate wings of the villa. The passage is long, the glass and white theme blinding, and we pass several closed doors on the way. Marta keys in a number on a pad, and opens a door leading out on to a small patio, off to the side of the large, marbled terrace.

'Oh. Thanks. What's the code, so I don't have to disturb you?' I ask.

She shakes her head. '*No problema*. Come and find me,' she says, already walking back along the corridor.

Despite the show-home appearance of the glossy walls, sleek tiled floor and spotless glass, why is my first thought of psychiatric hospitals? The keypad system is seriously freaking me out. How can I keep the door open when I go back upstairs to collect my swimming gear, without having to bother Marta again? The door is spring loaded, and doesn't appear to have a handle on the outside. If I don't somehow wedge it open, I'll not be able to get back inside. Marta must know this, but she's seriously creepy and is already starting to feel like a prison warden.

I stick one of my shoes in between the door and the frame to hold it open while I scoot back upstairs to collect my things. I can see my stay might need some forward planning.

I get my phone, my swimming gear, suncream and book, and hurry back down.

When I reach the end of the corridor again, my shoe has disappeared. WTF?

'Marta? Marta?' I look all round. I spot my shoe on the other side of the door. Did Marta kick it out, and close the door? Perhaps she wants to keep the house cool for Isaac, as he did mention he's not a fan of height-of-the-summer Spanish heatwaves.

The shuffle sound is back, and soon Marta is keying in the number again, with her free hand shielding the pad as if it's an ATM machine. I must remember to get the code from Isaac later.

'Thanks,' I say, but she's already gone.

Once outside, the heat is suffocating. It's an effort to walk down to the pool area, but I spot a sun-lounger at one end, covered by a huge umbrella. As I go to dump my bag, I notice a handwritten note on top of the lounger.

Have a great day. Enjoy the pool. If you need anything, ask Marta. If you need to go anywhere, ask Pablo. See you later. Isaac. X

I grin from ear to ear, slip the note into my beach bag, rip off my T-shirt and start to slather my body with suncream. Although I'm under the shade, I'll not take any chances. I check my watch. It's not yet midday, and I've got hours to kill before Isaac gets back.

All at once I hear a cutting noise, accompanied by the grate of a saw. On the other side of the small olive grove, I spot Pablo. He's working on the garden, trimming, lopping and tidying. He's got one eye on his saw, the other on me.

15

Isaac is back early. It's only six o'clock. Shit.

I fell asleep on top of the bed for half an hour after swimming thirty lengths, and luckily the patio door was cracked open when I headed back inside. I've been soaking in a tepid bath ever since, reading on my Kindle... a psych thriller about a deranged serial killer. I've got to where someone gets murdered in their bedroom, and it's set me on edge. It doesn't help that I'm in about the only room in the villa that doesn't have a lock on the door. Anyone could creep in without knocking.

I wandered round upstairs earlier, no sign of Marta, and tried all the doors along the length of the landing. The only other door that opened was the one for what I assume must be Isaac's room. The whole place is like a ghost house, everywhere is so tidy, and there are no visible signs of clothing, and a dearth of personal possessions anywhere. Either Marta's a brilliant, A-lister housekeeper, or Isaac is never here. There's always the possibility that he's one of those bachelors who is insanely tidy.

Mum tells me there are two types of bachelors. One who lives in a mess waiting for a wife-cum-mother to tidy up after them, and the other who is so anally meticulous, most women run a mile.

From the state of Isaac's room, he's obviously the latter. To give him his due, he probably works away a lot. Hopefully, over dinner, I'll learn more about him.

I lie deathly still in the bath when I hear a gentle rap on the bedroom door.

'Jade? Are you in there?' Isaac calls through a gap that he must have created by easing the door ajar.

'Yes. Sorry. I'm in the bath. I'll be down soon.' I yell, as if I'm telling an intrusive hotel cleaner to come back later. It all feels pretty formal. Hopefully it won't be too long till things lighten up.

'Okay. See you soon.'

I don't hear him immediately move off, but catch Marta's voice coming closer. I climb out of the bath, wrap the enormous bath sheet round me, and tiptoe into the bedroom. I can hear them talking. It sounds pretty heated. At least I now know Marta understands English perfectly, as she's having no trouble giving her side of the story.

'Sorry, Isaac. I'll clean up the mess now,' she says, in a loud whisper.

Why do I think it's a deliberately loud whisper? Possibly because my stomach knots when I realise she's referring to some sort of mess outside my bedroom.

When I came up from the pool, the muddy marks on the landing were still there, but didn't seem too bad. I assumed Marta would have cleaned them up by now, but apparently not. From their conversation, it sounds as if the trail of dirt is still there. Isaac is telling her that he doesn't tolerate mess in the house, and she surely must know that by now.

'It'll not happen again.'

Why does the dirt lead to my bedroom? I know I didn't trail it up, so how did it get there?

It takes about twenty minutes for me to dry my hair, put on a small measure of make-up (Isaac has owned up that he likes the natural look), lip gloss, subtle eyeliner and a large squirt of perfume... a half-price duty-free treat from Luton airport.

When I'm finally ready, I peek out from my bedroom and notice the landing is once again spotless. Marta was pretty quick, that's for sure. And scarily quiet. She was probably a mouse in a past life.

Over the iron railing at the top of the stairs, I can see Isaac sitting outside, the glass panels opened the whole way now. He beams at me as I glide down the staircase. I'm aware I've worn the floaty white cotton dress before, and it talks comfy rather than designer. But when Isaac lets out a wolf whistle, I know it's hit the spot.

'Hi,' he says. 'You look good.'

Good enough to eat springs to mind. His teeth have taken over his expression, and I think of the wolf in 'Little Red Riding Hood'.

'Hi. Thanks. You don't look so bad yourself,' I say. I mean, what am I supposed to say to a millionaire who has everything, is handsome beyond belief, single, and seems weirdly interested in me?

'Love the hair,' he says. He runs a hand down the back of his neck, indicating he likes the flattened length, rather than the wild piled-high scrunched-up style he saw last.

'What'll you have to drink?'

'What's on offer?'

I know exactly what's on offer, because I heard the pop of the champagne cork from upstairs. There's a full bottle of Moët in an ice bucket on the table beside him.

'Will this do?' He very carefully, not a drop spilled, fills a crystal flute and passes it to me.

My hand is so shaky that a little dribbles over the side.

'Marta?' he yells. 'No worries, Marta will clean it up.'

Jeez, it's only a few dribbles on the patio. You'd think I'd spilled a whole bottle of red wine over a cream-coloured carpet. But give Marta her due, she appears with a cloth and frantically sops it up.

Maybe it's because I can't warm to her, but Marta is definitely looking smug. Pleased that I've already done something to irritate my host.

16

Despite my unease around Marta, she's a first-class cook.

Isaac and I eat on the terrace. Well, on another terrace, which I didn't know existed. It's further on round from where I exited earlier and next to an outdoor kitchen which is hidden behind a festoon of pink and purple bougainvillea. Marta wanders back and forth with tapas, followed by grilled fish skewers, all variety of salads, and baked potatoes, and regularly tops up our wine glasses. I'm in heaven.

When a piece of tomato rockets off the end of my fork, Isaac rolls his eyes, but Marta's on it like a bonnet. She's ridiculously subservient, but seems to relish the role of general all-rounder. Eager to please. Of course, I'm attaching a healthy salary to her laborious efforts.

'Well, Jade. Tell me about yourself,' Isaac says, once our ice cream and fruit desserts have been polished off.

'What's there to tell?'

'Is there a Mr Jade?' It's an interesting first question, but easily batted away.

'No. Dare I ask if there's a Mrs Isaac?'

I typed in a list of questions on my phone to ask him, and this was, of course, top of the list. I'm not sure how far down I'll get, but it's as good a place to start as any.

'There was.' Isaac sets his glass down and leans back in his chair. Perspiration coats his brow, and his usual pristine cool appearance is slightly awry. His linen shirt has tiny sweat bands under the armpits, and his Brad Pitt hair could do with a trim. There are at least half a dozen wayward strands sticking out at angles.

'Oh.' I'm not sure what to say. Did she die? Did she leave him? Or did he dump her? Perhaps a third party was involved.

'She left me,' he says.

What? Why would anyone leave this guy?

I sit up.

'I'm sorry.' It feels awkward to pry, but finding out about ex-wives is number one on my list. I need to probe. If I'm to snare my millionaire, I need to know what makes him tick, and learn about his past.

'Don't be. We were going through a rocky patch. Well, that's what I thought it was.' He gives a wry smile. 'Things must have really got to her, because...' He takes a sharp intake of breath.

'Yes?' I'm all ears, willing him to hurry up.

'I had no idea she was in such a state. She suffered from depression, you see. I tried often enough to get her to seek help. But it seems she was too far gone.' He closes his eyes. 'She killed herself.'

'Oh no.' I'm genuinely shocked. Why would his wife kill herself when she seemed to have everything? 'I'm really sorry.'

He answers the next question, which is on the tip of my tongue, as if he can read my thoughts.

'Her name was Astrid.'

'Hence, Casa De Astrid. The name of the villa.'

'Yes,' he replies, raising a single eyebrow. 'She lived here before we got married. The plan had been to rename the villa, but it never happened.'

'I'm sorry.' The *sorry* repetition is hard to break, as I'm not sure what else to say. I want to ask how she killed herself, but again he beats me to it.

'It was less than three months ago. Astrid loved yachting, and speed-boats. She would sail or race around the coast on her own. The water was a passion.'

'She was a good sailor?' I've visions of a strong, athletic woman, tanned and windswept from the elements. I certainly can't compete with my imaginings. I feel proud that I wasn't seasick on the boat, let alone skipper on a one-woman catamaran.

'They found the speedboat she'd chartered, abandoned, a few miles round the coast.'

Isaac is surprisingly calm in the telling, but I'm in shock. OMG. She jumped overboard. I bite down on my lip.

Out of the corner of my eye, I notice Marta standing to attention. She's been listening, taking it all in.

When Isaac finally changes the subject, on to the dangers of the building heatwave and the need to keep cool and stay indoors, it's my chance to bring up the subject of getting in and out of the villa.

'I couldn't get outside earlier. Although Marta came to my rescue,' I begin. 'Could you let me have the door and gate codes, then I won't have to bother her?'

'I hope you're not trying to run away?' His playful twinkle is back. 'No worries. I'll write down the codes for you.'

'That would be great.'

'I'll also have to lend you a front door key, because once you've entered the code, you'll still need a key to open it.'

'Sounds like a plan.'

Sounds more like Fort Knox, but maybe he's hiding an expensive Rolex watch collection somewhere and is paranoid about burglars.

Marta suddenly reappears, having crept up on us, and starts to clear away the dishes. She asks Isaac if there's anything else he needs before she clocks off.

'No, thank you, Marta. We'll be fine from here. Catch up in the morning.'

'Thanks,' I echo, but she totally ignores me, and somehow manages to clear the table in one sweep. I'm scared she's going to drop the lot. Plates are balanced along both arms, and I can imagine her practising using her head. Her upper body is certainly strong, her arms muscled as if from working out.

When she's out of sight, I ask Isaac if Marta has been with him long.

'They moved in about the same time as I did. Astrid had been living on her own, but I persuaded her it would be good to have help around the villa. It is rather large.'

He's not wrong there.

'They?'

'Marta and Pablo. They're married, you know.'

I didn't know, and I wonder why I hadn't guessed. They're obviously very loyal to Isaac. Again, I wonder how big their pay cheques must be – or perhaps work here is hard to come by.

When Isaac tells me there's accommodation to go with their jobs, it starts to add up.

'If you go through the garage in the basement, there's a door at the back. They have a little self-contained annex with a small garden plot of their own.'

'Nice,' I say.

Very nice. That would explain their dedication, as I know property in this area is exorbitant.

Isaac doesn't seem to have a list of questions for me. He seems to know I'm a millionaire, a default assumption. If not a millionaire, at least a lady of means, but he doesn't pry. I rest more easy when I dare to believe it might not be my money that attracted him.

He asks if I'd like to walk round the grounds and have a proper look about before turning in.

'I'd love that,' I say.

He holds out both hands, and pulls me out of my seat.

'But first,' he says, 'there's something I'd like to do.'

'What?' I blush like a schoolgirl when he wraps his arms round me. His lips move gently over mine, until his tongue gets involved, and in an instant, the world of swimming pools, marbled patios and scented flowers feels like paradise.

Who'd have thought one scratch card could have found me Mr Perfect?

It's only as we untangle our bodies that I see Marta over my shoulder.

She's staring from the open kitchen door. Her eyes are narrow slits, her mouth buttoned up. Pablo comes up behind her, circles her waist, but she pushes him away, and snaps at him like a crocodile.

As Isaac and I walk away, I can feel her eyes following us.

What the hell is her problem?

17

I didn't need much persuading, that's for sure. When Isaac followed me up the stairs last night, he asked if I'd like a nightcap in his room. At first, I thought he was joking when he said he has a loaded minibar in his room. He certainly wasn't joking. His fridge is more jam-packed with goodies than the ones at the hotel.

By the time he popped the cork on a second miniscule bottle of fizz, I was already half-naked, and Isaac wasn't wearing much more. It all happened so quickly, so effortlessly, as if it was meant to be. Written in the stars.

When I wake up this morning, I feel as if the room is moving. And it is. The monster of a bed we slept in is huge, and circular. A remote control makes it move... round and round, and it's still revolving. I wonder if it's been moving all night, or if Isaac switched it on again before he left. It's certainly left me feeling spaced out, and completely disorientated.

I reach for the remote, stretching across the full diameter of the bed, and press *stop*. There's no sign of Isaac, but he told me after we'd made love (more than once, I might add) that he had an early start, and wouldn't wake me. He'd see me tonight. I must have been in a really deep sleep because I didn't hear a peep when he left.

Today, I'm to use Pablo as my personal driver if I fancy doing a bit of sightseeing or shopping. Isaac promised to message me places of interest. When I look at my phone, I notice I have six new WhatsApp messages. One from Mum, again, and another one from Connor. Apparently he's been kicked out of his flat and is begging me to let him temporarily share my bedsit. Over my dead body. I tell Mum all is great and delete Connor from my contacts. He's now officially history.

The other four messages are from Isaac, suggesting places to go. Marbella for shopping, and lunch perhaps. Mijas Pueblo, the white-washed village in the hills which is a magnet for the Brits. Perhaps the village of Ronda in the mountains if I'm not freaked by heights and hairpin bends. He's so thoughtful, and so trying to make my extra week a time to remember. I opt not to tell him I've decided to go back to Puerto Banus, as it's close by, and I never got a proper look around. There'll be plenty of time to do the other sights before I leave.

I linger in the shower in the en-suite to Isaac's room, making use of the free gel, soap and shampoo, which are in similar-sized containers to those I nicked from Los Molinos. Looks as if Isaac and I mightn't be too dissimilar, as there's a full, neatly arranged basket with a variety of hotel toiletries from all parts of the world.

The towels are like those in the guest bedroom, all white, soft and fluffy, as if they've never been used. I fold them neatly when I've finished, and carefully arrange them over the heated towel rail. It's a welcome feature in the bathroom, because the air-con is back on and the bedroom is freezing again.

On my way out of the bathroom, I notice a Post-it note attached to the inside of the door.

Good morning, Jade. Hope you slept well. Please leave bathroom floor dry, as it gets very slippery. Thanks. See you this evening. I xxxx

I slip the note into the pocket of my bathrobe, before ripping a few tissues out of the silver box on the wall, and wiping the drips off the floor. Isaac is right. The floor is like an ice rink.

By the time I'm dressed, my stomach is growling. And although it's not Los Molinos, I can't complain about the breakfast. On the marble-topped breakfast bar, croissants, brown and white bread rolls, a selection of cheeses, cold meats and a colourful array of fresh fruits are laid out. There's another Post-it note from Isaac stuck on the Nespresso machine.

Help yourself. Better than the hotel, I hope! Try not to leave any crumbs, as Marta is a stickler for cleanliness. Laters. xxxx

I'm so worried about dropping flaky crumbs from the croissant that I opt for a couple of fresh rolls and fill them with ham and cheese, and pop them in my bag. I also include an apple, an orange, and a banana. Once I'm away from the villa, I'll tuck in. For now, I stick to a couple of strong espressos, forgoing the milk and sugar hazards, and leave everything otherwise as I found it.

When I'm ready to leave, I set off to find Marta to let me out, as Isaac forgot to give me the key. I've got the door codes on my phone, but without a key, I still can't get out.

As I'm mooching around downstairs, she materialises in the foyer like a hovering ghoul.

'Good morning, Marta. Would you mind letting me out, please? And is Pablo by the pool?'

'Yes. He's by the pool,' she says, keying in numbers and jangling a bunch of keys.

'Thanks. Have a good day,' I say.

No point in us both being downright rude. If it's possible, she looks even more pissed off this morning than she did when I arrived.

Anyway, it's great to get outside, although the sun is already high in the sky, not a cloud in sight, and the heat is savage. I scrummage round in my handbag, and realise I've forgotten my suncream. But to be honest, I think the lobster look might be better than facing Attila the Hun again.

Pablo seems to share his wife's sixth sense, because the car engine is already running when I appear, and again, he's grinding a cigarette end with his toe. When he sees me, he lifts the butt, and stuffs it in his pocket. He bends down, and with his fingers swishes away speckles of cigarette ash by his foot.

Perhaps it is Marta who has an issue with cleanliness, but why am I uneasy that Isaac might be the one with the obsessive tendencies?

Pablo is like a personal bodyguard. Too short in stature to be threatening, despite his hard-iron muscles, but he's bloody determined. I tell him I'll text when I need picking up, but he shakes his head, holds up a palm.

'I come with you. Just in case.'

'I might be some while,' I say, wondering why he's got nothing better to do, and what does he mean *just in case*? In case of what? The possibility that Isaac might have asked him to spy on me seems ridiculous, but it does cross my mind.

'*No hay problema.* Is no problem,' he says with a dreadfully cheesy smile. At least it's one up from his wife's miserable pout. 'Wait five minutes, and I come with you.'

He goes off to park the car, but I don't hang around. I take a swift left, aiming to shake him off. On the way, I pass Isaac's motor yacht. The same skipper is standing at the front of the boat chatting to a young couple. He tips his cap at them, indicates for them to look around. I duck behind a wall, and watch what happens next. Five minutes in, the skipper starts up the engine, and the young couple settle on deck and pull out a couple of cans of beer from a rucksack.

I didn't realise Isaac chartered out his yacht. But then again, perhaps it's not his and he hires it out himself for guests. Guests to impress.

Guests like me. I assumed it was his yacht, the way he showed me round. Maybe I got it wrong.

The temperature is now so high, the heat is scrambling my thoughts, and I'm feeling decidedly on edge. I dig out my scrunched-up straw hat from my bag and pull it on, along with a trendy pair of Oakley sunglasses I picked up at the duty free along with the perfume. I decided to leave my fancy white-rimmed glasses at the villa, keen to avoid the spectacled-owl look for a second time.

If I buy a cheap T-shirt, swap it for my canary yellow one, perhaps Pablo will give up on me. Hopefully not report back to Isaac that I've given him the slip.

There's a narrow alleyway a few yards further on, and I dive into the shade. At the far end is a pavement board flashing up a picture of a frothing pint of Guinness. When I reach the entrance, the cool bar with whirring overhead fans entices me inside. It's on the dark side, but that suits, as Pablo will be hard-pressed to find me, even if he does look round. I may as well play him at his own game.

I order half a lager, then get out my phone to catch up on Wordle. I'm just about to take a sip of drink when I notice there are three new messages. All from Isaac.

Jade. Hope you're having fun. I hear Pablo dropped you off at the port again. Wonder if you'd do me a favour? X

The favour details come in a second message.

Would you mind popping to the motor yacht we took the other day, and speak to Mario, the skipper. I owe him excursion fees, and he's chasing them. I can't access my bank account for some reason where I am (Wi-Fi down, and phone signal sporadic), and wonder if you'd settle them for me. It's not much – £5,000, give or take. I'll reimburse you this evening when you're back home. Really appreciate. I X

WTF. Really? The third message leaves me no option.

Oh, and I'm missing you already. What say I take you out for dinner tonight? Give Marta a night off. I know a great Argentinian Steakhouse a few miles inland. XXXX

Common sense tells me to ignore him and get the hell out of here. But this is Isaac. We slept together. He's hot, wealthy and gorgeous. And it is only £5,000.

It's laughable that I think it is *only £5k*. A few months ago, this would have paid my rent for a full six months. As I drink the lager, knocking it back rather too quickly, I realise that if I pay out this amount, my bank balance will be down to £25,000. But my promise when I won the money was to enjoy myself. Live dangerously. I'm certainly living dangerously, but I'm no 007. Caution is in my genes, and I've been living hand to mouth for as long as I can remember.

Okay. Will do. I'll call and see Mario while I'm at the port.

I leave out the kisses. A reply bounces straight back. I shovel to the back of my mind the fact that he says he's out of Wi-Fi range – despite his protestations, his phone signal seems to be working perfectly.

Thanks! Really appreciate. Mario will give you the exact balance, along with a copy of the bill. Don't worry, I'll pay you back this evening. With interest! XXXX

I turn my phone off and attack the lager. I order another one, to help me relax. But it's really tough. The most I can pay out of my account at one time is £5,000 without changing my bank settings, and I've no idea of my log-in details. If it's over £5,000 I'm in trouble.

At least, hopefully I've given Pablo the slip.

19

I'm tipsy, to say the least, from lager, heat and nerves. I sit by the port for half an hour, hat pulled low, wearing a new blue and red striped top I've picked up from a T-shirt kiosk. I binned the canary-coloured one, as I need to downsize flying home, and it was much too tight.

I watch Mario steer the boat carefully into its berth before I get up.

I stroll over, and as I draw close, he instantly calls out.

'*Hola*,' he says. 'Jade?'

How the hell does he remember my name? Isaac didn't introduce us properly when we went out on the yacht, so it's more than likely that Isaac has contacted Mario since, and told him I'm on the way. I'd not be surprised if Pablo appears from below deck, and the way I'm feeling at the moment, I'd not be surprised if I'm taken hostage.

Mario is slick, I'll give him that. There's a printer next to the microwave, and in five minutes he hands me a copy of Isaac's latest invoice. For the months of June and July.

Five thousand one hundred and forty-two pounds. I don't ask why it's not in euros, as Mario doesn't seem in any mood for pleasantries. He tells me to take a seat on one of the leather benches and opens up a laptop for me to use to log in. He's thought of everything. When I say I'd prefer to pay by card, he produces a card machine with a flourish. Think white-rabbit slick.

He's not so accommodating when I tell him my withdrawal limit is £5,000. I suggest he adds the extra £142 to Isaac's next bill.

'There'll not be a next bill,' he snarls, but when he enters the exact amount of £5k, I enter my pin, and thankfully the payment goes through without a hitch. He tears off the payment slip, and plops it down beside me. I'm too wound up to wonder what he means by 'no next bill', and I scurry off the yacht like a criminal who has been in the process of settling a drugs debt.

There's a general buzz around the port. People are lazing everywhere. It makes me wonder how there's so much ostentation, alongside so much inactivity. I can't believe everyone is on their lunch hour.

At one end of the harbour, past the alleyway with the Irish pub, is a small seafood restaurant. My stomach is growling, and I'll pass out if I don't eat something. I remember the filled bread rolls in my bag, which I'll probably end up feeding to the seagulls. The smell of fish and the sight of huge pans of paella do their pitch. I look through the open door, deciding I'll eat inside as the temperature is still rising. It must have hit the mid-thirties because sweat is pouring off me, and my new top is already drenched.

There's a woman sitting alone at a table by the window. People are chatting, laughing all around her, but she's like *The Silent Patient* – a book I've just read. She's staring blankly out to sea. Why do I recognise her? She looks so familiar, but I can't place her.

Then I remember. It's Emmeline. The woman who accosted Isaac in the restaurant the other night. I don't remember her looking so old, but she's got to be in her late forties, early fifties. Her hair is grey, with fading highlights. She looks defeated, and all I can think of is the noise she made as she howled on Isaac's shoulders.

A waiter comes up to me and asks if I'll be dining.

'Yes, please. Give me a minute as there's someone I need to speak to first.'

I'm not sure the hunky young waiter understands, but he lets me past, and I head for Emmeline's table.

'Emmeline?' I ask. I aim for telesales polite, and an expensive jeweller's smile.

She blinks a few times, as if trying to bring my face into focus. She looks spaced out, as if she's drunk, or high on magic mushrooms.

'Yes. Who are you?' She speaks with clipped pronunciation and puts a heavy accent on the word 'you'.

'Jade. Jade Wiltshire. I think we sort of met the other night? Do you mind if I sit down?'

I put my hands on top of a chair, and she doesn't object when I slide in across the table.

'Where did we meet?'

'I was with Isaac. In a restaurant.'

Her face turns to one of horror. Her eyes widen and dart around in their sockets as she looks furtively from left to right. If she'd a sharp knife in her hand, I suspect it might come my way.

'You're his new woman. Good luck with that,' she spits, accenting the word 'luck' this time.

'I've only just met him,' I say.

'Where?'

'Sorry?'

'Where did you meet him?'

'On a flight to Malaga,' I say. 'And you?'

'I was staying at Los Molinos hotel. That's where I met the bastard.'

'Oh. That's where I was staying until a few days ago.'

'You're now staying at the villa?' Emmeline gives a weird hyena-type laugh. It could be her accent, but she definitely sounds unhinged.

I nod. My stomach is now lurching, rather than rumbling. I'm dreading what she's going to say next.

'Good luck with that,' she says for a second time. 'If I were you, I'd get out of there as fast as you can, before he locks you in.'

The waiter reappears and plonks a menu in front of me. At the same time, he sets down a plate of grilled prawns and battered calamari for Emmeline.

'If you don't mind, Jade, I'd like to eat. Alone.' She stabs at the cala-

mari, and manages to attach a piece to her fork, and nibbles on the end
with her small incisors.

I get the message and put a hand up to the waiter to indicate I'll not
be staying.

'One more question. Why did you and Isaac split up?'

'He conned me out of all my savings, and then threw me out.'

My heart starts to beat rapidly, and I come over all woozy. Anxiety is
mingling with an empty gut, and my head starts to spin. The sight of the
sea over Emmeline's shoulder makes me feel like I'm back on a boat.

'How much money?' I ask.

It's a loaded, nosy question, and while Emmeline chews on the calamari, I think she might ignore it.

'One hundred and fifty thousand euros. It was my life savings. I've got
nothing left.' She gulps on a long glass of water and waves a hand to tell
me she's had enough. 'Now if you don't mind, I'd like to be alone.'

'Sorry for bothering you, Emmeline, but thanks for talking to me.'

I scramble back out into the heat and can hardly walk. It's like a
sauna, and I tug my hat on again, stumbling back the way I came. At the
far end of the marina, I see Pablo talking to someone. He flaps a hand in
the air, letting me know he's not far away. Did he see me talking to
Emmeline? Or has he stayed at the same end of the port since he
dropped me off? It's like being trailed by a private detective.

Fearful of passing out, I sit down on a bench in a rare bit of shade and
dig into my handbag. As I haul out a squashed-up ham and cheese roll,
desperate for sustenance, a business card falls out.

I read the details printed on the card. *Marbella Inmobiliaria. Carlos
Fernandez.* I remember the slick sales agent from the hotel, and when I
check the address on the card, I realise the property company is less than
fifty yards away.

I don't know why, but I suddenly have an interest in Marbella property prices.

20

I walk with a swagger past Pablo. It's the only way to go, as I'm done with skulking in doorways. It's my holiday after all, and I've no idea why I've resorted to sneaking around. When he sees me, he does the grinding-cigarette-butt routine again. I feel like a Mafia boss's moll, minus the ostentatious gold and diamond accessories.

Outside the Marbella Inmobiliaria, I check out the properties on show in the window. The cheapest one on offer is a snip at 750,000 euros. When I know Pablo is looking (I can see his reflection in the shiny glass window), I trail a finger down the details of a penthouse apartment in the port, and take a photo. Might as well enjoy myself if I'm to be hanging out with Isaac for a few more days. Although, it's hard to be gung-ho when I'm in knots worrying about the money I've just paid across to Mario. It's clouding my drunken feel-good moment.

I keep having to wipe my brow, as a steady stream of water is trickling down my cheeks.

I decide to bite the bullet, and venture inside. I push open the thick gold-handled glass doors and am hit by a wonderful sheet of cold air. I stand under a huge ceiling air-con unit, whip off my hat, and flap a hand up and down against my face.

'Hola, señorita.'

Carlos greets me from behind an enormous desk, but stands up immediately when I walk in. As he approaches, he extends a hand. 'Ms Wiltshire, if I remember correctly?'

He's either got an incredible memory, or someone has told him I've a cool £20 million in the bank, and that maybe he should follow me round as well. It's a bit scary that I might be on the local Mafia's radar.

I ignore the outstretched hairy hand and wander over to a display board headed up *Apartamentos*. Before I have a chance to blink, Carlos is alongside, proffering a glass of sangria. Why not? My throat is parched, and it looks like nectar.

'Thanks,' I say and gulp down the cold raspberry-coloured liquid. I'm not sure quenching my thirst with alcohol is the best idea, but I remind myself, again, that I'm on vacation.

'Are you interested in a property? An apartment perhaps? There's plenty of choice.' Carlos oozes sales-agent slime, and is already licking his thick lips with a bulbous tongue.

'Yes, I am. Any bargains?' I mosey up and down the display, pausing and peering at a penthouse five minutes from the port. Seven hundred thousand euros. A snip.

'The one you are looking at has just been reduced in price. It is now only 680,000 euros.' He could be telling me there's a special offer at the supermarket on fresh eggs, or free-range chickens. I mean, what is 680,000 euros? 'How about that?' he says.

How about that indeed? I knock back the sangria, and he's already topping up my glass.

Pablo has been skirting back and forth outside, and is currently peering over the sea wall on bent knees, looking on to the deck of an obscenely ostentatious superyacht. It makes the motor cruiser Isaac chartered look like a boating-lake rental.

Carlos scuttles back to his enormous desk and pulls out a shiny brochure from a teetering pile.

'Here you are, Miss Wiltshire. May I call you...?' He's aiming for familiarity, to suck me into a friendship that will make it hard for me to resist his sales patter.

'Jade. That's fine, Carlos.'

My head is already more than a bit woozy, but I'm feeling much more relaxed than I've felt all day. The loss of £5k mightn't be the end of the world, although I know when I sober up, it'll feel like it. Anyway, I need to give Isaac the benefit of the doubt. Especially since I slept with him.

Suddenly my phone beeps with a new message. It's Isaac, again.

Hi. Hope you're having fun, and Pablo is looking after you. See you later. Have booked the Argentinian steakhouse as promised. Think you'll fancy it. Oh, and make sure you're hungry! Isaac xx

What's not to fancy? I'm not sure whether it's the sangria, or a sudden feel-good moment, but I'm now thinking I've been really harsh on Isaac. Mainly down to Emmeline. I've only got her word for it that he fleeced her out of so much money. I can't imagine what it would be like to lose your life savings. It feels bad enough that I've handed over £5k. But I need to hold the faith. It's Isaac after all.

I message straight back.

Sounds like a plan. See you then. Yes, Pablo being very attentive, and I'm starving!

I err on the side of caution and leave out the kisses. Isaac might appear really keen, but I feel a need to play at least a bit hard to get. My stomach gurgles with excitement, and I let myself imagine again what might be. Perhaps there is a chance of a future with Isaac. Who knows? And... last night was pretty amazing.

Don't look a gift horse in the mouth springs to mind.

Carlos stands very still, waiting for me to finish on the phone. His back is now to the entrance, and I'd need to sidle round him to make an exit. But I don't, as I'm starting to enjoy myself.

I sit on one of the large black leather sofas that face out towards the sea and the bright sunshine. I'm enjoying the heat from the inside looking out, momentarily forgetting its savage attack.

I thumb through the brochure Carlos has given me, and he's soon sitting next to me on the sofa, rather too close for professionalism. But what the heck.

'Looks amazing,' I say.

I've reached the last few pages in my book, *How to Live Like a Millionaire*, and I'm now using Carlos to put into action the sage suggestions, and yes, I do feel like a million dollars.

Embrace the life of a millionaire.

Go to the expensive shops. Browse.

Treat yourself, as often as you can afford, at the most expensive restaurants.

'You say it's been reduced?' I hold my glass up, sip, and raise a brow at Carlos with wide-eyed excitement. He's falling hook, line and sinker.

'Yes, indeed. It's now just 680,000 euros. It's most unusual for a sudden reduction, but the owners are very keen to sell. Family problems, I understand.'

Carlos speaks very good English, I'll give him that. He could be from Essex if it wasn't for a weird off-piste twang to his accent.

'You know what?' I say. Carlos has developed a tic on his jawline, no doubt through the excitement of a potential mouth-watering sale.

'Yes?' He smiles, a large toothy affair, and raises a monobrow.

'I'd love to see it. Have a proper look round.' I flick from cover to cover, and back again.

Carlos is quickly out of his seat. I turn my gaze back outside for a second and shiver when I see Pablo has his nose pressed against the glass. While staring at me, he's trying to operate his mobile phone at the same time. If I'm not mistaken, he's taking a picture.

'Of course. I'll get on to the owners now,' Carlos says.

'I'm not sure exactly when I'll get there, but it'll be in the next two or three days,' I say. I wave at Pablo, hold out my glass, and ask Carlos for a top-up.

21

I'm seriously squiffy by the time I head back out into the sauna. Not sure if I'm seeing double, but the concreted pavement around the port seems to be melting. I gingerly navigate over a couple of bubbling areas, feeling nearly as disorientated as when Isaac rescued me at Malaga airport.

Pablo is soon shadowing me. Maybe it's the mood lift from the sangria, but I finally slow down and let him catch up.

'Pablo. Can we make a stop on the way back?'

'Where would you like to go?' His smile melts away, a bit like the concrete underfoot. He stuffs his hands in his trouser pockets. I assume Isaac doesn't let him out in shorts, but he must be boiling.

'Los Molinos, if that's okay? I think I left a pair of sunglasses there, and want to see if they've got them.'

'That's fine,' he says. But it doesn't look as if it's fine. He checks his phone, and I wonder if he'll have to ask Isaac's permission to make a detour.

I manage the walk to the car, but each step in the now 38-degree heat is an effort. A red alert is out for the whole of southern Spain, and people are advised to stay indoors unless absolutely necessary. The gauge is now to hit 40 degrees by the weekend.

We drive off in silence, me in the back, and Pablo with one hand on the wheel. At least it's up from one finger. When we hit the AP-7, he does his customary weaving at breakneck speed through the traffic as if he's Lewis Hamilton. It certainly isn't helping the wooziness. I look out the window, but can feel Pablo's eyes bore into me every so often through the driver's mirror.

He slows as we reach the hotel, and the Merc cruises up to the entrance. A porter I recognise, whom I tipped over-generously, grins from ear to ear when I step out. He greets me like a long-lost cousin.

'I won't be long,' I tell Pablo, although I've no idea how long I'll be. It depends if I can find Logan or not.

I'm still feeling pretty mean at having ditched him as soon as Isaac appeared on the scene. It's much too early to go back and face Marta, so I'm hoping he might be on duty at the tapas bar and we can catch up. Also, I could do with some serious snacking to keep me going.

Pablo has left the car running, and the porter is trying to move him off. Out of the corner of my eye, I notice a brightly coloured euro banknote change hands. It's all really starting to get on my nerves.

I've no idea why it bothers me so much that Isaac wastes his money, but I suspect it's down to the fact that I've rarely had enough cash to buy a pint of milk. And the thought of the £5k I lent Isaac is seriously niggling.

I saunter out to the main pool area, and I'm in luck. Logan has a tray of empty glasses in his hand, and is heading my way.

'Logan,' I screech. No idea why I screech, but he seems like a friendly face in an otherwise tense situation. Also, he's looking pretty cool in a white shirt and hip-hugging black chinos.

'Jade.' He smiles, but it lacks enthusiasm. Okay, I get he feels peeved, but surely he'll let me make it up to him. Also, I want to pick his brains.

'Are you busy?' I ask, although I can see he's not. The place is deserted. There's no sign of even the most hardened sun sizzlers under the umbrellas.

I've no idea how Logan manages to look so cool, not a bead of sweat in sight.

'Not too busy,' he says.

'Well, I'm here to keep you company.'

He strides ahead as if he's trying to give me the cold shoulder.

At least the tapas bar is under shade with a couple of fans whirring their comfort overhead. I nestle directly underneath one, plonk my hat on the bar and turn my face upwards. Heaven.

Logan busies himself behind the counter, drying glasses, chopping lemons and limes, and doing everything possible to avoid conversation.

'What can I get you?' he asks.

I'm tempted to go for a white wine, but as I've got a hot date with Isaac later, I decide against it. I've had enough to drink, and I seriously need to sober up.

'Fizzy water, please.' Before he has time to get my drink, I add, 'Listen, Logan, I'm really sorry.'

Not sure what for exactly, other than bumping into the apparent millionaire of my dreams, but I do feel guilty. Logan seems like a good guy.

'What for?' he asks in a sulky tone.

'For disappearing when Isaac came on the scene. Do you know him?'

'Sort of. He's a regular at the hotel. Comes for dinner, drinks.' He doesn't look my way, but wipes a cloth across the bar in front of me.

'Do you know much about him? Anything you can tell me?'

He mulls the question over, takes a moment to answer.

'He's a millionaire. But I guess you already know that.' He lets out a sarcastic puff of air.

'I'm staying at his villa. For a few days.'

'Good luck with that.' This time the sarcasm is linked to a quiet, but distinct, laugh. He sounds scarily like Emmeline did earlier.

'What do you mean?'

He sets down my fizzy water and carefully attaches a slice of lemon to the rim.

My cheeks are so hot, I hold the iced glass to my face. 'That's better,' I say, before taking a long swig.

'He seems to like the ladies, that's all I can say.'

'Did you know Emmeline?'

His delay in responding sets me on edge. I can tell he did know Emmeline. It's in the grim set of his mouth.

'Vaguely,' he says.

'Any idea why they broke up?'

He looks round the pool area. A couple have appeared and are wandering aimlessly. He looks right and left, then drops his voice to a whisper.

'She accused him of stealing money from her.'

'Oh?' I wobble on the stool, sliding to one side before I manage to right myself again. 'Did he?'

'Well, he says she gave him money to help with the bills when she was living at the villa. He never stole it.'

Logan's crimson cheeks, and the shaky tremor in his hands, tell me he knows more than he's letting on.

'Do you know Isaac well then?'

'He drinks here, and he likes to chat. He's also a good tipper.' He gives a wan smile, hinting at mine and Isaac's similar millionaire habits. I wonder if Isaac tips as well as I do. The thought makes me want to giggle, but I hold it in.

'Did you ever talk to Emmeline?'

Logan turns to a very complicated-looking computer till, keys in numbers, codes, and whatever else a barman who has very few customers to serve needs to do. He prints off my bill, and sets it down in front of me.

'Listen. I need to get on.'

'Did you ever talk to Emmeline?' I repeat.

'Isaac told me not to.'

With that, Logan wanders off towards a lower pool terrace, where a few people are preparing to brave the rays.

I drink up, forgo ordering a plate of tapas, and head back towards reception. When I see Pablo sitting on the Moroccan bench inside the front door, I head to the desk. The pretty waitress whom I spotted talking to Isaac is waiting for me.

'Hi. I'm not sure if you remember me. I was staying here for a week and I think I left a pair of sunglasses behind. Could you check for me?'

She's not going to check. She's rooted to the spot.

'No, sorry, madam. There are no sunglasses in Lost Property,' she says with a closed-mouth smile.

How could she know if she doesn't look? Then I'm aware of Pablo behind me, standing up.

Of course, he's already asked. It's as if he's been checking up on my real reason for coming back to Los Molinos.

22

I breathe more easily when we get back to the villa, and as the gates slide open Pablo finally slows down.

I thank him, get a cursory nod in response, and head round the side of the villa to try to gain access. Anything other than having to alert Marta by ringing the front bell and staring into the security cameras.

No such luck. She's sweeping the patio, which is already spotless, and like Pablo, barely acknowledges my appearance. It must be a family trait, or else Isaac has warned them both against familiarity with guests.

Luckily, the patio doors are thrown wide, and I don't need to creep along the length of the villa looking for an opening. As I step inside, the cold blast of air is like an oasis in the desert, although, in less than ten minutes I've goosebumps up my arms and am shivering uncontrollably from the icy conditions. I head up to my bedroom, thinking it best to shower and change there, and not make assumptions about returning to Isaac's room. It feels as if a week or two has passed since we swivelled on the circular rotating bed, yet it was only last night.

I close the door, wishing there was a lock on it, as everyone seems to creep around the place. Even Isaac has a stealthy tread, and I'm not a fan of sudden unannounced appearances. Connor used to creep up from behind and boo on me, thinking he was hilarious. The more I freaked out, the more he'd carry on doing it.

Marta is the queen of creeping around, and it's off-the-scale unsettling, but at least she's unlikely to jump out and yell.

There's an unfamiliar scent in my room, and I realise Marta must have been in to clean and tidy up. It's like a five-star hotel experience, but to me, it feels like Marta is snooping. My suitcase has been lifted out from under the bed and is now sitting atop a strappy, luggage rack (which I don't recall being there before). I need to tell Isaac that I'm happy looking after my own space. I'll freak if there are chocolates on the pillows when we get back tonight.

The shower is fabulous though, and the jets assault me from all angles. There are tiny spray heads, which I didn't notice before, set into the sides of the shower walls. They come on without the need to turn dials. It crosses my mind that someone must have reprogrammed the settings because they definitely weren't working last time.

As I'm getting dried, I hear a text pop through on my phone. I scoot back to the bedroom and sit on the bed, water dripping from my hair.

See you in half an hour. Looking forward to it! I XXX

I reply with a thumbs-up. I'm still not at the XXX stage, even if Isaac has got there rather quickly. I've no idea why I feel the need to hold something back, as I've been pretty easily seduced. But talking to Emmeline, and then Logan, has left an uneasy feeling in my gut. The only way to shift it will be to find out for myself what really makes Isaac tick.

It takes a while to dry my hair, which seems to have grown a few inches in the sun, and definitely needs a good trim. It'll have to wait till I get back to England, as I'm not sure I want to ask Isaac for hairdresser recommendations. Marta's hair is so tightly drawn back that I don't suspect she's a salon regular.

I tidy round the sink, hang my towels up neatly and go dig out my sexiest outfit. In the heat, even at midnight, it might be too hot, but the skimpiest evening dress I've got hangs below my knees. The cream fabric swirls and the fine red straps match my sassy open-toed red sandals.

My heart is pounding and my stomach somersaulting as I leave the room and head towards the staircase. I see Isaac down below talking to Marta.

Oh.

I step behind the wall, peer round the corner and see him stab her in the chest with his finger. Three times. He's so not happy with her. I wonder what she's done wrong this time?

I let out a little cough, and Isaac steps sharply back. His smile lights up at my appearance, and he whistles using a thumb and forefinger. No worries about #MeToo with this dude. He can whistle all he likes. Tonight, he looks better than Brad Pitt has ever looked, if that's possible.

Isaac's trademark white linen shirt is ironed to perfection. I've never seen a linen shirt look so smooth, and his cream chinos have such an expensive cut. No idea how I know they're an expensive cut, but probably because they lack visible creases, other than a knife-sharp edge running down the centre of each leg.

How can he get back from a day's work looking so smooth and unruffled? He hasn't even been upstairs for a shower, but then again, perhaps he has one at work. I've still no idea where he works, and what he does for a living (something to do with investment choices), but perhaps, after a few drinks tonight, he'll tell me. I'm itching to get to know him better. He's certainly keeping a lid on the mystery.

'Jade. Wow. You look amazing,' he says. He stretches out both hands, pulls me close, and lets his lips linger on mine. His aftershave is subtle, but he looks concerned when I cough. It sort of catches in my throat. 'You okay?'

'I'm fine. Just a tickle.'

'Well, are you ready? Pablo is waiting.'

Bloody Pablo. I was sort of hoping we could have ditched him for the evening, but no such luck.

'Yep. Good to go.'

Isaac keeps hold of my hand as we head out. Behind a wall, I see Marta. She's watching us, and if I'm not mistaken (although I could be as it's just a glance), she's wiping away tears. She must have done something really wrong to get Isaac so annoyed.

Anyway, once we're in the back seat of the Merc, air-con on, soft music playing, I put Marta to the back of my mind.

Tonight, I'm going to enjoy myself.

23

The small, off-the-beaten-track restaurant is on the way to Mijas. It's not oozing five-star ostentation, with its wooden shell, barred-up windows, and tabletop electric fans, but Isaac tells me it serves the best food in southern Spain.

I don't remind him that's what he said about the first restaurant we visited, the one where Emmeline gatecrashed the party. I don't want to spoil the moment, as Isaac is soon visibly unwinding.

We get seated at another very cosy table in the corner, and Isaac stretches his long legs out to one side of the compact rickety table. Once again, he seems on very familiar terms with the overly enthusiastic staff.

'I've ordered paella. In advance. It's to die for,' he says, filling my glass from a carafe of cold white wine which has appeared on the table. Considering it's an Argentinian steakhouse, I'm gutted. I have been dreaming of red dripping steak, with all the trimmings, for the last couple of hours.

'Sounds good to me,' I say, totally unprepared for more paella. I've overindulged in seafood since I got here, and am desperate for juicy red meat. Somehow, I manage to paint on an eager smile to match Isaac's full-on happy face.

'I know their steaks are legendary, but I'm not much of a red meat eater,' Isaac says, stretching a hand on top of mine. 'Hope you don't mind if we stick to the fishy theme.'

My expression, when he mentioned paella, mustn't have gone far enough in disguising my disappointment. But I'm so hungry, I think I'll have less trouble than usual negotiating the fiddly shells and stomaching yet another plate laden with salty seafood.

The young waiter tells us it will take about twenty minutes, and Isaac assures him we're in no hurry. That's what I'm picking up by gestures and watch-pointing anyway. Must say, I'm impressed by Isaac's command of the lingo, as it definitely adds to his sex appeal.

'Anyway, Jade. Tell me how your day was. You've been busy, I hear.'

Bloody Pablo. I wonder if he has to do written reports.

'Yes, I've had fun. I went to the port, and paid your charter fees by the way.'

'Thanks. Mario has been getting pretty shirty, demanding payment, as if I'm not a regular client.' He tuts, rolls his eyes. I don't tell him Mario said it was to be his last bill. Instead, I sip steadily on the wine, wondering how long it will take for Isaac to ask for my bank details to refund the £5,000. Even though I paid the fees on his behalf, I feel uncomfortable asking how long it'll take to get my money back. In Isaac's millionaire world, £5k must be like reimbursing 50p. Thoughts of Emmeline aren't helping me keep things in perspective.

As if reading my mind, he says he'll repay me later. That'll have to do for now, but I'll not relax until I get the money back. Five thousand pounds is a huge amount where I come from.

'I hear you popped into an estate agent's in the port?'

'Yep. Thought I'd see what was on the market.' I sound like a casual window-shopper, but Isaac seems really keen to know if I'm serious about making a purchase.

'Are you thinking of buying in Marbella?' His eyes are aglow. Maybe he likes the idea of having a lady friend close by, without having her move in to his villa. The thought gets me twitchy.

'Toying with it. It was one of the reasons I came here.' I'm starting to believe my own spiel. Funny how one lie can balloon into a whole life story. But, what the heck? Where's the harm in playing the game?

'Property isn't cheap around here,' he says, staring at me rather intently.

'You can say that again.'

Why do I get the feeling he's itching to ask if I can afford it? Perhaps he'll try to sell me a mortgage. He's into high finance, although I've no idea what that means.

'Did you see anything you like?'

'Plenty,' I say, coughing and hiccupping from too big a mouthful of wine.

'If you want me to have a look with you, I'd be more than happy.'

Strange, I got so used to analysing everything Connor said, trying to second-guess his meanings, that I'm already doing the same with Isaac. He's asking pretty innocent questions, but why am I suspicious? Again, the chat with Emmeline springs to mind, as well as the throwaway comments Logan made. I definitely feel the need for caution, but it's too tempting not to carry on.

'I've seen a penthouse that's just come down in price and looks pretty stunning. I'm going to have a look round before I head back.'

'Oh. When are you heading back? I thought you'd be here a week or two.' He pulls himself up, as if I've made a very important announcement.

'Another few days, then I need to get back. My mum isn't too well, and I don't like to leave her on her own for too long. If I buy a property, she'll be able to spend time in the sun.'

Why am I lying? I'm well into the millionaire storyline, but the lie about my fit and healthy mother came a bit too easily. I certainly can't tell Isaac that I need to go home and look for another job. I can't go back to the nursing home, as it sucked me dry. The Covid pandemic took everything out of me, and now I need to find a new career. Although I've no idea what I'd really like to do.

'Well, let's make the most of your next few days,' he says. 'And let's get that apartment in the bag.'

The young waiter, Francis, and an older lookalike, his father perhaps, approach, pushing a trolley carrying the most enormous dish of paella. I think of the first restaurant we went to, the laden trolley, the sizzling pans. Isaac seems to be a man of habit, that's for sure.

The fishy smell ratchets up as the food nears our table. I'm now so hungry, I'd eat anything that was put in front of me.

'That looks amazing,' Isaac says, looking from Francis to the older guy, and to me in turn. He then repeats the sequence, and I have to push back the panic when I see the dish is full of mussels and clams. I like paella, but I'm not a fan of the fiddly shells. Mussels are piled high. At least if I make a mess over the tablecloth, or flip the shells on to the floor, Isaac can't complain. He'll not need to motion for Marta to clear up.

'Wow,' I say, with as much enthusiasm as I can muster. I'll need another carafe of wine to block out the smell and taste of the shellfish.

'*Muchas gracias,*' Isaac says, and when I repeat his words, he laughs and winks.

* * *

Once we've finished eating, Pablo appears out of nowhere, and motions to Isaac. Isaac gets up, tells me he'll just be a minute, and goes outside to speak with him.

When he comes back, there's no sign of Pablo, and Isaac suggests perhaps I'd like to go for a walk. Work off some of the food.

I'm not sure whether I'm more excited to dislodge some of the paella, which has sunk to the pit of my stomach, or to get Isaac to myself. The thought of a walk in the balmy night air sounds just the ticket.

24

We meet up with Pablo about an hour later. I'm feeling much better from the exercise, but I'm also relieved to see our driver as I'm now exhausted and ready to get back.

The journey only takes about twenty minutes. The car purrs through the gates of the villa around midnight, and both Isaac and I are in a relaxed, chilled mood.

'Fancy a nightcap?' he asks when we're back in the spotless surroundings of the eating area. 'Probably best we stay inside as the mosquitoes are rather busy round the pool.'

'Sounds good to me.' Although I'm not sure I could stomach another drink. But Isaac is so upbeat, and chilled. Funny, the way he is at the moment, it makes me realise how uptight he is generally.

It's very quiet inside the villa. There's no sign of Marta, and Pablo has turned in for the evening. I'm curious to see their annexe out the back; it's at the top of my to-snoop list before I head home.

I sit on a white – spotlessly white – chair by the small indoor pool. I've worked out that the shallow square of water is purely for show, not for using, although it looks very tempting, with its romantic underwater lighting and soothing wall jets.

'Let me make you one of my special cocktails,' Isaac croons, before he slips into the room where Marta usually lurks. I'm assuming it's a kitchen. It's just below the *annexe-through-the-garage* on my snoop list. I'll be poking my nose in there definitely before I leave.

Suddenly, all around, soft soothing music filters through what must be hidden speakers. Wherever he's gone to, Isaac must have turned on a music system. The melody sounds like waves breaking on the shore, it's that soporific, and threaded through the sleepy sounds are birds chirping. I feel as if I'm on a therapist's couch about to be hypnotised.

Isaac reappears carrying two V-shaped cocktail glasses. I don't ask what's in them, and decide *why not*. A single nightcap can't hurt.

He sits on the chair next to mine, and we both face the dip pool. Wall lights have come on and complement the underwater glow with their beams shining across the surface. I reckon the water is no more than a metre deep, but it's so magnetic that I'm sort of hoping Isaac might suggest a midnight swim. Okay, a midnight dip, but it's so tempting.

Then, without comment, he throws down a lumpy envelope on to the glass-topped table between us.

'For you,' he says.

My heart misses a beat. Could it be tickets to a sold-out show? Or, maybe, just maybe, flights to a Caribbean island? I'm now so squiffy from drink and excitement, my mind is in overdrive.

'What is it?'

'Your money,' he says.

My disappointment that it's not something more romantic is rapidly replaced by relief. I've been trying not to worry about the money, but I'm beyond relieved. Not only because I've got my £5k back, but that Isaac has come good on his promises.

'Thanks. I'd forgotten all about it.' I laugh. As if! If I'm to have a few more five-star trips, I'm going to need it. Not to mention, Mum is at me to find somewhere to live. I might not be able to afford the flat in Muswell Hill she's suggesting, but if I'm to get out of the bedsit I'll certainly need a healthy rental deposit for something bigger.

I take the unsealed envelope and peek inside. It's a wad of what look like unused fifty-euro notes. Even in my squiffy state, I wonder how many euros he's given me. I know that £5,000 is approximately 5,500 euros, but now doesn't seem like the time to check.

Nor does it seem the time to ask, *why all the cash?* It's more than welcome, but I was expecting him to ask for bank details to do a transfer.

Isaac's eyes are drilling through me, so I set the envelope back down.

'Cheers,' I say, holding up my nearly drunk cocktail.

'What say we go up?' Isaac's eyes shine. He stretches his hand out to take my empty glass and then straightens his chair (yes, really) before he disappears with the empties. A few seconds later, he's back, and when he sees I've aligned my chair neatly alongside his, he smiles.

'Thanks. I like things neat,' he says. An understatement if ever I heard one.

Once Isaac has turned off all the lights and activated the downstairs alarm, we head up the winding staircase. It feels so grand. I hover at the top, and he takes my hand and leads me towards his room.

'This way, young lady.'

I'm a bit unsteady on my feet, but I put a hand to my cheeks which are burning up. I follow in silence.

His room looks even larger than it did last night. Wall lights are already on, dim in their sconces. While I sit on the bed, butterflies in my stomach, Isaac disappears into the bathroom. Everything is really quiet, and after a couple of minutes, when no noise comes from the bathroom, no taps, or toilet flushes, I get edgy.

Something feels off-kilter. What is he doing, and what's taking him so long?

25

A few seconds pass, and then Isaac appears in the bathroom doorway, holding up a wet bath sheet in one hand and what looks like a sodden bath mat in the other.

'Jade?' His voice is low, almost a growl. Even in the half-light, I can pick up that he's furious.

'Yes?'

'What are these?' He sounds like a robot, emphasising each word in a harsh tinny voice.

'They look like towels from where I'm sitting.'

WTF.

'What did I tell you about leaving the bathroom the way you found it?'

I suddenly feel squeamish, nervous, like a child preparing for a full-on ticking off. Perhaps a smack on the bottom and grounded for a year.

'I hung up the towels and put the bath mat along the top of the bath. The way I found them.'

I did, didn't I? Yes. I did. I remember being meticulous in making sure the edges of the towels were aligned. Heaven knows why, but I'd already picked up that Isaac is a neat freak and likes a clean and tidy ship.

'Come in here if you don't mind.' He motions me over with a wagging forefinger and steps to one side as I enter the bathroom.

OMG. The place is in a state. Toothpaste globules are splattered around the sink. A few straggling hairs, the same colour and length as mine, are hanging over the edge. The tops of the shower gel and shampoo containers have been left *in* the bath, and there's a solid dirty ring around the porcelain as if someone bathed there covered in mud.

'Jeez. It's in a state,' I say. I put a hand over my mouth, actually shocked by the mess.

Isaac nudges my back with a stern finger towards the sink, and from a cupboard underneath, takes out a cloth and thrusts it my way.

He thinks I'm the one who left the place in this state.

'Perhaps you'd be so good as to clear up your mess.'

'It wasn't me,' I say, but I can tell he absolutely doesn't believe me.

'You were the last person to use my shower, so...' He widens his eyes. His lips seal in fury. I don't think I've ever seen anyone look so angry. Except Connor perhaps, when I told him to piss off, that we were over.

'I did not leave this mess,' I say, but Isaac has already stormed out. I listen to him stride across the bedroom, out the door, and slam it behind him.

I'm now seriously shaking, freaking out. How did the bathroom get this messy? I didn't even use the gel or shampoo, and I hate loose hairs anywhere. The sight makes me gag. I so did not make this mess.

Then it hits me. Marta. She's been following me round. She always makes a point of clearing up the slightest crumbs I drop in full view of Isaac. I remember the dustpan and brush appearing more than once.

Why? Why the F. does Marta want me to appear so slovenly? I know she doesn't like me, doesn't want me at the villa, but what is her game? Could she be jealous? Perhaps she and Isaac have history, and she's pissed off at the competition.

Whatever is going on, I set to cleaning the bathroom. One thing I do know is that I'll be going back to the guest bedroom. If Isaac thinks I'll sleep with him now, he's got another think coming.

As I set to scrubbing the surfaces, and refolding the towels and mat, I look in the mirror which stretches the length of one wall. All this luxury, potential, yet through smears coating the glass, I can see tears in my eyes.

This is not what I'm looking for.

26

I don't sleep a wink. I've had one ear pricked all night, half expecting Isaac to appear. Either to hand me a mop and bucket, or to beg me to come back to bed. Although, he'd be crazy to think I'd even consider the latter. Lustful thoughts have completely drained away.

When I do hear muted voices outside my room, I check the time. I must have finally given in to a couple of hours' sleep, as it's now 8 a.m. I slide out from under the duvet, then straighten it meticulously, sort of wishing I had a tape measure with me to make sure it hangs evenly. My jaw is locked in anger, and I'm not sure I'll be able to reel in the fury when I come face to face with Isaac.

Deciding against a shower in case I leave a rogue drip on the floor, I pull on a pair of shorts and a T-shirt. But it's so cold upstairs that goose-bumps stipple my arms and legs, giving me the look of an uncooked chicken, and I have to tug a sweatshirt over my head. Isaac is certainly not saving on electric bills, that's for sure. The air-con, if it's possible, is making the room feel even colder than it did yesterday.

When I leave the bedroom, there's no one about. I inch along the wall at the top of the landing and peer down at the scene below. At least the glass doors out to the terrace are open, if only by a crack, but there's no sign of Isaac or Marta. The silence is seriously creepy, a lot worse than hushed voices. If this is the millionaire lifestyle, then I'm out of here.

My bare feet inch down the stairs until I'm at the bottom. It's then I notice a huge multicoloured bunch of flowers in an ostentatious frosted-glass vase. Apart from a smattering of red roses, I'm at a loss to identify the other varieties. Propped up against the vase is a handwritten note.

Jade. I'm sorry for yelling last night. Just really tired, and I am overly obsessive when it comes to keeping the place tidy.

I sort of soften when I start reading. Okay. He's sorry.

But the next bit makes me want to pick up the vase and hurl it across the room.

Don't worry about tidying the mess. This time, I've asked Marta. She's an ace with a cloth and mop. Enjoy your day. Pablo is at your beck and call, and is awaiting instructions. I'm off to Malaga on business, so catch up later. Let me know when you'd like me to come and view the apartment with you.

Isaac XXXX

I put my phone down, deciding to let Isaac stew. I opt not to go near the croissants, ham and cheese, and leave the breakfast buffet, coffee cup and plate untouched. I'll not be blamed for any movement of the fine-boned china to either the right or the left.

Through the patio doors I can make out Pablo's outline near the steps down to the swimming pool. He's holding up a set of shears and is trimming overgrown foliage woven through a wooden arbour. He was probably tasked with putting together the bunch of flowers.

I decide to have a snoop around the villa before I summons him to drive me back to the port. Although I've seen some of downstairs, there's a corridor leading through to the garage which I haven't been down. Also, there's a set of stairs leading up to the roof terrace.

I remember Isaac telling me the views on the roof terrace are to die for.

'There are sun-loungers and umbrellas, and even a fridge filled with ice-cold drinks in the corner. Make yourself at home. It's totally secluded, so if you fancy going topless?' He'd grinned, and I'd blushed, feeling quite hot under the collar. Now the thought makes me shiver.

Rather than going out through the patio doors, I do a U-turn, and mosey down the long corridor to the left of the staircase. There are several closed doors either side, and again I think a hospital corridor or mental institution. The walls are bare, with small square windows every few paces. They're head height for people six foot plus, but I'd have to jump up and down if I wanted to get even a glimpse of greenery.

At the end of the corridor is a solid wall without windows. Off to the right is a large fire door, with a small plaque attached marked 'Garage'. I need both arms to haul the door open. It grates from effort. Inside, there's a concrete stairwell winding down a couple of flights, like stairs leading off a multi-storey carpark. The walls echo, and as I head down towards the basement, the heat ratchets up to a suffocating level, and by the time I reach the bottom I'm seriously sweating.

The garage is marked out in bays for at least ten cars, it's that large. But apart from the Merc that Pablo drives Isaac around in, there is only one other car. A Fiat 500, which I presume is Marta's. The walls are a dark, sombre grey, and the ceiling is so low it feels as if it's closing in. I certainly wouldn't want to get trapped down here. There are, what appear to be storage rooms off to the right, and at the far end a small, red-painted door. When I reach the door, I pull it open, and am instantly blinded by sunlight.

I jump back inside when I spot Marta standing in the garden of a small plot, talking heatedly on her mobile. She's out front of a compact, rustic-looking finca. What hits me though, isn't the low-stone-walled building, but the enormous, steep walls that surround the bijou garden and building. The only way out seems to be back through the garage, up the stairs, and along the mental hospital corridor.

I hover a moment and turn my ear outwards. All I can pick up through the smattering of Spanish conversation is the one word: Isaac. Over and over again.

* * *

I scurry back through the garage and up the stone stairwell till I reach the fire door. I push my shoulder against it, and start to panic when it doesn't open. Shit. I'm sweating buckets, and again use both arms to smash against it. It gives a few centimetres, then with a last effort, I manage to jam my foot into the opening and squeeze through. My ankle screams in agony.

Holy shit. I'll not be in any hurry to go back down there, that's for sure. How the heck does Marta come and go? There must be another way down to the garage, or else Marta is seriously strong from all the hard labour, not to mention all the cleaning.

By the time I get back to the marble-topped eating bar, I've calmed down, but only just. The breakfast food has been tidied away, and the surface is gleaming. Marta must have been very quick, and somehow got down to the annexe before I did. It's always possible Pablo popped in and lifted the breakfast stuff away, but it's unlikely. His working shoes aren't the cleanest.

I sneeze, my nostrils agitated from the stench of whatever cleaning agent has been used. It's been effective though, as I can almost make out my reflection in the shine.

I'm now shivering from the cold, and the panic. I walk past the indoor pool, my stomach knotted from the memories of me and Isaac sitting here last night, and all at once the water jets spring to life, making me jump. They must be on a timer system, but it's as if my movement has activated them.

I glance over my shoulder, a strange feeling I'm being watched. Last night the jets gave off a merry, welcoming effect, but this morning the sight only ratchets up the chill.

This time, I walk in the opposite direction, to try to find the door leading up to the sun terrace. Soon, I'm on a narrow staircase, that seems to go on for ever. When I reach the top, my heart is pumping, and I slump against the wall to catch my breath. I'll count the number of stairs going down, but the terrace is so high up, it must tower over the grounds and neighbouring properties. At least the door at the top pops open easily.

And voila!

Wow. The terrace is enormous. By the door is a huge cast-iron doorstop, so, taking no chances, I wedge the door open for a quick getaway. No idea who I think will be following me up, or chasing me down, but I feel safer with it that way.

The heat is heavenly, but then it is still early. I wander round, and round, wondering what views Isaac was talking about. The walls here, like those around Marta and Pablo's finca, are so high, and the area so secluded, that you'd need a fifty-foot ladder to see anything. Though it's definitely the spot for a bit of topless sunbathing. I decide one of the sun-loungers might be the place to settle later this afternoon. But only after I've been to see Carlos and arranged the apartment viewing.

I'm feeling more positive about Isaac, now I've come up with a plan to find out if there's any possibility of something more than a holiday romance between us. I need to know what makes him tick, and whether I can trust him. Emmeline, Logan, and the wagging finger incident have left me feeling decidedly uneasy. But I'm not ready to throw in the towel quite yet (especially as we spent the night together, and it was pretty amazing). One-night stands are not my thing. And as Mum says: 'There's more than one way to skin a cat.'

I know Isaac paid me back my £5k pretty quickly, but what if there had been more money involved? Would he have paid me back so promptly? There's still the niggling doubt (well, perhaps a tad more than niggling) that he's after me for my fictitious millions. Well, now's the time to find out. Last-chance saloon. I wonder if he'll be as trusting to lend me money. Mum's in my head again: 'Trust has to work both ways.'

I might enjoy looking at apartments, pretending I'm a serious buyer, and in the process upping my millionaire profile. But at the same time, I might just have come up with a way to test Isaac. Give him a chance to prove himself, and see what he's made of.

I skip back down the stairs from the roof terrace, deciding for definite that when I get back from the port, I'll do a few lengths of the pool and then go back up and doze on a secluded sun-lounger. Maybe I'll even get a chance to finish the last pages of my millionaire manual.

I might as well enjoy my last few days.

27

Pablo scurries across when I appear with a bag slung over my shoulder. It's nearly eleven, and the temperature is already rocketing. Warnings are out to stay indoors between midday and 4 p.m. At least the Merc is air-conditioned, as well as Carlos's offices. I can already taste the cold sangria and suspect I'll get a whole pitcher when Carlos hears I want to view the penthouse. Though I'll need to pick up a couple of pastries, and a coffee first, to line my stomach.

Pablo looks even worse than I did earlier. Despite his swarthy weath-ered complexion, in the driver's mirror I can see dark rings suffocating his eyes. He never says much, but today his mouth is even more zipped than usual, and he's not even watching me. He seems miles away. I know he must really be under the weather because he drives within the speed limit, gripping the wheel tightly with both hands.

When we get to the port, he doesn't ask where I'm going, but drops me off at the same place as before, and sits without turning off the engine. Yay. Looks as if he'll not be following me, but I'll not count my chickens.

I pick a little café at the far end of the port and eventually perk up after three strong coffees. I feed crumbs from my pain au chocolat to the hovering gulls. I giggle thinking that perhaps Marta should keep a gull as a pet to assist with speedy clear-ups.

Relaxed, replete and feeling more like myself, I stroll back towards the action.

Carlos is standing by his window when I approach and moves quickly to throw the door wide.

'Jade. How good to see you again,' he enthuses with a very cheesy grin. Estate agents seem to have a genetic smarminess, but that's okay. Today, I'm going to give him even more than he was hoping for.

'I'd like to see the penthouse property. The one that has been reduced in price. How soon can we see it?'

'"We"? Oh, is there a Mr Jade?' he asks, his smile more twitchy now there might be a second person to schmooze.

'Ha, ha. No. Definitely not. I've a friend I'd like to come and look round with me.'

'Another pretty *chica*?'

'No, a gentleman. Not a husband, just a good friend.'

'*No hay problema*. No problem at all. It's good to get second opinion. When would you like to view the property? I can arrange now.'

'Later today would be good. I'll text my friend and see when will suit.'

'And your friend's name?' Carlos raises an eyebrow, which soon droops when he hears my reply.

'Isaac. Isaac Marston.'

Carlos's face is a picture. Of course he'll know Isaac. Puerto Banus is a rather cosy place, and I suspect local millionaires have reputations. Judging by Carlos's expression, Isaac's isn't too hot.

'Oh, I see. Are you buying on your own, or together?' he asks. His smile has evaporated, along with the gushing mannerisms.

'Yes. I am indeed buying on my own. Isaac is purely giving me advice.'

I'm back on the sumptuous leather sofa while Carlos makes a couple of calls. As an afterthought, he pours me a rather mean measure of sangria, but it still tastes amazing. Every sip is pure nectar. My glass is empty by the time he comes back to confirm that he can show us the penthouse around 4 or 5 p.m.

'Perfect,' I say, wiggling my empty glass.

'More sangria coming up,' he replies.

I get out my phone as it's time to message Isaac.

Appointment lined up to see the apartment. Can you meet me at the port at 5? We can walk with Carlos from his office. Thanks. Jade

I dither whether to leave kisses, but decide against, opting for a professional tone. If Isaac comes good, there'll be plenty of time for kisses.

A couple more sips of sangria, and I add a second message.

Oh, and thanks for the flowers. Lovely.

When I pat the padded cushion beside me, Carlos sits down. He suddenly seems to come over sweaty despite the cool of his office, and I nearly burst out laughing when I realise he thinks I'm coming on to him. In his dreams.

Yet I get his full attention when I start talking. Telling him of my plans, and milking his obvious dislike of Isaac for all it's worth. I also let him talk, and OMG. He certainly doesn't keep a professional lid on his tongue.

There's more than one way to get what one wants, and Carlos is soon eager to help. It's amazing what 1,000 euros can buy. Especially, 1,000 euros in clean, crisp banknotes, slipped into his back pocket. It's a lot of money, and Mum would go crazy.

But it's my money, so let's see if it'll get me some answers. It could be my future we're talking about.

28

I am pretty drunk by the time I leave Carlos's office. What with the sangria, the heat and nerves, I'm decidedly wobbly. Rather than going back to the villa, I spend the next few hours sightseeing further along the coast and stop every so often to find a spot in the shade. I even crash out on a very comfortable sun-lounger, falling asleep under an enormous parasol until a guy comes and asks me if I'm a guest at the hotel. I look aghast when he tells me I'm on a private beach and I can't sit on these particular stripy sunbeds.

After a few mumbled apologies, I scrabble my things together, before checking my watch. Jeez. Lucky the guy did accost me because in half an hour I'm meeting up with Isaac.

I walk back the way I came, refreshed from the doze, but butterflies are battering my insides with thoughts of what I'm about to do. It mightn't have been the best idea to suggest meeting Isaac in the Sea Bream Bar, a five-minute walk from the property agent's, but I'm in desperate need of a couple of drinks for Dutch courage. It's the only way to go or else I might back out.

I'm under a large blue and white awning, clutching an enormous glass of Viña Sol, when I see the Merc pull up. Isaac, for a change, is sitting in the front. He's usually happy to lounge in the back when Pablo ferries him from A to B, but for some reason he's not today.

A couple of girls, millionaire-pulling tourist types, sitting at the next table, do a double-take when Isaac gets out. He does look drop-dead gorgeous, sporting a light-blue shirt and navy slacks. Despite the heat, he looks amazingly cool. The navy tinted sunglasses ratchet up the film-star appearance. He walks so upright, he could be a Hollywood A-lister. There's a definite swagger, and the girls are now giggling behind their hands. They've no chance unless they've a few million in the bank. Maybe it's the drink, but my cynicism is growing by the mouthful.

Perhaps I should just have fun with Isaac before I set off on my next adventure. But I'm not into casual sex. I'm after Mr Right, Mr Perfect, and I need to find out if Isaac is going to cut it. I'm not excited about tiptoeing round a neat freak, one who waggles admonishing fingers, but he is really hot. And Mum tells me often enough, that relationships are all about give and take, and only loose women engage in one-night stands.

'Hi. You been waiting long?' Isaac bends, kisses me on the cheek and glowers at my half-full wine glass.

'No, just got here,' I lie. Despite the head start on the wine, I'm feeling ridiculously nervous. There's something dangerous about Isaac that seems magnified by the drink, rather than diminished. He's got a sharp-edged dagger look in his eyes. He's either disapproving of me drinking on my own, or disapproving at how much I drink. Either way, it doesn't matter. After Connor, I promised no man would ever again tell me what to do. Maybe the wine and sun is making me paranoid because Isaac asks if I'd like another one.

'Before we go and see the property?'

I'd love another one, but I know it's time to stop.

'No, thanks. Maybe have one after we've done the viewing?'

'Fine by me. Do you want to lead the way?'

About fifty yards from where I'm sitting (Isaac is still standing), I spot Carlos outside his office. He waves, jiggles a set of keys in the air, and starts heading in our direction.

'Oh. It's not that crook Carlos Fernandez, is it?' Isaac laughs, stuffs his hands deep in his pockets and sneers.

'Why? Do you know him?'

'Who doesn't know Carlos? A property shark. Anyway, let's go.'

Isaac stretches out a hand and hauls me to my feet, gripping me tighter than usual. We set off, but I'm in no hurry, a panic attack threatening, and Isaac has to hold his long stride in check. We pass the motor yacht we cruised on, and Mario is on deck, staring our way. He's wearing a white flat cap today, trimmed in red and blue. He's switched from the Spanish flag colours of red and yellow to those of the Union Jack. Maybe he alternates colours, depending on the nationality of his clientele. He turns his gaze in the opposite direction when we walk past.

As Carlos approaches, Isaac releases my hand.

'Isaac. Good to see you,' Carlos announces, extending a hairy, dumpy hand that gets swallowed up by Isaac's slender manicured fingers.

'You too, Carlos. Business good?'

Isaac has no interest whatsoever in Carlos, but at least he's making an effort.

The three of us walk the few yards back the way Carlos came and then take a right turn into a side alley. It's narrow, but the walk up is steep, and none of us talk until we reach the top, where a small white apartment complex houses the penthouse property.

Carlos keys in a code (what's with all the codes?) on an outer gate, covering the pad with his free hand. When there is a loud click, he motions for us to go in, but promptly calls us back, and points up to the third floor where a glass wrap-around balcony envelopes a large property.

'That's it up there,' he says, indicating the position of the apartment with one hand, while shielding his eyes against the sun with the other.

'Wow. Let's get inside.' I scream like an excited child, while Isaac's hands are back stuffed in his pockets. His expression is deadpan, as if he's seen it all before. But then perhaps he has.

Carlos filled me in on the number of properties Isaac has viewed over the last couple of years. At first, Carlos thought Isaac might be a competing property agent, but when Isaac always came to viewings with pretty women, he changed his mind, wondering what his game was. All

Isaac's girlfriends couldn't be looking for a property, surely. That said, the women Carlos showed around all looked once, and never came back.

Anyway, now certainly isn't the time to worry about Isaac's past girl-friends, or what his game might have been. Now, I need to have a look around, and see if this is the anything like the penthouse I've always dreamed of.

And, more importantly, to find out for myself what Isaac is made of.

29

The lift up to the apartment is miniscule – think another sardine can – and even though it's only three floors up, when Carlos presses his finger on the button, I ask directions for the stairs.

'Not a fan of enclosed spaces,' I laugh.

So not a fan. I'm panicking just looking at the metal death trap. If it did break down, I'd never cope with being trapped inside with Carlos and Isaac. That would be worse than being trapped in on my own.

'The stairs are this way,' Carlos announces, and takes the lead.

Three flights up, he slots a key into an unmarked door and flings it wide open.

'Voila!' He sweeps an arm across his body and steps aside to let us in.

'Wow, wow, wow,' is all I manage.

There's a huge living/dining area, kitted out with plush grey linking sofas with white cushions. The kitchen is fitted out with built-in Bosch appliances, half of which I don't recognise. But they'll do. There is a separate shower room with toilet on the corridor leading through to a master bedroom, which has an enormous en-suite, and two guest bedrooms that share a bathroom.

But it's the terrace that does the selling. It is enormous and wraps around the whole property.

'South facing, except the small, shaded side section.' Carlos again does a sweeping-arm-gesture thing, this time pointing out the Mediterranean in the distance. It doesn't need pointing out; I'd buy the place for the view alone. I have trouble swallowing back several more wows.

We look over the balcony wall, and down below is a huge community pool. Apparently, there is also an indoor pool and gym. What's not to like?

'And... there is 24-hour security,' Carlos says. He's certainly doing a very slick sales pitch.

Isaac wanders round on his own, looking serious. His brow is slightly puckered, but I bet he's loving the cleanliness and sleek lines. Not a crumb in sight.

'Well? What do you think, Isaac?' Carlos asks.

'Really? It's good.'

Understatement or what, but I have to remind myself Isaac lives in a £5 million property where nothing has to be shared.

We're all pretty quiet for a bit, wandering, mulling and staring out at the views. Then Carlos pops his sales folder onto the beige marble-topped table. He clears his throat with a husky cough.

'I need to tell you both that we have had an offer this afternoon – twenty thousand euros under the already-reduced asking price.'

I manage my horrified face, and even plop both palms against my cheeks.

'Oh, no. You mean it's already been sold?' I stare at Carlos. 'Why didn't you tell us before we came to view?' I add a bit of grit to my tone.

'How much?' asks Isaac.

'How much? You mean how much was the offer or how much is it on the market for?'

'Either will give me an answer to both questions.' Isaac laughs. He's got that scornful look again. He really doesn't like Carlos, that's for sure, but their mutual dislike is a bonus where I'm concerned.

'On the market at the already-reduced asking price of 680,000 euros,' Carlos snaps.

'Has the offer been accepted?' Isaac asks.

'Not yet. We haven't been able to contact the vendors, but have emailed and texted them the offer.'

Isaac looks at me. My lips are pouting, downturned, and my eyes glaze over with tears. I won't start sobbing, until it definitely appears like a total no-go.

Carlos is now wandering round the living area, back and forth to the glass wrap-around doors. He's lathered in sweat – think mangrove swamp – and his receding black curls are stuck to his head in moist clumps.

'The only thing I could suggest is that if Miss Wiltshire pays a deposit today, then I'd take it off the market.' Carlos doesn't look at me, which is a good thing, as I'm finding it hard to keep a lid on it.

'How much of a deposit?' Isaac asks.

Good old Isaac. Bet he's tough in business.

'Twenty-five per cent.' Carlos is sharp with his reply, but Isaac is already working out how much is needed to get the property off the market.

'That's 165,000 euros. Presuming the owners are willing to accept the offer of 660,000? I am assuming you already know they will.' Isaac expels a puff of scornful air without looking at Carlos.

Instead, he comes up to me and tilts my chin with a finger until I'm looking into his glassy blue eyes. Carlos moves outside, and with his back to us, stares out to sea.

'Well, Jade? Are you going to go for it? It's a great property, and the price is competitive.'

I slump on a dining chair, as if my knees have given way. My heart is pounding in my ribcage and the apartment is toasty hot. No air-con blasting to cool down prospective buyers.

'It's not that easy. I'd love to go for it, but...' I cover my face with both hands.

'But?' Isaac sits down beside me. 'What's the problem if you like it? It's a great investment and a fantastic holiday home. All-year-round sunshine, what's not to like?'

I consider that Isaac might be in cahoots with Carlos, and they're doing a double-pronged sales pitch to persuade me to buy. But despite

Carlos's seedy appearance and slick patter, I trust him more than I trust Isaac. Call it gut instinct. Also, I've already greased his palm, and am certain he will play ball. Especially as there's more cash dangling.

'The maximum I can withdraw, without giving forty-eight hours' notice, is £20,000. The bulk of my money is locked away in bonds and other investments, and I'd need even longer to access serious amounts.'

To my own ears, I sound ridiculous; the £5,000 I lent Isaac was a serious amount from where I come from.

'Oh.' Isaac pulls back, his eyes scanning the lounge as if for clues. Not sure clues for what, but his mind is definitely ticking. 'Carlos?' He summons Carlos as if he's a slow-moving waiter who needs to get his skates on.

'Yes, sir.' Good old Carlos. He's pretty quick at getting his professional hat in place.

In a second, he's alongside me.

'Would you accept a £20,000 deposit as Miss Wiltshire could transfer this amount across immediately?' Isaac asks.

'No. I'm really sorry, but that's not how we work.' Carlos is now talking in a low whispering tone. Think Mafia, under-the-mattress-money sort of tone. He's assuming Isaac will know how shady deals work. 'I would need the whole 165,000 euros paid today, or I'll have no option but to accept the other offer.'

There, he's said it. I now start to cry, amazed at how the tears flow. My cheeks are soon sodden, and I wipe my fingers across moist nostrils.

'How long did you say it would take you to get the money, Jade?' Isaac's eyes are intense and bore through me.

'It would be two days before I could have the full amount. The whole 660,000 euros.' I do great puppy-dog eyes. Connor used to hate it when I pleaded with droopy jowls, but it never failed to work. Let's see what Isaac's made of.

It's as if time stands still, and no one moves. Until Isaac breaks the silence.

'Listen. I could perhaps pay across 145,000 euros, Miss Wiltshire 20,000 euros...' He turns to me, 'And Jade...'

'Yes?' I'm scared to smile.

'You can pay me back in forty-eight hours. Perhaps with interest?' He's smiling, but he's not joking. A few seconds pass, and Isaac goes quiet, as if he's regretting what he's just said. I can sense a big but coming up.

Now is the time I should pull out. Say that I can live without this property. There'll be plenty more, but I've got Isaac where I want him, and I mightn't get another chance.

'Did you know Mario is selling the yacht?' I ask, not daring to look at Isaac. But it doesn't take him long to twig.

Isaac raises a bemused eyebrow. 'And?'

'If you lend me the money for the deposit today, I'll buy you the yacht. To say thanks.'

I think Isaac's laugh might be audible all along the Costa del Sol.

'Deal. You're on.' He whips out a hand in my direction. All his doubts about lending me the money are buried in an instant. I hesitate, for a nanosecond, before shaking on the deal. We may have slept together, but this is no sweetheart deal; where Isaac is concerned, this is business.

'Great news, Miss Wiltshire. And Isaac. What say we go back to my office, draw up the paperwork, and seal the deal?' Carlos is already jangling the keys, eager to get on with the next part of our agreement.

Carlos is making easy money, but who is going to turn down the chance of another envelope bulging with clean, crisp bank notes to the value of 1,000 euros?

But first, he has one more favour to do me. As soon as Isaac has paid the money across into Carlos's business account, Carlos has promised to pay it all over into my personal account.

Carlos knows I've no intention of buying the apartment.

Once I've got the money, I'll see what Isaac is made of. If he's cool and trusting about me paying him back, then we might have a future together. Either way, I'll pay him back every penny as soon as I get hold of my bank and explain the situation (that I'm on holiday without my log-in details). If Isaac trusts me enough to wait until I've sorted things out, then we could be in business. We can laugh about it later.

Of course, if Isaac really cares, he might even buy the apartment for me when he finds out I don't have any money.

OMG. Who am I trying to kid? And as for the promise of buying Isaac the yacht for helping me out... this could have been a big mistake. It's likely down to the heat, but I might have seriously lost the plot.

On the way back from Carlos's offices, Isaac announces that we will be staying in tonight, and Marta will be making her signature risotto. At least it's one up from paella, and apparently will contain chicken rather than seafood.

'Oh, nice,' I say, biting my tongue against sarcastic jibes about the dangers of rice grains littering the patio.

'Her risotto is to die for,' Isaac says as he keys in the combination on the front door. I know the combination, but I still don't have a key. Yet when I squint, Isaac seems to be tapping in a different code to the one he gave me.

Once inside, he asks if I could leave my white trainers by the front door.

'No problem,' I say, slipping them off. He does likewise with his loafers and slips on a pair of what look like brand-new deck shoes from a cupboard. He hands me a cellophane-wrapped pair of flip-flops, funky pink and purple. Nope. Not my colours, but again with Isaac, there doesn't seem to be a choice.

The villa is like a morgue. Silence echoes off the cavernous walls, and as yet, there's no sign of Marta doing her feral-cat-sneaking-around thing.

Isaac suggests we have a swim, to cool off. This sounds like a genuinely great idea, and I instantly agree. We're both wrung out from the heat, and even though it's almost six o'clock, there's no let-up in the temperature. The villa inside is cool, soon ratcheting up to freezing, so when Isaac rolls back a large section of glass door, the heat instantly smacks us back in the face.

'Yes, definitely,' I say, before wondering how I'll dry off without bringing a water trail back inside. What the heck? We can lounge by the pool for half an hour before getting changed.

'Why not get ready, and I'll meet you back down here in ten minutes?'

'You're on.'

I leave Isaac standing, a hand shielding his eyes, and scouring the grounds. No doubt checking up on Pablo, or Marta. Or both.

In the bedroom, I dig out my red one-piece, Marks & Spencer's best, and tug it on, then match it with a red sarong. I scrunch my hair on top and dab on a dollop of cherry lip gloss. Might as well look my best. In the bathroom, I lift down a huge bath sheet and stuff it into my enormous pink canvas pool bag.

By the time I'm back downstairs, it's so cold, I feel I've got into an ice bath. I'm not sure the extremes in temperature can be healthy, but I'm now desperate to get back into the heat.

Through the glass patio doors, there's no sign of Isaac. I wander out, and make my way over to the steps that lead down to the pool, and there he is. Already in the water doing lengths. And, WTF. He's wearing a bathing hat and goggles. So much for lounging on lilos sipping cocktails.

'I've left you goggles and a bathing cap on the side.' Isaac pauses at one end of the pool, shouts up to me, and points.

'Thanks.' I give him a thumbs-up.

I pick up the bathing cap, which, like the flip-flops, is wrapped in cellophane, and goggles that are so thick they could be used for scuba-diving. I doubt Isaac hosts many swimming parties. Playboy mansion this is not.

Somehow, I manage to tug the very snug-fitting cap on to my head, stuffing my already tangled hair inside, but I ignore the goggles. I'll just have to keep my face out of the water.

The water is heavenly. It's like a tepid bath, easy to slip into, but wonderfully cooling. Isaac swims across and wraps wet tentacles round my waist. Strange – rather than feeling tingly and lustful, I stiffen. When he rubs a finger across my cherry lip gloss, wiping it off, I have the most dreadful urge to slap him away.

Even though Isaac put the deposit down on the apartment, and I should be excited that he's taken a leap of faith, reality has quickly returned to hit me in the face. I watch him pound up and down the pool, and realise it's all been an illusion. He might be film-star handsome, and wealthy, but unless he has a personality transformation, I couldn't live with such a control freak.

There's no point in pretending any longer. I breathe more easily when I make the sudden decision it's time to go home. Any thoughts of a happy-ever-after with the millionaire of my dreams have been well and truly quashed. That last wipe of my lip gloss was the final straw. And I'm already freaking out about how I'll get back upstairs without leaving some hint of mess.

When I'm in my room, I'll book a flight home for tomorrow. I can be at the airport before Isaac notices I've gone. I'll get Pablo to drop me off in Malaga, tell him I'm shopping, and then get a taxi for the evening flight. As soon as I'm back in England, I'll get on to the bank and transfer Isaac back all of his money.

Decision made, I feel much happier, and Isaac will be easier to put up with this evening. He doesn't need to know it'll be our last meal together, so I may as well enjoy it.

Soon the buoyant water has me in its thrall. I swim up and down, Isaac lapping me every few lengths, until we finally come to rest, side by side again, at one end.

It's the first time I notice the large blue dolphin at the bottom of the pool. It's marked out in light blue tiles, several shades lighter than the deep blue of the rest of the area. The dolphin's fins are picked out in a sunny yellow.

'A dolphin. Cool,' I say. My head is seriously hurting from the rubber cap, and I have to keep slipping a finger under the rim to loosen the constriction.

Isaac is a master at ignoring what he doesn't want to acknowledge. I'm not talking about the tightness of the cap, but rather about the dolphin.

'Why a dolphin?' I press, but he's already doing a final few Olympic lengths.

We get out at the same time, and Isaac hands me a huge blue towel.

'Keep the white ones for the bathroom,' he says. 'The blue ones are for around the pool.'

In the corner, I spot a pile of pristine blue towels stacked like at Los Molinos. He's definitely going for the five-star hotel feel, but why bother?

'Thanks.' I tug it round me, flip off the ghastly cap and hand it to Isaac.

'Pop it in the dirty basket by the towels. Marta cleans the caps.'

OMG. I need to get upstairs and book my flight. Now. But I can't take the chance that I might drip water through the villa, so I give in to a luxurious twenty minutes on a sun-lounger. Once my costume is dry, and I feel confident that there'll be no water trail, I head back inside.

Isaac has already gone up, and as I pass through the villa, I spot Marta standing in an open doorway. She's staring at me, stony-faced as always. I don't bother engaging – too much effort – and scuttle on up towards my room.

I collapse on to the bed, guessing that my chlorine-coated costume should probably have gone in the dirty basket as well. Who cares? I'll soon be out of here.

The first thing I do before heading for the shower is boot up my laptop and check for flights. Seat 2A isn't available tomorrow night, so I decide I can cope with one more day. It's free on Saturday, along with seat 2B. I'm too late to get 2C as well, as it's already booked, but with no other choice, I go ahead and click *buy now*.

I'm not sure which is worse: dealing with Isaac or having to sit somewhere different on the plane. Any further back than row two isn't an option, and I'm somehow going to have to cope with another person in my row. After the near-death experience getting to Spain, I'm still freaking out about having to do the return journey, but for now, I need to shovel the thoughts to the back of my mind.

Flight booked, I decide to make the most of my last day tomorrow – perhaps get Pablo to take me up to Mijas Pueblo, the whitewashed village in the hills, or to Ronda, the mountain-top city with spectacular views, historic bridges and mouth-watering tapas. Two must-see places, according to my mammoth pre-trip googling sessions. Alternatively, I could slope off to the beach with my Kindle, and top up my tan with a last few sangrias to keep me company.

As I'm getting dressed for our risotto extravaganza, I hear noise from downstairs. It takes a moment to realise it's music. I inch back the door and catch the definite sounds of classical music. Good old Isaac, but I'm afraid he's a bit too late with the romance.

I tone down my outfit, opting for linen bootleg trousers and a button-up blouse. So not sexy, more secretary functional, but it should put out the right message. *Sex is not on the table.*

Heading downstairs, I see Isaac talking on his phone. He's holding the end to his mouth, and the phone projects at right angles. The way Connor likes to talk, always at the top of his voice, about some mundane subject. Football, online gaming, or about his favourite female contestant on *Love Island*.

Isaac is having a heated conversation and when he spots me, he moves outside and strolls off in the direction of the olive trees. The table is set outside, and I cringe at the sight of red candles, red serviettes and red roses. It looks as if Isaac has romance on his mind, but hopefully the sight of my bootleg trousers will calm him down.

Marta is hovering by the door to the kitchen, hands behind her back, as if awaiting instructions. Again, I wonder why she's so subservient, but the pay really must be that good. Also, live-in accommodation has to be a big plus. At least I won't have to put up with her sourpuss face much longer.

'Jade. Have a seat.' Isaac reappears, the phone nowhere in sight, and pulls back a chair. I feel more like a potential new client for some large hedge-fund manager. Despite the red romantic theme, Isaac is acting very formally. Maybe he's not good at romance, but why do I feel it's all got something to do with money?

'This is nice,' I say, nodding at the fancy place settings.

'Hm. Yes. Good old Marta. I told her to make an effort.' He laughs, and nudges my chair forward as I go to sit down. He clicks his fingers and, lo and behold, Pablo appears in a black-and-white waiter's uniform. He has a white serviette hung over one arm, the way Logan does at the tapas bar, and is holding up a bottle of white wine.

'Your Marqués de Riscal, sir,' Pablo announces, turning the label towards his boss. 'Would you like to taste?'

'Thank you, Pablo. Yes please.' Isaac sniffs the taster, swills it in the glass and knocks it back. 'Perfect.'

Pablo proceeds to fill my glass and then Isaac's.

'Cheers. To us,' Isaac says, clinking his glass against mine.

'Cheers.' What else can I say? That I'm leaving the day after tomorrow, that he's a seriously weird guy and I'm not remotely hungry?

Pablo returns ten minutes later, pushing – with effort – what seems to be a very heavy trolley. It seems to be the way things are done in Marbella. My first thought is: where's Marta? Surely with her strong arms, she could have managed the pushing.

On top of the trolley is an enormous pan of risotto, looking more like school rice pudding than an Italian must-taste recipe. Lumps of chicken are sprinkled through with peas. I'm seriously wondering if paella might have been favourable, the sight of lumpy rice turning my stomach.

'Wow. This looks amazing as always, Pablo. Compliments to the cook. Where is Marta, by the way?'

'She's battling a migraine, so I'll be serving up tonight.'

'Well, let's get at it.' Isaac's eyes light up like a kid having his first Big Mac. I can almost see drools of saliva.

'A small plate for me,' I say, looking with pleading eyes towards Pablo. He winks and I have an urge to hug him. We're on the same page. I'm just hoping the risotto isn't laced with arsenic.

* * *

At least the wine is wonderful. It'll now be my favourite white wine of all time. Even better than my up-to-now favourite Marlborough Sauvignon Blanc.

I manage to do damage to the risotto, and with the wine to help, it slips down without too much trouble. Marta certainly isn't a bad cook, although, like Isaac, I'm wondering why she's not serving up. The migraine explanation was a bit too random, and a bit too sudden.

I wipe the corner of my lips with the edge of a starchy, well-ironed napkin, the sharp creases knife-edged like those in Isaac's shirts and trousers. I fold it over when I've finished. No doubt it will be joining the rubber bathing caps in the laundry basket.

'I was thinking at the weekend, we could take a trip somewhere,' Isaac says. 'Gibraltar, perhaps? Have you ever been there?'

I fiddle with the serviette, before straightening my fork on an almost empty plate. And then I take a very deep breath.

'No, I've never been, but perhaps another time. I'm having to head back the day after tomorrow, as my mother isn't too well. I was hoping to be able to stay longer, but I'll certainly be back.'

Isaac goes eerily quiet and motions for Pablo, who appears instantly – think genie in Aladdin's lamp – with a second bottle of wine.

As Pablo pours, I get an uneasy feeling. Telling Isaac that I'm heading back to the UK so soon hasn't gone down too well. Did he really think I'd want to stay here?

'Oh, and don't worry, I'll be paying back the money you lent me before I go. No worries there. Tomorrow, I'm popping down to the port to check out my new property, and to meet up with Carlos.' I bite the inside of my cheek and wait. I sense that telling him I'll transfer the money when I'm back in the UK, might not go down too well. Hopefully, I'll be long gone before he twigs.

Isaac seems to visibly unwind. It could all be about money, after all. He can't be skint or else he wouldn't be able to afford this villa, and he did readily lend me 145,000 euros without too much blinking. Perhaps he did blink, but the mention of a yacht as an interest payment seemed to knock aside any doubts he might have had.

'I'm sorry you're going. I thought we might have had something special going on,' he says.

'Me too.' I did think so in the beginning, before the wagging finger incident, not to mention the rubber bath cap and goggles. He's gone from hot to creepy pretty quickly. Also, no matter how hard I've tried, I can't forget Emmeline's tales of woe and deceit, or Logan's throwaway warnings.

'I appreciate you paying me back so promptly,' he says. At least he doesn't mention the yacht, which is a minor brownie point. 'Anyway, you'll need to come back soon to sign off on the apartment. If you need a good solicitor here in Spain, I can give you details.'

Night draws in, and we make small talk. Spain versus England as a place to live. As a place to work. English versus Spanish football teams. For a while, things seem quite normal, and I have a few serious moments of doubt. Perhaps Isaac isn't that bad after all, and I'm just being paranoid.

It's only on the way back up the stairs, that all hell breaks loose, and I fear Isaac is going to throw me over the banisters to certain death.

32

I see it before Isaac does, even though the lighting throughout the villa has been dimmed by remote control.

My first thought is that Marta is going to be in real trouble. There's a distinct dusty line of shoe marks in the middle of each stair tread. There's no let-up in the trail.

Behind me, I hear Isaac brake. Yes, I hear him stop in his tracks, as if he's skidded.

'What the hell,' he snaps, turning on the torch on his phone. I look round, and follow his eyes which rake up and down the staircase.

I carry on walking, slowly, sucking in my breath, scared to make a noise. Scared Marta might appear and be verbally attacked, or worse. It suddenly dawns on me that Marta lives in a completely different part of the building, out the back, below stairs, and out to one side of the under-ground garage. Why would she be leaving trails of dirt up the main stair-case? Surely she's clocked off for the day. Or sleeping off the supposed migraine.

Holy shit. The trail of dust leads to the guest bedroom. At least it can't have been left by me, as my shoes are by the front door. I saw Isaac with my own eyes put them in the closet, and I'm still wearing the 'non-sexy' pink and purple flip-flops from earlier. If the bootleg trousers haven't managed to tone down the sexy look, the shoes have it.

Isaac nudges past me and pushes open the door to my guest bedroom. Even in the half-light I see a vein throb in his neck. He goes ahead, and bends down inside the door. I swallow back the bile, knowing something is up.

He lifts up my white trainers, no longer white but with a loose smattering of a clay-coloured dirt coating the uppers and presumably the soles as well.

'Are these yours?' Isaac narrows his eyes, his voice dropped to a dangerously low level. Think sharp-teeth-baring Dobermann.

'They look like my trainers, but...'

Isaac hurls them across the room before I can finish my sentence.

'I left them by the front door. Remember?' I'm seething with his assumption that I made the mess, but my body is shaking so badly that I know to rein in the reactions.

'Well, obviously you put them on again and trailed this filth upstairs.'

I stare at him. This is the guy who has just wined and dined me, lent me an obscene amount of money to buy a property and fifteen minutes ago made me think I should maybe hang around a while longer.

Over my dead body.

'I did no such thing. It must have been Marta.'

'Why the hell would Marta wear your shoes and trail dirt upstairs? She'll only have to clean it up. Well, this time you can get to work.'

He storms into the bathroom and digs out the dustpan and brush (again), along with bacterial floor wipes. He hurls them at me, narrowly missing my head.

I feel like a battered wife, despite the fact that I've only known this guy for a little over a week. We're not even in a relationship. I've no idea who he is, but I'm petrified. It's all in his expression. I can't see his eyes properly, but I know they've likely turned red.

I stand completely still for what must be at least ten minutes and listen to Isaac go back downstairs and slam a door somewhere. Then I lift out my suitcase, fling it on the bed, and start packing. Tomorrow, I'll be getting the hell out of here. I'll sleep on the beach if I have to.

Only problem, I don't have my bank log-in details, and know I need to pay Isaac back immediately. At least Carlos texted, confirming he's transferred the money Isaac paid into my bank account. It must be all about the money. About *my* money. Isaac has never had any romantic notions, and this is the first time I realise for certain that all he's after are my fictitious millions.

Who the hell told him that I was a millionairess? They're going to be in big trouble when Isaac learns I've now got only about £20,000 left in the bank account... Well, £20k after I pay him back his 145,000 euros.

If I want to get out of here alive, I'll have to find a way to pay him back.

33

I don't sleep, at all. The villa is deathly quiet, and it's only around 7 a.m. that I hear scuffling noises outside my room. The footsteps gradually fade, as whoever it is makes their way downstairs.

I skip any notion of a shower in case a single drip of water might hit the floor. Although I've packed all my belongings, I leave my case under the bed. If Isaac pops his head round, contrite or apologetic, I don't want to wind him up again.

This time there's no way I can forgive him. I am *out-of-here*. I'm so freaked that the villa feels like the Bates Motel.

When I dare venture down to the breakfast bar, a single croissant is set out, along with a glass of water. No sign of coffee, ham or cheeses. It looks like a prisoner's breakfast. The thought makes my insides revolt. I slip the croissant into the pocket of my shorts and head for outside.

WTF. Everywhere is closed up.

'Marta? Marta?' I repeat her name over and over as I traipse through the villa. My voice rises in panic when I can't see a way out. I peer through the glass doors which are already baking to the touch, and it hits me that the air-con isn't up full-blast as usual. Sweat is pouring down my face, and the increasing panic isn't helping.

I wander down the long corridor, past the unopened doors, until I reach the end. Yes. Yes. Yes. There's a crack like before, and I have to wriggle my hips, along with every other part of me, to get through.

Even though it's still early, it's like stepping out into a sauna, the coals fiercely sizzling. I head for the pool, which looks really inviting, and might be the only option for today's activities. Unless I can find Pablo, and get him to take me away from here.

Pablo is nowhere in obvious sight. Usually, he's got an eye out for me and is generally working round the pool area. He comes scurrying when I appear, offering up his chauffeur services for the day. But as I wander round, through the olive grove, down the steps to the property boundary, there's no sign of anyone.

I get out my phone, and sit on a small parapet near the steep drop down to the road. I don't think I realised until now how steep it is. Any chance of shimmying down without breaking your neck would be impossible. Even for the most seasoned abseiler.

I check for messages. There's a new one from Mum and two from a number I don't recognise. I read the second two first, but delete them immediately when I realise they're from Connor on a random number. Even though I've deleted him from my contacts and blocked his number, it looks as if he isn't going to give up easily.

There's also one from Logan. Hoping he might have forgiven me for dashing his hopes of anything between us, I read it next.

Jade. Hope all is well. Let me know everything is okay. Logan

His words make me even more panicky. If he'd asked to meet for a drink, a coffee or even for a stroll along the beach, I wouldn't feel quite so uneasy. Why does he want to know if everything is okay? Why wouldn't it be?

Mum is still at the property thing.

Have you checked out the property details I sent you? Check out the links. I've been to see numbers 1 and 2. Amazing. Let me know all good in Spain. Mum xxxx

Mum always asks if everything is good, but it sounds as if she's in cahoots with Logan. Mum can sense when I withdraw and when there's a problem without needing to be told. *That's mothers for you*, she tells me often enough.

Rather than engage, I send through a single thumbs up. At least she'll know I'm still alive.

As I'm sending the thumbs up to Mum, another text pings through. It's Connor. Again.

Shit, he says he's coming out at the weekend to talk to me. Ha, ha. We'll probably pass in the air. Serves him right.

I notice my mobile battery is almost flat, but before I head inside to put it on charge, I tackle the croissant. Although I need to eat, it tastes of sawdust and must be a few days old as it's impossible to swallow. The dry hardened flakes make me gag every time they hit the back of my throat. It takes me at least ten minutes to get it down.

A faint movement through the arbour makes me look up. It's Pablo, with his head down, and he's tiptoeing. FFS. Why? It's obvious that he doesn't want me to see him, but why all the secrecy? I hop up, scurry across the rocky landscaped area, but by the time I reach the arbour, there's no sign of him.

As I head back to the villa, I hear the purr of a car engine.

I race across the patio to the driveway where Pablo usually waits for me, but I'm too slow because the Merc is already slipping out through the electric gates. The Colditz-high gates with spikes on top. I frantically wave my arms, but if he sees me, he has no intention of stopping. Before I get to the end of the driveway, the gates are closing, and a final clunk tells me that I'm officially locked in.

34

Inside the villa the heat is building. I scout around for the air-con remote control, but it's not in its usual place. The small black gadget holder that sits on top of the glass-topped table by the indoor pool (today looking decidedly murky) isn't anywhere to be seen.

The only option will be to go for a swim to cool off. My costume is already packed, as I had been planning on a trip to Mijas, or Fuengirola to visit the Castillo Sohail. Today was to be a last chance to tick off another 'must visit' place from my list. No chance of that now. I could google local taxi firms after my swim and get as far away from this hell hole as possible, but how would I get out of the villa grounds? I don't know the outdoor gate code. Unless I can find Marta, I'm trapped.

Back up in my room, I go to plug in my phone, top up the charge, but notice the adaptor plug that I've been using has also disappeared. My charging lead is on the bedside table, but I can't plug it in without the adaptor. Isaac gave it to me when I arrived, amused that I didn't have one of my own. I told him that Logan, the guy at Los Molinos, had lent me one, but I forgot to bring it with me.

Why has he taken the plug away? Or why has Marta removed it? My battery is already on its last bar, about to die at any moment. I boot up my laptop, and it's the same. The battery is almost flat.

I slump on the edge of the bed. My heart is starting to race, and I'm feeling almost as anxious as I did on the plane when I thought we were going to crash. I've no idea what to do, who to call or how to get out of here. Isaac hasn't been in touch.

I could use my last breath of battery life to try to contact him, but something tells me I'm safer when he's not around. He suddenly seems like the villain. Only problem: if it's the money he's after, making sure I pay him back before he lets me go, I can't get hold of the bank. I would be more than happy to pay him everything left in my bank account if it'll get me out of here. But without a phone, or laptop, how the hell can I even try to contact my bank?

I slip into my swimsuit, throw a light sarong over the top, and gripping my own towel (heaven forbid I wet one of Isaac's), I head down towards the pool. There's still no sign of Marta, although she must be around because the plate that held the croissant has gone, and the water glass with it.

The grounds and pool area are still heavenly, but I'm not so excited about being alone in the Garden of Eden. I slather myself in factor 30, and suddenly remember I'm not supposed to use suncream in the pool. Shit. Shit. Shit. I stand under the shower by the steps, for at least ten minutes, scrubbing until my skin is raw. I'm a lot cooler when I turn the jets off, but without soap, it's almost impossible to get rid of the fine oily layer. At least I've remembered the rubber bathing hat, which appeared back in the guest bathroom after it had been through the laundry.

I head to the far end of the pool, count to ten and dive in. I flow under water, skimming across the dolphin marked out in light blue tiles along the bottom. It's the first time I notice the tip of its tail is picked out in red. I'll be able to tell Mum I've been swimming with dolphins. I giggle, and for a moment, everything doesn't seem so bad. Once Isaac comes home, I'll charge up my phone, tell him I've decided not to buy the property and will phone the bank and arrange to pay him back immediately. Sod the yacht.

Ten lengths in, and out of the corner of my eye as I turn, I see Marta. I think it's Marta but she disappears from view so quickly that I can't be sure. But who else could it be? I need to get hold of her, find a way out of the grounds. If I can, I'm tempted to head straight for Malaga and spend the night there before my flight tomorrow. I could find a small guest house in a backstreet somewhere.

Suddenly it feels good to have a plan. Isaac will never be able to track me down. I doubt Marta knows I'm leaving. Unless... Pablo might have overheard me telling Isaac my plans last night, and reported back to Marta.

After I've towel-dried, I lie in the sun for half an hour and try in vain to relax. I nearly jump out of my skin when water jets spurt violently up from the bottom of the swimming pool. It's like with the indoor dip pool, and the bathroom shower. I feel someone is watching me and deliberately turning on hidden taps.

My head starts to spin when I try to get up, telling me again I need sustenance. Marta. She's my only hope.

* * *

With my sarong over my now-dry costume, I circle back round under the villa's central staircase and down the corridor that leads to the underground garage. I hump my body against the fire door to heave it open and once again find myself slithering through the gap.

The garage is even hotter than the house, the dreary grey walls not helping. The metal shutter grilles in the garage, which Pablo has to open so that he can drive the Merc up a ramp to ground level, are closed, and the Merc isn't back yet.

For the first time, I notice a small door leading off from the ramp. Shock. It opens, and my eyes are assaulted by sunlight. I walk up until I'm standing by the exit gates. But without the code, or the zapper Pablo keeps in the Merc, I'm no better off.

I go back into the garage, checking the ceiling and wall corners for security cameras, but there's nothing. I creep to the end, feeling like a burglar up to no good.

I pass through the door that leads out to Marta's and Pablo's bijou finca. It looks even more bijou than I remember. One storey, likely housing no more than three rooms.

It looks as if I'm in luck, depending on which way you look at it, as the windows are all thrown wide. Marta is likely around somewhere. Although, perhaps not, as Pablo and Marta have little reason to keep the windows or doors locked: no one is likely to be trying to break in as a burglar would need a really long rope ladder to get down from the top of the perimeter walls.

I peek through one of the windows, but there's no sign of life. I rap at the front door, poke my head round, and call out.

'Marta? Marta? Are you there?'

The silence is worse than in the villa. It feels spooky. Signs of life are all around: washing floating on a line to one side of the property and a pair of woman's shoes by the door.

Where the heck is Marta?

The door creaks as I nudge it open, and I dare wander in. The stone floor is icy cold, and even with the flip-flops on, my feet freeze up. I mosey round the lounge, with its large faux-leather sofa and a pair of well-worn rattan chairs, and come to a stop at a series of photographs on a wooden trestle table.

There's a huge head-and-shoulders portrait of Marta and Pablo, all smiles and togetherness. Their rapt expressions are a far cry from their regular dour expressions, which makes them hard to instantly recognise. But it's definitely them. Pablo has an arm round Marta. Also, there's a picture of them in the grounds of Los Molinos if I'm not mistaken. Perhaps they were guests, but more likely they were working there. I set the picture down and start shouting out again.

'Marta? Marta?'

Still nothing.

I don't feel comfortable hanging around. If Marta hadn't been such a cow leaving a trail of mess with my name on it, I might wait a while longer. But something tells me to get back to the villa. Marta could be even more deranged than Isaac for all I know. She's certainly off-the-grid creepy.

Looks as if I've a lot of time to kill. I need to forget my pride and anger at Isaac, and use the last bit of battery life to contact him.

And ask him what the hell is going on.

35

I hurry back upstairs, and make a grab for my phone. The battery is now in the red, with possibly only enough charge for one swift call or a couple of texts.

To be on the safe side, I key in the words.

> Isaac. I can't get out of the villa, and no sign of Marta. Or Pablo. When will you be home?

A second after I press *send*, a reply bounces straight back. Minus kisses, concern, or answers. Only a veiled threat regarding the money.

> I won't be back until tomorrow, around midday. Marta will look after you till then. Don't forget to transfer the money in the morning. Forty-eight hours I think you said? Isaac

As if on cue, after I've read his message, my battery dies. I'm now officially stranded. I feel my heart race and am desperate for a brown paper bag to cushion a full-blown panic attack. Sweat is pouring off me as the heat cranks up. There's still no hint of the air-con, and unless I spend the rest of the day in a cold shower, or in the pool, I've no idea how to stay cool. I'm not hungry in the least, but without sustenance, I'm likely to pass out.

I fling my phone aside and go out on to the landing. I lean over the grey railing and notice food has been set out down below again. Marta must be somewhere nearby. The thought should calm me down, but it doesn't help. Where is she hiding? Why is she ignoring me? No doubt she's following instructions from her boss, as no one could be so callous.

My mind is all over the place, and I'm starting to question Marta's motivations. Why leave all the mess around the place unless she badly wants rid of me? The only reason I can think of is that she wants Isaac to herself. Perhaps they share history. This thought spooks me even more, as I've no idea how far she'll go. Pablo likely has no idea either.

The lunch is spartan, not much better than breakfast. A slice of ham, a bread roll and an apple – it all looks even less appetising than the solid croissant, but I have to eat. It might be all I get until tomorrow. At least there's another full glass of water.

I take the plate outside to the patio, find a small space in the shade and drag a chair across. The roll is so crusty that each mouthful is almost impossible to swallow, but with endless sips of water, I manage to get it down. The ham smells rank, like Connor's feet on a bad day, but mixing small strips with bites of apple, it's soon gone.

It's only when hiccups kick in that I start to cry.

This is not the way it was meant to be. So much for a millionaire's life-style. Rather than sun, sea, sex and sangria, I feel like a prisoner on death row. How am I going to survive the next twenty-four hours on my own? Even being with Connor would be better than this.

* * *

I do a few more lengths of the pool, then decamp to the sun-lounger where I dig out my Kindle. I stick to a light-hearted romcom, having completely lost the appetite for psychological thrillers. I'm certainly not in the mood for spooky cliffhangers.

Although the afternoon soon passes, and this time tomorrow I should be at Malaga airport preparing for lift off, I can't shake the unease. One thing's for sure, I'll never be back here.

I wander upstairs, strip off my costume, which at least is now bone dry, and stuff it back in my suitcase. I don't dare shower, but I feel clean enough after being so long in the water, and decide to change into the clothes I'll wear for travelling.

Suddenly, I hear voices and muted conversation. The fact that I'm no longer alone should cheer me up, but instead I start to hyperventilate. I feel as if I'm suffocating, and my heartbeat is now irregular as well as racing. I'm dreading coming face to face with Isaac, as I've built him up in my mind to be a total psychopath. And Marta isn't coming off much better.

I inch my door slightly ajar, and press my ear to the gap.

I hear Marta talking to someone in Spanish, and a few seconds later, I pick up Pablo's husky tones. Suddenly, there's a loud crash, as if something has fallen from a great height. It's coming from near the stairs up to the roof terrace.

Then there's total silence, before Marta starts screaming at the top of her voice. She could be angry, or shocked. I've no idea what's going on. What has happened to Pablo? He's not responding. Has Marta attacked Pablo? The way I'm feeling, I wouldn't put anything past her.

I sit on top of the bed, hug my knees to my chest and rock from side to side. I should go and find out what's going on, what's happened, but I'm far too scared of what I'll find.

Five minutes later, I breathe more easily when I hear Pablo's voice again. It's weak, wobbly, but at least he's alive.

There's more movement, as if stuff is being moved around the villa. If Isaac has got back early and is involved, he's being unusually quiet. I'm shaking so badly, that I stay where I am for another half an hour before I pick up the courage to leave the bedroom.

Spying over the balcony (my default place to find out what's going on), I see what I suspect is my supper. A meagre glass of what looks like white wine, a green, very sad-looking salad, with yet another crusty bread roll. But again, I feel sick rather than hungry. I'm like an inmate being teased with five-star luxury, but given underground bunker treatment.

Once I've eaten, I'll start counting down the minutes until tomorrow. Until I can escape this hellhole.

36

It's around 10 p.m. before I get into bed. First, I double-check I haven't forgotten anything and that everything is packed: passport, wallet, credit cards and my book, *How to Live Like a Millionaire*. I'm tempted to chuck it, but as the villa is void of waste bins of any sort, I tuck it in the bottom of my suitcase with all manner of assorted rubbish: tissues, cotton wool balls and even used dental floss, along with a couple of empty plastic shampoo bottles from the hotel. I won't risk having Isaac give me a parting telling-off for leaving trails of normality around the place.

All the swimming and nervous energy send me into a fitful sleep, and I manage about five hours uninterrupted, before I start to toss and turn. I wake shortly after 3 a.m., but can't get back to sleep. I try to read, but have the concentration of a gnat.

Around 6 a.m., I get up, splash water over my face, avoiding use of soap and hairbrush, and get dressed. If I could leave for Malaga straight away, I'd be gone. I dither whether to take my packed case downstairs and leave it by the front door, making it clear to Isaac when he returns that I'm on my way. He'll be able to go back to living germ free as if in a sterilised IC unit. I'm furious and desperate to let rip, tell him exactly what I think of him, but I'm far too scared. I could be standing outside the headmaster's study, petrified of what's about to come.

I opt for leaving my suitcase in my room, under the bed. As soon as I get the all-clear, I'll bring my stuff down.

Marta doesn't see me or know I'm watching her from the landing. She's mopping the floor, her hair scrunched up under a white butcher's hat, and she's covered in a bodysuit which reminds me of Covid lockdown. The only thing missing is a mask. I'm surprised Isaac lets her breathe inside at all.

'Marta,' I say in a raised voice, as I march down the staircase. The mop flies out of her hand, and she looks as if she's seen a ghost. In a second, she's disappeared, and returns with another stale croissant. I think I can see a faint coating of blue mould around the edges of the pastry. As my tummy is seriously rumbling, I've no choice but to force it down. Again. When I see a milky coffee in her other hand, things feel as if they might have taken a turn for the better.

What if the whole thing has been a big misunderstanding? That she's just not allowed to talk to house guests? I've no idea why she won't talk to me, but then I know nothing about Marta and her relationship to Isaac.

'Thanks,' I say when she sets the mug down. She gives me a faint smile and hovers, as if she's going to speak to me, but seems to change her mind.

I put the coffee to my mouth, desperate for the comforting taste of warm liquid, but when a couple of drips fall on to the marble surface, Marta doesn't offer to clean it up. Instead, she scuttles off. I tug out a couple of tissues from a pocket and frantically wipe away the mess. The soggy tissues will have to join the rest of the rubbish at the bottom of my case.

I'm definitely getting a sense of what solitary confinement must feel like, but at least today I'll be out on parole. The place is in total silence again. The momentary, if illusory, comfort of having Marta around has quickly dissipated.

I eat up as quickly as possible and head outside, through a welcome crack in the patio doors, with my Kindle. The romcom might be light-hearted, an easy read, but it may as well be about a serial killer, all the good it's doing.

At 11.10, I hear Isaac's voice. I freeze. He said midday, but he's back early. Shit. Shit. Shit.

I hop up off the sun-lounger and scurry back across the terrace to the crack in the door. I can hear him near the staircase as I creep down the long corridor.

'Jade? Jade? Where are you?' His voice booms my way. He sounds cross, his words clipped. What is up with him now?

When I turn the corner into the breakfast bar area, he's standing there, staring at the marble surface. Marta hasn't taken away my plate and mug as usual, and WTF? There's a new wet coating of milky liquid dribbling from the countertop on to the floor. Croissant crumbs are everywhere, scattered at random around the room.

The bitch has been at it again.

'Come here. What is this?' He stares at me as if I've committed a heinous crime.

Okay, I know he doesn't like mess, but he's looking at me as if I've again done this deliberately.

'I've no idea. Marta must have left it like that,' I say. My words come out in a seriously hoarse whisper, and my legs are shaking so badly that I'm scared they might give way.

'Marta? You've got to be bloody joking me,' he yells, lunges for me and grabs both my wrists. 'You will clean this up now, pay me my money and get the hell out of here. You're no better than a pig.' He spits the words in my face.

My wobbly legs give way to bottled-up fury, and when I slap him hard across the face, he shoves me so violently with both his hands that I fall back against the table and bang my head. He stares at me, and if looks could kill, I'd be dead long ago. He is beyond angry.

I rub at my head and feel a small bump developing on the side that took the impact. But now isn't the time to worry about concussion, or blood clots. Holy shit. I need to get out of here. But how?

I struggle up and grip the edge of the table until the dizziness subsides.

'You don't need to worry about your bloody money. If you hadn't taken the adaptor, my phone battery would still be charged, and I could have sent the money across.'

This is, of course, a lie, a dangerous lie, as I have no idea of my log-in or telephone banking details, and talking to someone on a Saturday wouldn't be easy. Also, without ID, if I did get through to the bank, they're unlikely to allow a random voice on the other end of the phone to transfer 145,000 euros into a strange bank account.

Isaac reaches into his pocket and hurls an adaptor my way, which narrowly misses my face.

'You've got half an hour, tops, then you're on your own. I'll check my bank account before I let you go. And you'd better not forget the yacht money. Why else do you think I lent you the money in the first place?'

He's spitting in my face again, like a viperous snake, and is totally out of control. I've no idea how I'm going to pay him everything back. Even when I get to England there's still no way I'll be able to pay him the yacht money. I'll pay back what he lent me, and hopefully when he gets that, he'll be willing to forgo the rest. How could he force me to pay the extra anyway? It was only a gentleman's agreement. What the hell was I thinking?

Why did I ask for the deposit in the first place? I must have been really drunk when I came up with the ruse to test the trust issue. See if Isaac would readily lend me money, the way I had when I paid Mario his charter fees. It's hard to believe I wanted to see if we had a future together. I must have been crazy. Poor Emmeline. I guess she was telling the truth all along, and the bastard really did rip her off.

I never had any intention of keeping the money, but it felt good to act like a millionaire. Play their games.

Act as if you have money. As if you have money to burn. Make ostentatious gestures. Look as if you fit in.

I'll definitely be binning *How to Live Like a Millionaire* now, that's for sure. Why the hell did I believe the straplines?

37

I've never been as scared in my life. When Connor hit me once, I was scared, but this is in a whole other league. Toying with millionaires is very different from toying with guys from North London council estates. Sicilian Mafia versus high school bullies.

I plug in my phone and stare at the screen as the charge slowly builds. I've got half an hour to come up with a plan, an excuse, anything to convince Isaac to let me go. I haven't got my log-in details for my bank account and won't be able to transfer any money at all until I speak to someone at the other end. Even then, without identification, I doubt I'll be able to get into my account. But I need to try. The thought makes me hyperventilate, until I'm gasping for air.

There's a deathly silence all around the villa. There's no sound at all. No soft footsteps, no whispers. Nothing.

Until suddenly... all hell breaks loose.

'What the fuck is this?' It's Isaac, screaming again. His yell is booming through the building, bouncing off the walls. I've no idea where he is, but he's so loud, it sounds as if he could be outside the bedroom. Then his voice gets a little quieter, as if he's moved further away. 'JADE? Where are you? *Get out here now.*'

I want to crawl under the bed, or better still, crawl into a hole and bury myself alive. My insides turn to liquid as I hear him march around.

Then Marta's voice, calm, steady breaks through. Isaac must have asked her something.

'Jade. The trail of dirt is from her shoes, sir. You can see where she's gone,' she says.

WTF. What is she thinking? Doesn't she realise I am in serious danger if Isaac suspects I've left a deliberate mess anywhere in the house? She must surely have picked up that this isn't some mild temper tantrum. He's got murder in mind. I can hear it in his voice.

Then it hits me. This has been Marta's game all along. She's the one who wants me dead, and it looks as if her wish might be about to come true. She's banking on Isaac finishing me off. OMG. Or perhaps she's planning on doing it herself. Either way, I'm totally on my own.

I can hear footsteps, banging noises, and then an eerie quiet. WTF is going on? I've no idea, except that I'm in danger.

Somehow, I manage to move and I know there's no other choice now but to face the music. Whatever the music is. It'll not be good, but hiding away isn't going to help.

Before I leave the room, there's enough new charge on my phone to leave one last message. Mum keeps her phone off at work, but she'll check her voicemail later. I'm trembling so much, it's hard to sound upbeat.

'Mum. I'm fine. Will be home tomorrow evening. Love you and miss you.'

It's like a death-bed message, but if anything bad does happen, there's a chance the call could be traced back to the villa. I really do miss Mum, and I promise myself, in this one second, that I'll make it up to her. She can come on my next trip. If there is one.

I leave my room, wheel my case along the landing, and hump it down the stairs. I leave it at the bottom, then follow in the direction of where the noises came from. Marta's voice is just audible, and then I see what the issue is. There is a trail of wet muddy footmarks leading up the stairs towards the roof terrace.

The bitch has done this deliberately. But why?

I quickly do a U-turn, nudge my case under the stairwell, and head for the small downstairs cloakroom. I pull the door to, flop back against the wall, and pray.

My senses are so alert, I could hear a pin drop. I daren't move. I think of *Waiting for Godot*, when nothing happens, and the seconds feel like hours. An eternity seems to pass. There are faraway noises, a door being slammed and then a scurry of feet heads my way, stopping right outside the cloakroom.

38

'Jade. Are you in there?' Marta's clipped tones make me jump.

She is right outside the cloakroom. Even in my petrified state, it hits me that she's talking in very clear English.

I freeze when she rattles the handle, and pushes the door open. It narrowly misses my face, and I've no idea how, but I manage not to make a sound. I feel I might be already dead, as I can't seem to breathe.

Thankfully, she doesn't linger. She leaves the door open, and is soon walking away, demanding in a loud persistent voice that I have to come out. Or else...

'Where are you? Come out, come out, wherever you are.'

It's like a horror movie where the villain is in relentless pursuit of his victim.

Her voice fades as she moves off. Well, I think she's moving off, but she could be hiding not far away. Perhaps she's deliberately quietened her voice, to trick me into appearing. She could be lying in wait under the stairwell. Shit. I've left my case there. If she sees it she'll know for definite that I'm downstairs.

It's then I remember my handbag is still upstairs in the bedroom. Shit. Shit. Shit. It's got everything important inside. Phone, passport and wallet. I need to get it, and get out of here... *now*. I've no idea how. Isaac changed the door codes recently, and there was no way he was ever going to share them after he lent me the money. But it doesn't matter anyway, as I still don't have a key.

I peer round the door, and my body is shaking so badly, my bones are rattling. As I sidle along the wall towards the stairs, there's no sign of Marta. There's an eerie silence everywhere, and Isaac seems to have gone off-grid. He's likely gone outside to find me, murder on his mind.

It's as if I've come face to face with death for a second time in a little over a week. The near-death experience on the plane was one thing, but this is even scarier. Isaac, if he really is Marbella Mafia, likely owns a gun. Or two.

He and Marta are possibly in cahoots and are doing a two-pronged attack to bring me down. But why? If Isaac wants my money, it's not clear what Marta's motive is. All I can think of is that she wants Isaac to herself. They must have history, as I can't think of any other explanation. It's beyond weird, but I've no time to work it out.

There's only one place I can think of going that might give me some time. But first I have to pick up my handbag.

It's hard to tiptoe quietly and quickly up a marble staircase, as my feet try to keep pace with my hammering heartbeat.

I dive into the bedroom, and do a quick check of my handbag. My phone charger, and adaptor are still plugged into the wall, so I rip them out and chuck them in my bag.

It's then I notice my trainers by the window. In the urgency to pack, I must have forgotten them. So I rip off my sandals, squeeze them into my bag alongside my phone and documents, and pull on my lace-up trainers. The need to move quickly is uppermost in my mind.

My ears are pricked for the slightest sound as I sidle back out on to the landing. The coast is clear.

But as I start my descent, Marta suddenly appears at the bottom of the stairs. She's been waiting. She must have heard me go upstairs.

OMG. One of her hands is clutching the banister, and the other one is behind her back. It might be my imagination, but I think she's gripping something. Keeping it from my gaze. Is it a knife? A gun?

'Jade, come with me.' Her voice is dangerously low.

She lifts her hand off the rail, and slowly walks up the stairs towards me, her fingers outstretched. She looks deranged, her eyes wide, and her hair, devoid of any tie-back, is wild and frizzy, as if she's had an electric shock.

Sweat pours down my face, and into my eyes. My vision is blurred, and my head is seriously spinning. Marta is going to kill me.

39

Marta suddenly glances over her shoulder, as if she's heard a noise. If Isaac appears, it's all over.

This could be my one chance. It's now or never. As she turns her head, I race down the stairs, and when I come level, my shoulder bag smacks against her head and causes her to lose her balance.

We are halfway between the landing and the ground floor. As in the movies, everything seems to happen in slow motion. Marta falls backwards, tumbling like a dead weight to the bottom. Her scream turns to silence, and for one awful moment I think she might be dead.

I rush to check her pulse, and slide two fingers on to the side of her neck. But suddenly a hand shoots up and she grabs my wrist. WTF. I needn't worry about Marta. It'll take more than a tumble down a flight of stairs to finish her off. She's very much alive.

Without looking back, I careen down the long corridor towards the fire door that leads to the garage. There's no way I can take my suitcase with me, so I abandon it under the stairs. My only concern now is getting out of the villa alive, and there's a slim chance that if I reach the garage I can escape.

The small door I found earlier, which leads up the ramp and out into the garden, is where I'm heading. Assuming it's still unlocked, I should be able to get outside the villa and see if there's somewhere along the property perimeter with a gap, so that I might be able to call out to passers-by. It's a pretty weak plan, but I can't think of anything else. I need to try.

Somehow I navigate down the stone stairwell, but stop in my tracks near the bottom. I throw a palm up against the wall when I hear a humming, purring noise, coming from the garage. It must be the Merc. Please God don't let it be Isaac.

It's the first time in my life that I almost give up. About to collapse on to the ground and hold my wrists out in surrender, I realise this could really be it.

Up ahead, I see the car running, and freeze when I notice the front passenger door is open. Perhaps Isaac is going to take me away from the villa to finish me off. It's too late for me to turn back and retrace my steps. And what would be the point?

Slowly, I inch forward, and see eyes looking at me through the driver's wing mirror. Through the open window, an arm appears, the hand flapping at me to get a move on. It takes a second to register it's not Isaac's hand. The hand is rough, calloused with thick black hairs up the back.

'Pablo?' My voice is a hoarse whisper.

'Get in. Hurry. There's no time.'

What choice to I have? I crawl in beside him, and when I pull the door closed, I hear the click of locks.

Pablo pulls down a thick pair of black sunglasses from the top of his head, but not before I notice bruising along the bone of his right cheek. He also has a small bump on the side of his head. The glasses provide meagre camouflage. I remember the noises, the banging, the screaming. Marta must have really attacked Pablo.

'Seat belt,' he says pointing, before he zaps the controller to open the grilles. We slowly drive up the ramp, Pablo's eyes straight ahead. A flicker of hope kicks in. If Pablo is kidnapping me, surely he wouldn't be too worried about my seat belt.

'Where are we going?'

'You see.'

I'm scared to ask anything else. I don't really want to know if I'm on my way to a gruesome end. Yet, a sixth sense tells me Pablo is as scared as

I am. He looks as if he's taken a beating, and is as desperate as I am to get away. How did he know to wait for me in the garage? Maybe he wasn't waiting. Maybe he was trying to escape from Marta, or Isaac, and I just happened to turn up as he was preparing his getaway. Whatever, for some reason, I feel safer alongside Pablo than I've felt in the last twenty-four hours.

As we drive up to the main entrance, the villa gates slide open. In the passenger wing mirror I watch as the steel grilles of the garage close behind us. My heart pumps, expecting Marta or Isaac to appear at any minute, and I'm half expecting a ricochet of bullets against the back window.

When we're safely outside, Pablo speeds up and heads for the motorway. If I thought his driving was reckless before, this time the danger is off the scale. My heart's in my mouth, yet I've never enjoyed speed more. My stomach is rolling and lurching as if on a big dipper.

It's as if we've masterminded a bank heist, and are on the run from the enemy. One false move, one wrong turn, and we're both dead. From Pablo's stony expression, I suspect we are fleeing for our lives.

Ten minutes in, I guess where we're headed, and relief washes over me.

'Are we going to the airport?'

'*Si. El aeropuerto.*'

Yes. Yes. Yes. The airport.

It's all I need to know.

PART II

MARTA

PART II

MARTA

40

THREE MONTHS PREVIOUSLY

It's hard work being a chambermaid. Los Molinos might be a five-star hotel, but cleaning up after other people, changing sweaty bedding, picking up soggy towels and throwing out stale food rifled from the breakfast buffet is really tedious.

At least when I get to George Stubbs' room each morning, I can take a breather. His room is bizarrely tidy. It's as if he's sleeping somewhere else, as there's no sign of life inside room number eighteen. There's no indication that he's used the bed, the bathroom or the toilet. I'm tempted to count how many sheets of toilet roll he uses, as the roll always looks untouched.

I first spoke to Mr Stubbs a few days ago. I am the regular cleaner for his room, and I always wait until he leaves for breakfast before going in. I often hang around once I finish, eager to see him. Last Tuesday, he suddenly appeared out of his room and made me jump out of my skin.

It was the first time we'd had a conversation. Well, a conversation of sorts.

'*Hola*,' he said, scaring the life out of me when he opened his door and appeared in front of me as I hovered in the corridor.

'*Hola*. Would you like me to clean your room now?' I knew there wasn't much to clean, but he tips really well, gently stuffing a pristine, unused twenty-euro note into my pocket once a day. He usually gives me a knowing wink, but never engages in conversation. Generally, he gives me the note when he gets back from breakfast and after I've finished cleaning, but occasionally before. Once, he even slipped me the note when he caught me off duty late one afternoon in the hotel foyer.

I aim to have my trolley outside his room before he sets off for breakfast. It's not a sneaky move; Pablo and I are just really hard up, with Pablo still out of work.

'Yes, that would be good, Marta,' he says with his wide, perfect smile and easy manner. 'Thank you.'

The first day he spoke to me took me completely unawares. He proceeded to hold up both hands balled into fists. My face always flushes when he stuffs the euro note in my pocket. At first, I thought he was having fun, toying with me, before giving me the tip. But no. This particular morning, it wasn't money in his fists. It was an assortment of Lindt chocolate balls. The ones we are instructed to leave on guests' pillows each night.

'I don't need these, thank you, Marta.' He squinted at my name badge. 'The thought of chocolate melting onto the bed sheets is a bit disturbing. Don't you think?'

He smiled, all teeth, oozing humour. I really thought he was joking, but I couldn't have been more wrong.

'No problem, Mr Stubbs. Let me take them.'

In an instant, his mouth clamped tight, and a tic pulsed in his neck. He rubbed fingers from one hand across his baby-smooth chin.

'It's Marston,' he said.

'Sorry?' I had no idea what he was on about.

'My name is Marston, not Stubbs. Isaac Marston.' He smiled, but something about his glassy stare made me know not to question him.

'Oh, I'm really sorry, Mr Marston. I must have got confused with another guest.' I lowered my head, looked at the ground and clasped my hands behind my back.

'That's no problem, Marta. Now, if you'd like to take the chocolates, I'll head off for breakfast.'

He dropped the balls into my pockets, on both sides of my white chambermaid's coat, no sign of the usual twenty-euro note. Small comfort that Pablo likes chocolate.

I watched Mr Marston, his broad shoulders and muscled biceps straining through his gleaming white linen shirt, stroll down the incline towards the restaurant.

I was furious that I'd made such a gaffe. On the first day he arrived, I dared sneak a peek at his passport, which hadn't yet been locked away in the safe. It was sitting on his bedside table, and the name printed below his picture was definitely George Stubbs.

Well, if he wants me to call him Isaac Marston, that's fine. I'm more concerned that he knows I must have been snooping. It is one thing the hotel management tells us we mustn't do. No looking in suitcases, no rifling of pockets and no gossiping about the guests to other members of staff.

But there's something odd about this guy, something weirdly unsettling. He's too handsome by half, and Pablo loathes him. Says the creep is coming on to me.

As I go into Mr Marston's room and close the door behind me, I'm very tempted to have a proper snoop. See what really makes him tick.

41

Since the chocolate-balls conversation with Isaac Marston, the atmosphere between us is distinctly frosty. He's not so smiley. It has likely got nothing to do with the chocolate balls, but more to do with me calling him Mr Stubbs.

Isaac is a strong man's name, a mysterious biblical character. Although, from where I'm standing, George Stubbs is a much better fit for this guy. His obsessive room cleanliness is bizarre, and he's got a really disturbing vibe about him. But the most annoying thing is that he's stopped slipping me a twenty-euro note each day. Pablo is furious with me that I was so stupid. He's always telling me I'm much too nosy, and need to keep a lid on the gossiping. He's petrified I'll lose my job – well, at least until he's back in work.

After I finish my shift this morning, I get changed, and before going home I take my book out onto the patio area by the small children's pool. It's the one area that staff can frequent when they clock off duty. The other three pools are completely out of bounds as there's a rule that we mustn't fraternise with guests when we're not working.

Luckily, today it's pretty quiet. I can't face Pablo just yet as he'll be mooching round the house, waiting for me to come home so that he can start moaning again about not having a job.

I lie under an umbrella, it's so hot. Only the English guests sunbathe, but everyone else – the Germans, Dutch, Americans, and especially the pasty-faced Scandinavians – are all slathered in suncream wearing enormous wide-brimmed hats.

It's then that I see Isaac talking up close to Logan. He's really close up, like his nose is almost touching Logan's. He seems to be having a go at him. Perhaps Logan left chocolates in another unwelcome place. Goodness, Isaac Marston is really laying into him, and Logan hasn't said a word in response.

I like Logan. He's a decent guy, taking time out from a serious job to do downtime in Spain as a waiter, and sometimes on reception. He always chats to me, but as I watch the pair conversing, it dawns on me that recently Logan has been avoiding me. At first, I thought it was because he was busy, but watching Isaac with him now, a strange thought hits that his avoidance might have something to do with the guest in room eighteen.

When Isaac strides off, the only guest dressed so formally in slacks and shirt, I get up and head Logan's way. He used to be really pleased to see me, but as I approach he moves faster until he speeds inside the hotel and promptly disappears.

I then decide, before heading home to Mijas, that I'll scout round the hotel once more to see if I can bump into Isaac. It'll be the first thing Pablo will ask me. About the twenty-euro note. He's thrilled that we've been able to save a little for the first time in months. He even manages to swallow back his suspicions of Isaac, and not a little jealousy, each time I plonk a fresh note on the table. I'm praying that Isaac will soften and restart the magnanimous gesture. As he's a regular at Los Molinos, I'm guessing he's not short of money.

When I can't find Isaac anywhere, I take a last wander down the corridor where his room is. There's a lot of activity coming from the room next to his, room seventeen, and the door is thrown wide. I hover behind an enormous range of potted greenery, not a fan of the spurting water feature in the middle of the corridor which makes me shiver, and on each rotation spits in my face.

A middle-aged lady, probably mid-forties, is bustling in and out. A couple of men look as if they're keeping guard by the door. I'd suspect they're her friends, except one of them is mouthing something into a handset. They're both mightily bulked up, with hardmen facial hair. They look like minders for *The Godfather*.

'Go. Go. I'm fine here now.' The solid lady shoos the guys away with a flick of a hand. She smiles, a bright bubbly, happy smile, and blows them silent kisses. 'I'll call if I need you.'

I've no idea who the guest is, but I can have a quick chat at reception, a curious enquiry as to when I should clean the room. Perhaps this evening, when I come back for my second shift, I'll leave her a couple of chocolates. She can have Isaac's. Judging from her waistline, she's probably a fan of all things sweet.

42

I can't believe it, but the lady in room seventeen really is Norwegian royalty. Well, a distant relative of the Norwegian royal family, according to a mammoth googling session I did earlier. Also, through a series of Chinese whispers, as the hotel-staff grapevine has been working overtime.

'Go on. Check her out.' I swivel the screen towards Pablo who has been sulking in front of the TV since I got home. 'Astrid Olsen. She's a distant – okay, very distant – relative of King Harald of Norway.'

Pablo reluctantly mutes the TV screen and scans the article. With a couple of fingers, he flicks back a floppy fringe which has collapsed over his eyes. I snuggle up close, kiss him on his stubbly chin, still amazed how the smell of him sets my pulse racing. Even if he never worked again, I'd still love him. Pablo is my man, loyal with his life. He smells of wood chips and linseed oil. Every day a different smell attaches to him, depending on what has been keeping him busy. He's good with his hands, in more ways than one.

'You're right. Perhaps she'll tip well. Do an extra special job.' He takes my face, and curls my thick hair behind my ears. Then pretty quickly, he unmutes the telly.

'Guess what room she's in,' I say.

'No idea.' He's really not interested, but there's a minor movement when I tell him.

'The room next to that weirdo Marston. The one feeding me twenty-euro notes.'

'Maybe they'll get together. Wouldn't surprise me.'

Before I've a chance to ask why wouldn't it surprise him, Pablo's eyes are again glued on the TV screen. The football match is under way, with Real Madrid already kicking ass against Sevilla FC. There's no way I'll get back his attention now.

As I wander out to our small allotment at the back of our ramshackle finca and collapse on to the rickety chair by the wall, I get a sixth sense following on from what Pablo has just said. Why do I think Isaac might make a move on his neighbour in room seventeen? I've no idea why he's staying at the hotel, it's anyone's guess, but I know better than to ask.

There are a couple of supergrasses amongst the hotel staff, MI5 moles, who are told to look out for unsavoury gossip about guests. It's like a major criminal activity, and hotel staff are threatened with the sack if they partake. Yet, I'm now so curious, I'm not sure I'll be able to resist finding out more about the guests in rooms seventeen and eighteen.

* * *

I've stopped rushing to wait outside Isaac's room. What's the point? The euro tips have dried up, and Pablo says I need to direct my attention (and *sexy smile*) elsewhere. Before I left this morning, he followed me round and kept suggesting (at least half a dozen times) that I should concentrate on Queen Astrid.

'She's not a queen, and I doubt she'll be turned on by my sexy smile,' I snapped.

At first, Pablo's suggestions made me chuckle, but by the time I got into my Fiat 500, he was seriously getting on my nerves. He's so desperate for extra money and so downbeat and doubtful he'll ever find work again.

If only he hadn't punched the lights out on the Barcelona fan for taunting him with their 4–0 victory over Real Madrid, he'd still be in a job. He's the best pool maintenance man in the business. Before his three-month prison stint, he'd also started up in pool construction. His second new-build, sadly, had to be left unfinished when he got locked up, and it certainly hasn't helped his CV.

This morning when I get to the hotel, I decide, for a change, to start on the second-floor landing. I'm no longer so eager to bump into Isaac. He usually leaves the hotel after breakfast and doesn't get back until supper time. I've stopped wondering where he goes with his fine-leathered briefcase that looks like a throwback from twenty years ago.

Around 11.30, I make my way down to the first floor. There's no sign of anyone. I decide to start with Isaac's and Astrid's rooms and then work my way round.

I get the usual creepy vibe when I enter room eighteen. As always, it's like a show room. Nothing has moved since yesterday. Even the remote control for the television is aligned at right angles to the screen, as the chambermaids are instructed to leave it. One thing I do spot is that a packet of tarragon-flavoured pistachio nuts is missing from the basket of snacks on top of the minibar. I make a mental note, as the charge will have to go on his bill.

Emptying the bins is easy. There's never anything in them. Even when I pull out the one from under the long table in the bedroom, there's no sign of an empty nuts packet. As always, the bathroom is pristine. The towels haven't been used, save for a small hand towel that is slightly askew. A few millimetres askew, but I'm attuned for any changes. How sad am I?

The duvet is straight, pulled right up, and the pillows are plumped. It's a huge double bed, and I'm tempted to flop on top and get twenty minutes' shut-eye.

All of I sudden, I hear voices on the other side of the door. *Mierda*. Oh no. Isaac is back. What is he doing back so early?

I hear him talking in the corridor. He's laughing rather too loudly at something. He must know I'm in his room because my trolley is parked between rooms seventeen and eighteen. Exactly halfway. I shouldn't have closed the door, but he's not usually back until much later.

When I appear, empty bin bag in hand, Isaac jumps. His painted smile is nowhere in sight. Of course he's been talking to Astrid. Who else would he be talking to? Looks as if Pablo might have been spot on.

'Sorry, sir. I can come back later.' I bustle towards the trolley.

'Thank you, Marta,' he says. A fake smile appears, no doubt for Astrid's benefit. He's aiming for casual sexy, with one hand leaning against the wall and one knee bent in a relaxed pose. He's like the plastic hero in a Mills & Boon romance, lounging against the door jamb.

Astrid is rosy-cheeked. I can't believe it, but she really is falling for it.

She's giggling, pouting her fulsome lips, and fiddling with her rather lank blonde hair.

'Would you mind doing my room now?' she asks me. 'That is, if Isaac doesn't mind.' She raises pleading puppy-dog eyes his way.

'Of course not. Why don't we grab a drink by the pool while Marta gets to work?'

'Ooh. That sounds a great idea,' Astrid coos.

Isaac takes her arm and leads her down the incline before they turn left and head towards the pool. As my eyes follow them, Isaac glances back over his shoulder.

If looks could kill, I'd soon be dead.

43

Astrid's room is a mess, as if it's been rifled by burglars. I have to pinch my nose against the unsavoury stench.

If Isaac is a neat freak, Astrid, for all her connections, lives like a pig. I don't think I've ever dealt with a bedroom in a worse state. Certainly not in a five-star hotel. There are piles of clothes, all styles and colours, flung over every possible surface. There's a blouse hanging off the television set, and a pair of lacy knickers under the remote control.

Wet towels are on top of the bed, and the bathroom is like a quagmire. When I check the snacks basket on top of the minibar, there are only the chewy pink sweets left. Peanuts, pitted olives, cheesy crackers, sesame thins are all gone. Astrid has eaten the lot. All the wrappers are strewn in the waste bin along with tissues, wet wipes and random chocolate-bar covers.

The Nespresso machine already needs replenishing, along with tea bags, mini milk cartons and sugar sachets. It's like a student's bedroom. A really rebellious student at that. Also, the rancid smell is being circulated by the air-con which is still running. I turn it off and open wide the patio doors.

I step outside and take in a few deep breaths before I set to work. If

Astrid has her sights set on Isaac, she desperately needs to get her act together.

I change the bedding, despite the hotel's rule to only do so every second day if the guests are here for a prolonged period. According to reception, Astrid Olsen is here for one week. I wonder where her bodyguards are staying, as I now assume that's who the two men were.

Forty minutes later, twenty minutes longer than the maids are supposed to take, the room looks ready for a new guest. Apart from the mountain of clothes, each piece of which I've folded like an origami expert and arranged on top of the pristine bedding, everything else is back in its place. If Isaac pops his head round, or suggests Astrid invites him in for a nightcap, she'll still be in with a chance. I get the impression that Isaac isn't particularly tolerant and would freak if he'd seen the state of Astrid's room.

I head for the hotel kitchen at lunchtime and grab a quick sandwich from the platter made up for the staff after the guests have finished breakfast. I don't linger, as I still have a mountain of work to get through.

I methodically tackle the rest of my rooms, leaving the two either side of Astrid's and Isaac's till last. When I finally start on room nineteen, where I'm preparing for a late arrival, would you believe I can hear Astrid and Isaac's voices coming from next door? Room eighteen.

Each of the hotel ground-floor rooms have glass doors that lead out on to a private patio area kitted out with two sun-loungers, a small table and a couple of chairs. A wall, a little over head height, divides each guest's patio. You can only see over the wall if you stand on one of the chairs. Even if you are six foot plus, you'd have trouble. But you can hear over the top, that's for sure.

I sneak outside through the already-cracked-open patio doors of room nineteen and quietly hover. Isaac's and Astrid's voices filter through, and I imagine them lying on the sun-loungers. But when I hear the scrape of chair legs, I suspect Isaac is sitting upright. Probably looking down at Astrid in her voluminous yellow swimsuit which I earlier hung up in the bathroom to dry.

The conversation is very merry. They're speaking in English, as I suspect Isaac doesn't know much Norwegian.

I might be misjudging him, but despite his suave appearance, he's totally synthetic – *Stepford Wives* style, or in this case, *Stepford Husbands*. Everything about him is beyond perfect. From his neat, Antonio Banderas-in-the-early-days hairstyle, closely cropped, not a strand out of place, to his clean-shaven skin which likely reeks of carbolic soap.

I move around the patio with a cat-like tread, but keep close to the wall. I'm tempted to stand on one of the chairs and peek over the top, but I couldn't do that without the crowd round the pool seeing me. The walls divide the private patios to each side, but there is no wall across the ends. Guests can wander at leisure straight across the artificial grass to access the swimming pool.

Luckily, Isaac is talking in quite a loud voice and Astrid is virtually yelling. She sounds so excited, and when I hear the cork pop on a bottle of something fizzy, I suspect she's celebrating what might happen. What she's hoping might happen. No doubt both her and Isaac's minibars will be empty by tomorrow.

I glance out towards the pool and spot Astrid's two minders trying to fit in with their surroundings. Despite their casual dress, they are lousy at mingling. Both are gripping very antiquated walkie-talkies, the sort used by American cops in the eighties. They look completely out of place.

'Have you been to this hotel before?' Isaac asks Astrid.

'Noooo. I'm only here because I'm having work done on my villa.'

'Villa? You live in Marbella?' Hard not to miss the interest in Isaac's tone.

'Of course not. I'm from Oslo. But I have the most amazing holiday home here.'

She suddenly coughs, as if the fizz has hit the back of her throat. I imagine she's drinking quickly, the excitement too much. I own up that when I first saw Isaac, I was pretty excited. Although I'd never be unfaithful to Pablo, the sight of Isaac would turn any girl's head. Certainly, Astrid seems smitten.

'Oh. How amazing,' Isaac says. Even from my eavesdropping position, on the other side of the pretty sturdy dividing wall, I'm picking up the vibes.

'Yes, it is. I have workmen in, painting and decorating, so I thought I'd treat myself and stay here. I am soooo not a fan of sweaty workmen. The villa is my little secret from friends and family in Norway. No one, other than my two private minders, know where I am. How cool is that? Also, I bought the villa with my own private money. Everyone needs a little escape route, don't you think?'

'I absolutely agree with you.' Isaac laughs as he speaks.

I bet he's not a fan of sweaty workmen either, or sweaty anyone for that matter. He doesn't look as if he ever sweats. The escape route comment makes me wonder what Isaac might be escaping from, as he seems to be a confirmed bachelor. Maybe if Astrid plays her cards right, she might change all that. What an odd couple they'd make.

'Do you really need the two guys? I assume there's no Mr Olsen to look after you?'

Dios mio. My goodness. I can't believe it. Nosy or what. He's definitely trying to wheedle information.

'No. No Mr Olsen. Not yet.' She giggles, a girly behind-the-hand-sounding giggle.

'I see.'

I bet he sees. Why do I sense he's smiling?

'The only thing that's missing at the villa is an infinity pool. I have a really mean-sized dip pool, but a huge infinity pool is the next thing on my list. Perhaps once the inside work is done. Who knows?'

Astrid is sipping so loudly now, in between intermittent bouts of hiccupping, that I imagine her emptying the newly opened bottle in seconds. I hear it being lifted out of an ice bucket (I'm assuming it's an ice bucket, as I can hear the crackle of ice cubes).

'Thank you, Isaac. Help yourself. Why don't you drink?' She's too excited to be peeved, but I bet if they get together there could be an issue here.

'I'm happy with one, or two, glasses. I like to keep a clear head. But you enjoy yourself.' His tone is so patronising.

When I spot one of the bodyguards, or minders, or whatever, walking away from the pool in our direction, I scoot back inside and slide the glass doors across and secure the lock.

The guy, six foot six inches, give or take an inch, stares my way. It's a warning to get back to work.

Anyway, I've had my fun for the day. Wait till I tell Pablo!

44

I avoid both Isaac and Astrid for the next couple of days, making sure there's no sign of them round the hotel before I tackle their rooms. They're *polos opuestos*, total opposites, with regards to the mess. Astrid lives in a pigsty, and Isaac like a hermetic monk.

However, today is Pablo's birthday, and I've got the day off. The first day off in two months. I've been working Saturdays, Sundays and most evenings, without a break. The rent on our tiny finca has recently doubled, and the utility bills have sky-rocketed. But today is our time. Mine and Pablo's, and we decide to drive down to a beach restaurant a short distance from Los Molinos and treat ourselves.

'I've got the twenty-euro notes saved. Let's enjoy ourselves.'

'Thanks. I love you, Marta. I'll make it up to you, I promise. Something will come up soon.' Pablo kisses me. He's such a great kisser even after six years of marriage, and I still can't get enough of him.

We head for a stretch of beach along Marbella's Golden Mile, where the Squid Bar sits out on stilts in the shallow surf. It's what Pablo calls 'a little bit of heaven'. The restaurant isn't cheap, but still serves the best-priced and best-cooked seafood for miles around. Pablo knows about food and cooks every evening for when I get home. Today is my treat.

The table I reserved is by the window and looks right out over the

Mediterranean. The waiter has remembered to put my birthday card propped up against one of the wine glasses. Pablo's face lights up, and for the first time in months, he smiles properly. Not just for my benefit to show appreciation, but through joy. And relief that there's more to life than mooching around the tatty finca watching TV.

It's exactly 1 p.m. when we take our seats, and the restaurant is already filling out. No one is clambering to sit outside as the summer heatwave has begun. Inside is so cool, I could stay here forever.

'The lunchtime menu, *señora*.' The waiter hands me a menu, and then one to Pablo.

I order a carafe of white wine, which the waiter brings to our table before pouring large measures into our glasses.

'To us.'

'To us,' Pablo echoes.

As we clink glasses, mine nearly slips from my grasp.

'Don't turn round. But guess who's just come in.' The question comes out as a splutter.

'Who?' Pablo is not interested, but ignores my warning and turns round anyway.

'I told you not to look,' I hiss and instantly regret it. It's Pablo's birthday, his special day.

'It's that *imbécil*, Isaac, from the hotel, isn't it?'

'Yes,' I whisper, amazed how quickly Pablo recognises Isaac. He's only seen him once, hating him on sight. He was convinced the guy was coming on to me.

'Is that Astrid with him? She looks twice his age, and could do with losing a few kilos.'

Pablo rolls his eyes and knocks back what's left of his wine. He's topping us both up again when I realise the new arrivals are heading our way.

'*Mierda*. They've seen us.' I lower my eyes, but it's too late. The waiter is bringing them over, and it seems their table is next to ours.

'Hello, Marta. I couldn't place you for a moment.' Isaac is now standing right beside us, and he's holding Astrid's hand. That didn't take him long.

'Hello, Mr Marston. This is Pablo, my husband.'

Pablo doesn't extend his hand, keeping both palms round the large glass. He simply nods.

'And this is Astrid,' Isaac announces. It's as if he's forgotten that I clean her room as well. 'Astrid Olsen.'

Astrid smiles, a real girly smile for someone who must be nearing fifty. At a pinch, she could pass for Isaac's mother.

'Hello. Pleased to meet you.' Astrid looks from me to Pablo and back again.

It's only then that she manages to place me. Out of my constricting hotel cleaning clothes, I look quite different. Well, that's what Pablo says. He hates my uniform and says, every night after I take it off, that he's glad to have his *hermosa mujer* back. His beautiful woman.

I'm dressed in a light summer frock. White and blue, and wearing open-toed sandals. My toes have had a fresh coat of red nail paint, and I've done my fingernails to match.

I can feel Isaac staring at me as I engage with Astrid. I'm not sure if he's undressing me with his eyes, or trying to work me out. I feel uncomfortable, especially as Pablo is watching.

'You work at the hotel.' Astrid whoops, turning to Isaac. 'I've only just realised. Lovely to meet you properly.'

Not sure this is meeting properly, but she's no snob. She seems really happy, pleased to be part of a couple.

When Pablo finally opens his mouth, I kick him under the table. But I'm too late.

'Why don't you join us?' he suggests, already motioning for the waiter to push the two tables together.

This feels such a bad idea.

45

When Pablo suggests seafood paella for four, Astrid's eyes light up.

'Yes, please. I love paella.' After she speaks, her tongue sweeps over her glossy lips. I can almost hear them smacking in anticipation.

Astrid loves her drink, that's for sure, and she's already waving her empty glass at Pablo for a second time. From where I'm sitting, she's my sort of woman. Even Pablo seems to be enjoying her company, laughing at her witty anecdotes.

'Not for me, thank you.' Isaac looks out over the top of the menu, sets it down and points towards the fresh fish options. 'I'd like the grilled sea bream. Green vegetables and new potatoes.'

'Pablo?' I ask, looking at my husband. It's his birthday after all. 'Shall we go for paella for three?'

'Good idea. It's the specialty of the house, and I'm starving,' Pablo says. He certainly won't bow down to Isaac, especially not on his birthday.

'Paella it is then,' I say.

Astrid beams.

Isaac seems to stiffen. No idea why. He's sipping red wine, having declined the white as it's too acidic, but isn't yet relaxing. Astrid is positively purring and suddenly makes a grand announcement.

'Today, I officially got rid of my bodyguards. Well, minders really,' she explains. 'Isaac says he'll look after me, and I won't need them going forward.' She blushes until her cheeks match her rosy lip gloss.

She keeps flicking her hair back coquettishly, and I sense Pablo trying to keep his chuckle under wraps. I want to warn her that she hasn't known Isaac that long, and ask, *Is that a good idea?* But Astrid is obviously smitten.

Isaac sits close to her and stretches a proprietorial arm along the back of her chair. Their legs are in contact. I'm sacred to look at Pablo, and even more scared that he'll make some sarcastic remark. I dig him in the shins with my foot and give him a threatening look to make sure he keeps a lid on it.

By the time the three of us have devoured the paella, Isaac is still deboning his fish. He sears the flesh with the fish knife and chews every mouthful at least fifty times. Watching him makes my skin crawl, and I have visions of him dissecting a body.

But Astrid is a bundle of laughs. She's one of a kind, hilarious, free-spirited and very irreligious with her joke telling. She'd be a really fun girlfriend.

'You have a villa near here?' Pablo asks.

'Yes. Ten minutes from Los Molinos. I've had it for nearly five years. I needed somewhere in the sun. Norway is sooo cold.' She does a theatrical shiver and looks at Isaac for attention.

'I'm looking forward to seeing it,' Isaac says, finally placing his knife and fork neatly on an empty plate (apart from the skeletal filleted bones). His smile is wide, his teeth perfect, his jawline chiselled, and his eyes steely blue. He'd be a great Gucci or Chanel model, or better still, one of their stiff mannequins. He's that rigid.

'After lunch, I'll give you a guided tour,' Astrid says directly to him.

Isaac dons another type of smile, one with that patronising edge I've also picked up in his voice. But Astrid is oblivious, and also very drunk.

'The only thing missing at my villa is an infinity pool. I have a tiddly little plunge pool, which is no use at all. There is plenty of space in the grounds for a huge one though, where the views of the ocean are magical.

I dream of floating on a water bed with a book in one hand, and an iced cocktail in the other.'

'Very expensive,' Pablo says. 'I've worked in pool construction. Infinity pools are ten times the price of an ordinary one.'

He seems to have forgotten that Astrid is a multi-millionairess, and the rest.

I want to hug Pablo, wrap my arms round him, and tell him he'll get a job soon. But no need, Astrid jumps straight in.

'Did you? Are you still in the business?' Her eyes light up. Perhaps the sun has dimmed, but Isaac's blue eyes have lost some of their shimmer. They are now more of a dull grey.

'Why don't we take Pablo's number, and once I've had a look round, I can advise you on what might work?' Isaac suggests, snarling at Pablo.

Isaac doesn't look at me, but proceeds to put his finely manicured hand on Astrid's lap. I cringe when I see him nudge his fingers through a gap in her flouncy skirt and caress her flesh.

'What a good idea. It's so great to have Isaac to guide me,' Astrid sings.

Who is she trying to convince?

To give Pablo his due, he motions the waiter for a pen and jots his number down on one of the restaurant's business cards which he picked up on the way in.

'Here. Call me if you're interested.'

'I will do.' Astrid puts her hand out to take the card, but Isaac gets there first and slips it in his expensive-looking wallet.

It was this conversation about infinity pools that sealed mine and Pablo's fate. Not to mention Astrid's.

46

I'm late getting to work this morning. Too much wine, but certainly not too much love-making. It was like the old days. I hate to admit it might have had something to with our lunch with Astrid and Isaac.

When we got back from the restaurant, Pablo was on a high. He was buzzing, not only from birthday celebrations, but with thoughts of building an infinity pool for Astrid.

'Let's wait and see,' I said, trying to bring him down. I reminded him that a local contractor in Mijas is desperate for on-site labourers, and he should call them anyway. I felt mean afterwards, as if I was damping his boyhood dreams of playing for Real Madrid.

He was still in a sulky mood when I left the house, and his birthday hangover certainly wasn't helping.

I scoot through the front entrance of Los Molinos around ten o'clock and get a frosty glare from the manager who points at his watch. It's then that I see Isaac and Astrid at the reception, both with packed suitcases. They seem to be settling their bills.

Part of me is sad to see them go, likely because they're both so wealthy, and partly because of Pablo. There's no chance now they'll contact him about the pool. Out of sight, out of mind.

Isaac sees me before I have a chance to head up the stairs and get ready for my shift.

'Marta,' he calls, in a louder-than-usual voice.

Astrid is still busy with her bill; she seems to be questioning all the extra items. Minibar. Snacks. Champagne by the pool. Mid-morning tapas, and bike hire which she never used. I suspect she makes big plans to lose weight when she's drunk. Don't we all?

Isaac strolls over and dips his hand into his top jacket pocket. He must be off to work because again he's overly dressed for the heat. I wonder where he goes all day and what he does for a living, although he has the sheen of a very slick insurance salesman.

'For you, Marta. To say thank you.' He hands me an envelope, the contents bulging.

'What for?' The question is genuine because there was so little to do in his room. I saved at least twenty minutes on my round each day when his room was on the list.

'Looking after me, of course.' He's got his plastic smile in place, and I wonder if he's deliberately making such a show of tipping me well in front of Astrid. Pablo tells me I'm a cynic, likely due to far too many stingy, arrogant and rude guests. He says I need to get back to the world of trust. But I don't trust Isaac Marston at all.

That said, it doesn't stop me from accepting.

'My pleasure.' I slip the envelope into my bag as Astrid approaches us.

'Marta. What fun yesterday. It was nice to meet you and Pedro.' She links arms with Isaac, warning me off any ideas I might have (as if?), and I don't bother correcting her over getting Pablo's name wrong.

'We may be in touch about the pool,' Isaac says.

I wonder what he thought of Astrid's villa and if he enjoyed the guided tour. He must have because I suspect he might be moving in with his new girlfriend. According to the hotel register, he was due to stay on at the hotel for another week.

'Pablo would be delighted to come round and run through possibilities,' I say.

He would indeed.

'Bye...' Astrid purrs, already motioning for the porter to bring her luggage. She's got five leopard-skin cases, piled high on the gold-plated trolley, being rolled out through the front entrance, and a taxi driver is holding a car door open for her.

For a minute, I forget that Astrid is Norwegian royalty, albeit several generations removed. She's playing a role that she's not confident in. She may be wealthy, but she's like a kid underneath, unsure, desperate to please, and clinging to Isaac as if he's the answer to all her problems.

When their taxi drives away, I think it's the last I've seen of them.

* * *

I finish work earlier than usual, and when I get home, I rip off my sturdy shoes and chuck them across the room. I can smell Pablo's signature fish stew, and realise I'm starving.

Pablo turns from the cooker and blows me a kiss. Before I say anything, I throw the loaded envelope at him. With a side lunge, he catches it, but not before he smashes into the edge of the table.

'What? *Santa mierda!* You've got to be kidding me,' he says, counting out the notes, then repeating the sequence a couple more times. 'Five hundred euros. Wow.'

I'm not sure what to say. It's a huge amount, considering Astrid didn't tip anything. I have no idea how wealthy Isaac is, but the tip is definitely over the top for the meagre role I played in his hotel stay. It still bothers me that he likes to be called Isaac when his name is George. I haven't told Pablo this yet, as the hotel is so strict on confidentiality issues. Even with regards to family.

'I know. I'm not sure I should have accepted it,' I say, wondering if Isaac always tips so handsomely. What's in it for him?

'You must have done a good job,' Pablo says. 'Or else...'

'Or else what?'

I know what he's going to say. That I led Isaac on.

Pablo's face clouds over and he throws the envelope on the table.

'He fancies you. I told you.' He stomps outside, picks up a bottle of beer on the way and breaks off the lid with his teeth.

'Don't do that!' I yell. 'You'll break your teeth and I'm not spending my hard-earned tips on a dentist.'

'Whatever,' he snaps.

We are sitting in moody silence outside, each cradling a bowl of stew, when Pablo's phone goes off. He doesn't get up, assuming it's my phone and that it'll be for me. No one ever phones him.

'Aren't you going to get that?' I ask.

'Get what?' He looks left and right, not sure what he's supposed to be getting.

'Your phone,' I yell, popping back inside and then flinging his phone at him.

'*Hola,*' he says, accepting the call, assuming a wrong number. But suddenly he sits up a bit straighter, reeling in his long legs.

'How nice to hear from you. Yes... I'd be pleased to come round. When would suit?'

I can only hear one side of the conversation, but I know instantly who the caller is. Pablo winks at me, the phone locked on his ear.

Why do I feel so uneasy? I should be sharing Pablo's excitement. But it's all a bit too quick, a bit too random, and something doesn't feel right. I shiver in the evening sun, wondering what I'm so worried about.

47

I pick Pablo up after my shift, and we drive the ten-minute journey to Casa De Astrid. A fancy blue ceramic name plate is attached to the villa entrance.

'Wonder when it'll be Casa Isaac and Astrid.' Pablo laughs as the metal gates slide open to let us in. We're pretty much in tune, Pablo and I, because I was thinking the very same thing.

'Who knows?'

Who knows indeed?

I park up against the perimeter wall, in a small area of shade. I'm dripping in sweat, and anxiety isn't helping. I hope Pablo behaves. He's a talker and not impressed by money the way I am. It's one of the reasons I love him so much. He knows he's as good as anyone, despite being down on his luck. He calls it a temporary blip. If only.

Isaac strolls across, no sign yet of Astrid, and extends a hand towards Pablo.

'Pablo. Good to see you. Let me show you around.' He smiles at me, but lays a familiar arm round Pablo's shoulders and leads him off in the opposite direction to the villa entrance. Pablo visibly winces, but winks back over his shoulder at me.

I wander towards the front door and see Astrid bustling around inside. Heavens! If I thought her hotel room was a mess, this is on a whole different scale. The inside of the villa looks as if a tornado has hit or as if it's been thrashed by an army of burglars. A small side table is upturned and a colourful lamp is lying on its side on the floor. Every surface is strewn with papers, clothes, books, and all manner of paraphernalia.

The first thing to hit are all the colours. The walls are covered in paintings, possibly original artworks, made up of gaudy splodges of thick colour. Like they were painted by a child at nursery with their first paint set.

'Do you like them?' she calls from a far corner.

'Yes,' I lie. What else can I say? Obviously they're Astrid's choice.

'I painted them all myself,' she announces, pride beaming from a childlike smile. Again, she's after confirmation that she's doing well.

'They're amazing,' I say, walking from picture to picture, wall to wall. There must be at least ten canvas splatterings.

'I'm at my happiest when I'm painting. I have an easel on the roof terrace, and when it's cool, early mornings, early evenings, I set to being creative.' She giggles. If these are creative, I wonder what they're meant to represent. I dread to think. 'Isaac thinks I have real talent.'

I bet he does, but I'm not sure what to say.

The villa's layout is amazing though. The ceilings are so high you'd need a really tall ladder to get into the dust traps in the corners. This is when I wonder who looks after the place. Although the mess is everywhere, it's made up of possessions. Random bits of furniture, clothes (yes, mountains of clothes, even in the living area) and half-empty (or half-full depending on how hungry you're feeling) plates of snacks. There's a platter of freshly cut, and half-eaten, fruit. As Astrid talks, she dips in and crunches on a slice of apple.

But despite the mess, there are no signs of scuff marks, mould, or peeling paint. The structure is solid, the painted walls a gleaming white, and if I look closely enough, I'm sure I can see my reflection in the shiny cream marble floor tiles.

Astrid seems to read my thoughts.

'Sorry, it's a bit of a mess. I'm not very good at keeping home, but then

I only have myself to look after.' She blushes. 'Until now, that is. Isaac has mentioned the mess is not really his thing, and suggests we get a housekeeper.'

'Oh. Yes, it might help. Especially while you're busy painting.'

I'm saved from saying any more by the arrival of Pablo and Isaac strolling through the long expanse of glass patio doors. Pablo is sweating from head to toe, but Isaac looks glacially chilled. His skin is smooth, not a hair on his head out of place, and neat doesn't do justice to his appearance. For once, he's in shorts, but like his longer trousers, they have a knife-edged crease running down the front, and his linen shirt is ridiculously smooth (no idea how, as my linen dress creases within a minute of pulling it on). In fact, everything about him looks oddly symmetrical. Like a perfectly built robot.

Astrid races over. 'Well?'

'Well, Astrid. I think Pablo could be our man.'

'Really? Oh, Isaac, that's amazing,' she gushes, as if Isaac is going to build the pool himself.

While Astrid is swooning over her new boyfriend, and what looks like an exciting future together, I can't help wondering at the speed at which Isaac has taken over the household management.

'And...' Isaac gently nudges Astrid's clinging hand to one side and directs his unsettling stare my way.

I swallow hard. I guess what he's going to say. Pablo has folded his arms and is watching me as if he's won *la lotteria*. My heart speeds up, and I come over clammy, as if I'm about to receive bad news.

'As well as Pablo undertaking construction of our new pool, along with a bit of garden maintenance, I think Astrid and I would like to offer you the job of housemaid. Double your salary, double whatever you're earning at Los Molinos. What do you say, Marta?'

Pablo is beaming from ear to ear and has clasped his hands together. Not sure whether in prayer – praying that I'll accept – or in a congratulatory pose. But I'm in shock, not prepared for this at all.

When I don't respond straight away, Pablo's hands drop to his sides, and a pleading expression takes control of his features. I don't know what to say. I like my job at the hotel, even though double the salary would give us whole new opportunities. Problem is, I don't like being railroaded, and feel as if Isaac has deliberately trapped me in a corner.

'Also. Astrid, you remember we mentioned the annex round the back, through the garage?' Isaac looks at his girlfriend intently.

She takes a moment, pursing her lips. It seems like she's trying to work out where the annex is.

'The annex?' she asks.

'Perhaps we could offer accommodation as part of the employment package for Marta and Pablo. They could live in. Well, live in, but living outside.' Isaac's laugh echoes off the ceilings and walls. The noise sends a chill through my bones.

Astrid takes his hand again and whispers behind a palm. But Isaac again nudges her away, seemingly ignoring whatever suggestion she might be making, and extends his long skinny, bronzed fingers once again to Pablo.

'What do you say, Pablo? Would you like to move in?'

'Marta. What do you think?' He looks at me, desperate for me to agree. It's a dream come true for him. I can't tell him what I really think. Also, like I think Astrid does, I have a sense of being coerced into something I'm not sure of.

Instead, I say, 'If that's what you want, Pablo, then count me in.'

'Great. When can you start?' Isaac asks.

While Pablo is intent on Isaac's every move, I notice Astrid has moved further away from our little band.

I suspect this wasn't on her agenda. It's her villa, after all, and no doubt she was looking forward to having Isaac all to herself.

It seems as if he has other plans.

48

Pablo and I have already been working at the villa for a whole week. It's been hectic, but we've finally moved in, lock, stock and barrel, to the little annex round the back. It's an old rustic finca which must have been built years before the villa. It's certainly in stark contrast to the white, modern behemoth. But for us, it's beyond perfect.

The small garden is so secluded, and Pablo is already planning to plant a lemon tree and a satsuma tree. It really is a little bit of heaven. It's certainly safe and secluded because it is surrounded by the most enormous walls. Only the birds can see in.

Astrid is agog with excitement. I don't think I've ever seen anyone so happy, and for the first couple of days, she makes me coffee, plies me with all sorts of soft drinks during the day, and sangria and white wine in the evenings before Isaac gets home. But as soon as she hears the car purr through the gates, she makes some excuse that she has things to do, and Isaac's supper to prepare. Despite the fact that I've done most of the preparing, not to mention the shopping, chopping ingredients, and cooking whatever Astrid requests.

Tonight, as soon as Isaac appears, I scarper off in the opposite direction and only make my way back when it's time to start cooking. And serving. Isaac keeps adding to my list of responsibilities. He's determined to get his money's worth, that's for sure.

While on the surface everything seems to be going well with the lovebirds – plenty of spontaneous kissing, hand holding and eye contact – Isaac always seems stiff. As if he's keeping something back. Astrid doesn't seem to notice, although she's definitely making a real effort not to make so much of a mess.

'Looks much tidier today, Astrid,' Isaac says as his opening gambit when he appears. 'Well done you.'

I wonder if he'll give her a gold star. He's so bloody condescending.

'I'm really trying,' she simpers.

'That's all that matters,' he says. 'At least we're trying.'

He proceeds to pat her on the head like a puppy, but I know better than to hang around gawping.

I disappear into the kitchen and set to getting supper ready. Grilled fish, spinach and new potatoes. It's Isaac's staple diet request each morning. Astrid has dared override him this evening with the choice of starter, and now I'm witnessing the first little argument between them. Well, an argument of sorts. All calm voices and innuendoes rather than yelling like me and Pablo with our occasional item hurling.

'What's this?' Isaac demands, pointing at the macaroni cheese.

'Something different. You'll love it. Marta has done it exactly the way I like it. Go on, try.' Astrid has already got her fork into a couple of pasta tubes coated in cheese.

'No. I'll not be eating this. Sorry, Astrid, but I did tell you I like plain, good food. And non-fattening,' he adds. He dares lift his shirt and pat a very lean, corrugated-iron stomach.

'Oh. Sorry,' she says, her fork and mouth dropping at the same time. 'I won't eat it either.'

What? I've spent ages working with Astrid's recipe to get it exactly right. She was so happy in the kitchen with me, as she glugged on the cooking wine. She couldn't wait for Isaac to try it.

'That's a good idea,' he says. 'Now, what is the catch of the day, Marta?' he asks, motioning me from sentry position by the kitchen door.

'Sea bass, Isaac. It's very fresh.' I feel like it's my fault that the macaroni cheese wasn't well received. I'd love to tip the whole plate over his head.

'Good. Sounds lovely. And, Marta...'

What now?

'I think it might be better if you referred to me as Mr Marston, or sir, perhaps, while you're working here. Don't you?'

No, I bloody don't.

'Of course, sir,' I say.

Astrid is pretty quiet for the rest of the meal. It's as if she's sitting on the naughty step. Isaac is eating his fresh fish with gusto, every so often cleaning the corner of his full lips with the edge of a crisply ironed white serviette.

Strange, because I've remembered seeing him eat paella, and even steak and chips, at the hotel. The grilled fish thing, now he's moved into the villa, is likely an effort to rein in Astrid's less than healthy eating habits. He's being overly mean though.

'That was delicious, thank you, Marta. What say you tidy up, and Astrid and I will sit out on the patio. Perhaps top up the carafe of wine?'

'Certainly, sir. Coming up.'

Isaac goes round to Astrid's side of the table, plants a kiss on top of her mousy blonde hair and pulls her chair back.

'Come, darling. Let's go and sit outside and put the world to rights.'

Astrid nods, and her smile slowly returns. She's clinging on to his arm as they disappear.

Why do I think 'sinking ship'? She'd be better clinging on to something else other than this creep.

Isaac is far too slippery, and makes my blood curdle.

49

Isaac isn't around much for the next few days. Astrid tells me he's working away and shares how much she misses him.

Alas, Astrid's earlier promises to tidy up seem to have been a bit too rash. I seem to spend most of my time a few steps behind, and picking up after her.

There's no doubt she's happiest in her painting overalls, which consist of a hard clump of what-was-once white material, now stuck together with thick daubs of paint. She is desperate to show me her latest work, but I'm under strict instructions not to have a peek up on the roof terrace until she gives me the nod. It's her best work yet apparently.

Pablo has started sourcing materials for the new pool. Tiles. Hard core. And mechanical excavators. Isaac has also asked him to look after the gardens, a big ask, as they ramble higgledy-piggledy all over the place. Pablo is busy all day, every day, grabbing a quick sandwich at lunchtime, but I've never seen him so excited. Or so happy. He reports on his progress to Isaac most evenings, and is asleep five minutes after his head hits the pillow.

I freeze when I hear a key in the front door as it's not yet 3 p.m. Isaac has got home early, in fact, a full day earlier than expected, and I don't think Astrid knows. She's on the roof, merrily chucking paint on a canvas, when his voice booms round the villa.

Although I've managed to tidy away most of her mess, I notice small paint daubs on the floor. There's a little trail of bright blobs leading all the way up the stairs to the roof.

No. No. No.

I scoot into the kitchen, fill a bucket with warm soapy water and pray the paint will rub off before it sets. Astrid must have only left the trail when she popped down to use the bathroom.

When I come out with the bucket, Isaac is staring at the floor.

'What the hell?' he growls, in a menacingly deep voice.

He bends down, rubs a finger across a yellow blob and looks at me. My legs are like jelly. I can sense his anger, and disgust.

'Did you do this?' he spits at me.

What can I say? That Astrid left it? Surely, he'll know it was Astrid, as she's the one who paints. She's also the one who owns the bloody villa.

'Astrid is on the roof terrace. She's painting,' I say, ignoring the question.

He throws his briefcase on the sofa (usually he sets it neatly in the downstairs cupboard) and strides along the corridor. I hear his feet march up the stairs and then a door slam when he steps out to join Astrid.

I feel sick. So sick, in fact, that I find scrubbing at the paint makes me worse. I've had to use a small amount of paint thinner, and the smell of the turpentine is overpowering.

The silence seems to go on forever. It seems like forever, but the door from the roof terrace opens after only a few minutes. I hear sobbing, large convulsive sobs, and Isaac's footsteps returning.

He's soon standing over me, where I'm now on my hands and knees sopping up the loosened paint mixture. Thank goodness I'm getting the worst of the paint off. He doesn't say anything, just watches. Again, I have the most almighty urge to chuck the bucket of water at him. His pristine cream trousers are screaming out to be ruined. *Bastardo*.

But I know when to hold my tongue, so I keep my eyes peeled on the work in hand.

After about five minutes, which feels more like a couple of hours, he finally moves off. I hear him climb the grand, winding staircase to the first floor. He'll be having a shower and hopefully washing away some of the fury.

When Astrid finally appears, her eyes are swollen, and there's no sign of her painting overalls. She's shaking like a leaf.

'Are you okay?' I whisper.

She simply nods, before going outside and slumping down on top of a sun-lounger. Even from inside, I can hear her quiet but consistent sniffling.

* * *

I pop back to the annex before preparing Isaac's and Astrid's supper. Pablo is inside having a long glass of water. He looks exhausted but relaxed. I doubt Isaac treats him the way he does Astrid, or me for that matter. I suspect our boss is a latent misogynist. Okay with the men, but not so okay with the women.

I tell Pablo what happened, but instead of siding with Astrid, he dares to say, 'Well, she is a bit of a slob.'

'It's her house. She can do as she wants.' My voice rises several decibels.

'But why should you have to clean up after her?'

'Because it's my job. And I'm getting well paid.'

'I do wonder what Isaac sees in her. He's a cool guy, and she is rather a mess.'

I've never felt such a strong urge to slap my husband. My Pablo. And I blame Isaac. It's one thing to treat his girlfriend badly, but when it comes to putting a wedge between me and Pablo, that's something else entirely.

I'm starting to really hate the man.

50

* * *

When I return to the main villa to prepare supper, the place is much tidier. And, an even bigger surprise, Isaac is laughing and working alongside Astrid to get the place in order.

'Hi, Marta. Thanks for cleaning off the paint,' Isaac says.

'No problem, sir.'

'Astrid has apologised and says it won't happen again.' He looks at Astrid as he speaks. His big white teeth are on show.

How can she stay with this man? Isn't it time she threw him out? If Pablo dared belittle me like this, especially in front of other people, I'd pack his bags for him.

'Thank you, Marta,' Astrid says. 'I need to be more careful.'

Her eyes are still swollen, but it looks as if the pair have made up. Isaac, on cue, puts his arms around her, wrapping her up from behind and snuggling his cheek into her neck. Really? He's got to be kidding.

Pablo has warned me not to get involved in their domestics. It's not my place to comment. Their relationship is their affair. And he keeps reminding me we've landed on our feet. Pablo is so happy, at last looking forward to the future, a spring in his step. I should be so happy for him, but nothing feels right.

'I'll start preparing supper now,' I say, and head for the kitchen. Inside the door, I slump against a wall and try to control my ragged breathing. At least things should be calmer at supper. Grilled salmon, in-season vegetables and baked potato are on the menu this evening. Again. I know Astrid will crave butter with her baked potato, but I'll be leaving it in the fridge.

At least Astrid seems to be losing a bit of weight, which surely must be a good thing. Yet I can't help thinking, at what cost?

The evening goes to plan. No major hiccups. Isaac is particularly attentive, and if I didn't know better, I'd think he was regretting his earlier behaviour. But I'd bet my life on him doing it again. And soon.

Then the strangest thing happens. I've just hung up my apron and am about to head off, when I catch a glimpse of something odd. Round the edge of the kitchen door, I see Isaac get down on one knee.

Noooooo.

He can't be. Surely not?

'Astrid.'

Before he says another word, I see Astrid clasp her hands to her face. She lights up like a Christmas tree.

'Astrid Olsen,' he continues, 'would you make me the happiest man alive and be my wife?'

Isaac is on bended knee, his legs and body all at right angles, sharp and unwieldy. I cross my fingers and say a silent prayer that she'll say no, it's much too soon. But no. She's falling for it.

'Isaac. Of course I will. I love you,' she screams and throws herself at him.

I'll have a long wait if I'm expecting him to say he loves her back. All he says is, 'You make me very happy.'

I suppose it will have to do. But I can't believe what I'm seeing. Astrid must be really desperate.

51
_____

Astrid is in a flurry of excitement for the next few days. Isaac has booked
a honeymoon in France, of all places. No expense spared, I heard him tell
her. If Astrid was hoping for a more romantic destination, the Seychelles,
the Maldives, or even the golden beaches of Thailand, she's not showing
it. She's beside herself with excitement.

Isaac seems to be in a rush to seal the union, and Astrid is thrilled to
be getting married. *The sooner, the better*, she told me.

'What clothes should I take? What should I get married in? Marta,
you need to help me.'

'Of course. Let's see what your options are.'

Astrid has, in total, twenty wardrobes dotted around the various
bedrooms in the villa, and each one is packed (like sardines in a can) with
weird and wonderful outfits. Tatty market purchases are cheek by jowl
with top-of-the-range designer wear. Every time I lay a suggestion on the
bed, she squeals, telling me what great taste I've got.

'Why don't you and Pablo take a few days off when we're away?' she
suggests.

'Maybe,' I say, reluctant to admit that we're only now managing to pay
off a backlog of debts.

Astrid comes up to me, takes both my hands.

'It'll be my treat. Would a couple of thousand euros cover it?'

What?

'Oh, I couldn't,' I say.

I sooo could.

'That's settled then. I'll get some euros from the safe, and we'll hear no more about it.' She's almost hysterical from what's happening, and I think, if I played my cards right, I could up the two thousand euros to a couple of million. I've never seen anyone so excited.

As she goes back to folding, ordering and selecting outfits, she whispers, 'Just one thing. Let's not tell Isaac. We'll keep it to ourselves.'

She gives me a theatrical wink and turns back to what she was doing.

I certainly have no intention of telling Isaac.

Later, when I catch up with Pablo and tell him the good news, he's thrilled. But cautious.

'Let's not splash it all,' he says, rubbing his finger over unshaved stubble. He's been too tired and busy to shave.

'Of course, but I've always fancied a trip to Italy. Rome, perhaps for a few days.'

'If that's what you'd like. Has she given you the money yet?'

I pat my dress pocket.

'Yep. I've even counted it. But Pablo...'

His face puckers. 'What?'

'Not a word to Isaac. She doesn't want him to know she's given us the money.'

'My lips are sealed. Though, I'm not sure secrecy is the best start to a marriage.'

'I couldn't keep a secret from you if I tried,' I say, meaning every word.

The difference between Isaac and Astrid, and me and Pablo, is that we're soulmates. I have no idea what Astrid is to Isaac, but I've a pretty good idea it's not soulmates.

Pablo doesn't disagree.

52

A few days later, Astrid and Isaac are heading off.

As Astrid waits in the car for Isaac, who is driving them to France for a ceremony in a chapel in Lourdes, of all places, he pops back inside to have a word.

'Please make sure the villa is spotless when we get back,' he says.

He sweeps an arm round the chaos that has invaded downstairs. Astrid was far too excited to tidy up anything and went from one thing to the next in preparation for the wedding and honeymoon. In preparation for the rest of her life.

Isaac scowls at me, as if I'm in some way responsible and he is definitely trying to rein in his irritation at the mess. I don't tell him I've been in a frenzy clearing up after Astrid at every turn.

'Of course, sir. I'll have it gleaming for your return,' I say through gritted teeth.

Pablo and I aren't leaving for a couple of days, plenty of time for a late spring clean. We're aiming to be back a few days before the newlyweds, when a quick dust round should be all that's needed.

'One other thing,' Isaac says.

'Yes?'

What now?

He moves in very close, too close for comfort, and taps me conspiratorially on the shoulder.

'Astrid's paintings. Please take them all down, and ask Pablo to fill in the hook holes on the walls, and paint over them. They're a bit trashy, don't you think?'

I am so close to smacking this bastard's face. Instead, I stare at him, unable to smile as my lips are in early-onset rigor mortis.

'Okay, sir.'

Once he's gone, and I hear the car drive off out through the metal security gates, I race outside to find Pablo, who has started on the pool excavation.

What am I going to do?

Astrid has been so good to me, and Isaac such a pig. Do I take the paintings down or not? I have no idea.

'Pablo! Pablo!' I yell towards my husband who can't hear me for the noise of the digger. I shield my eyes from the sun and frantically wave with the other hand to get his attention.

When he sees me, he cuts the noise, and I hear that he's whistling. I hope I'm not going to ruin his day, as well as mine. But I need to tell him, so we can decide what to do.

Pablo always tries to avoid confrontation, and it takes him five minutes to come up with a compromise on the paintings.

'Why don't we take them down? I'll refill the holes and paint over, and if we line them up neatly, then they can decide what to do with them.'

'Hmm. It might work,' I say, but I'm not at all convinced.

'They need to sort this stuff out themselves, and we *must not* get involved,' he repeats for the umpteenth time, eager to get back to digging. He's hoping to have the main excavation work done so that when we get back from Rome, he can start putting in the foundations. He's currently eating, sleeping, dreaming infinity pools.

For my part, I'm already having nightmares of what's going to happen when the lovebirds get back from honeymoon. I can't quash a really dark sense of foreboding.

53

Rome was magical, so magical, that I don't want to come back. It's not that the villa isn't fabulous, but it's the thought of having to face Isaac and Astrid.

We get a taxi from Malaga airport, and although I'm tense, and Pablo and I don't talk much, I'm so glad we decided to come back a couple of days before the honeymooners. I've got two days to get back into role play, dust over all the surfaces and plan the week's menus. Hopefully, Isaac will have eased up on what he expects his new bride to eat, but for now I'll stick to tried and tested meals. Grilled fish, green vegetables and new potatoes drizzled in olive oil, mixed with garlic as a special treat.

The taxi drops us off outside the gates, which always make me think of prison gates they're so sturdy, and for the first time I notice a security camera attached under the parapet of the first floor of the villa.

'I could swear that wasn't there before,' I say, pointing it out to Pablo.

'It must have been, you just haven't been looking.'

Pablo looks so relaxed – not at all worried about getting back. Why is my stomach in knots and why am I so anxious? I'm so alert, it's as if I've had ten cups of coffee.

Pablo presses in the code on the gate keypad, and as the gates slide back, I shriek.

'Oh no. They're back early. Look, there's Isaac on the terrace.'

No. No. No. Thank goodness we cleaned thoroughly before we left, but I can imagine Isaac's errant finger has already wafted over surfaces checking for dust.

'Bugger,' says Pablo, but he's already wheeling his suitcase over the path towards the front. I'm more inclined to motion for the taxi driver to come back and drive me away. Anywhere other than here.

I make quite a noise entering the villa, not wanting to startle Astrid by my sudden appearance. I needn't have worried because she's nowhere to be seen. Also, there's no sign of her paintings which Pablo and I lined up downstairs against the wall after Pablo refilled the hook holes and made good the paintwork.

'Astrid? Astrid?' It takes me a moment to work out what's different. It's the lack of mess, the lack of life. There's the feel and smell of a hospital in the air. The subtle scents of potpourri have been replaced by undiluted bleach.

As well as a lack of photos on the wall, Astrid's knick-knacks have been moved. There's nothing on any surface. The large glass-topped table is bare, as well as the small side tables. And the welcoming water feature is turned off.

My first thought is that perhaps they've decided to sell up. Move on to pastures new. I'm not sure I'd be that disappointed as the place is seriously getting to me. Astrid's homely warmth has been obliterated.

I creep up the stairs to look for Astrid, welcome her home and apologise for not being here.

'Astrid? Are you there?' I rap on the master bedroom door a couple of times, and then try the handle.

'What are you doing, Marta?'

Mierda. Isaac is behind me, only a few paces. I nearly jump out of my skin, and my heart starts to race. I put a hand against the wall to steady myself.

'I was looking for Astrid, sir.'

Isaac looks really weird. His hair is thickly gelled, the trademark soft waves stuck in place, and his skin is unusually pale. He looks as if he's been sucked bloodless by a vampire.

'Astrid is lying down. I'd prefer if you didn't come upstairs, except when cleaning.'

He pushes past and lodges himself between me and the bedroom door.

'Will she be down for supper? I have your favourite sea bream in the freezer. I didn't realise you'd be back, or I'd have got it fresh from the Mercadona.'

My voice is very shaky, and my legs are like jelly. I feel as if I'm being told off by a wicked stepfather before he whips off his belt.

'No, not tonight. Astrid won't be down. Sea bream sounds fine, although you know I prefer it fresh. I'll eat on the patio, and you can leave Astrid a small portion outside the bedroom door.'

Seriously?

'Is she okay?' I narrow my eyes.

I needn't be scared of this guy. Pablo and I can get the hell out of here anytime, but I'm worried about Astrid. She's so full of life, and I really like her.

'Of course she's okay. Now if you can set to work, I'd be grateful. I'll have supper as usual at seven.'

With that, he stands with his back to the door and waits for me to descend the staircase.

I grab my suitcase, which I left at the bottom of the stairs, and hurry down the long corridor, through the heavy fire door down to the basement, and don't stop until I'm safely through the garage.

When I reach our house, I yell out, 'Pablo? Pablo? Where are you?' I rush inside, and out again, until I find him. He's opened a bottle of beer and is relaxing round the back in the shade.

'I'm here. What's up?'

Where do I start?

54

Pablo, of course, tells me I'm blowing things all out of proportion.

'Am I? Why then do I feel so bad? Something is going on.' I'm so breathless, it's hard to speak.

'What like?'

'I think Isaac is abusive – and only married Astrid for her money.'

'You don't say.'

Pablo is not worried. I know he agrees it's likely Astrid's money was Isaac's main reason for getting married, but as far as Pablo is concerned, it's nothing to do with us. He wants the work, and that's the end of it.

'Do you think she could be in danger?' I don't know why I think this, but it's the way Isaac talks to her. I can't bring myself to tell Pablo how uneasy Isaac also makes me feel.

'Marta, I think you're really building this up into something it's not.'

'Didn't you notice how tidy, and bare, the villa is since they've been back? It's as if Astrid's past has been wiped from memory. There's nothing of her on show any more.'

'Maybe they're going to put a new stamp on the place. Together.'

I sigh. Pablo has been taken in by Isaac. He's a man after all.

'Well, I'm off to prepare supper. Astrid is eating in her bedroom, you know. Isaac told me.'

This gets Pablo's attention.

'What do you mean? Is she ill?'

'She could be dying for all I know. When I take her tray up, I'll try and speak to her.'

'Marta. I've told you. Keep out.'

'Fine.'

But it's far from fine, and I am definitely not keeping out. I'm worried for Astrid, and I need to know she's okay.

Pablo is too relaxed, so I don't hang around. He's clocked off for the day, and I leave him chilling outside. I take a quick shower, get my apron on and head back through the garage, up the stairs and through the fire door into the villa. It's like two parallel worlds.

There's no sound anywhere. No sign of Isaac. I peel some new potatoes, season the fish which I left out to defrost, and prepare the vegetables.

At 6.55, I hear footsteps.

'Marta. Is my supper ready?' Isaac sticks his head round the kitchen door and presents his plastic smile.

'It'll be on the table in five minutes. Shall I do a smaller portion for Astrid?'

He's already walking away, choosing to ignore me.

I get his food ready, decant his favourite red wine and carry it all out to the patio table, which I set earlier.

Isaac has his legs stretched out to one side, a serviette resting over his pristine shorts and, if I'm not mistaken, he's humming. Tempting as it is to upend the food over him, I set it down. I remember what Pablo said. Keep out of domestics.

'Looks good, Marta. Pablo is a lucky man,' he says, knife and fork poised for action.

'I'll leave a portion outside the bedroom for Astrid,' I say, raising my voice at the end as if in a question.

'Okay. But just a gentle rap in case she's asleep. I'd prefer if you didn't become too familiar with my wife.'

He's already tucking into the fish, deboning it expertly like a fishmonger, and taking regular sips of the red wine. *Pig in shit* comes to mind. It's at this moment that I know, for certain, Isaac has married Astrid purely for her money.

55

I rap gently at the bedroom door. When Astrid doesn't respond, I try again.

'Astrid? It's me, Marta. Are you okay?' I hold my breath, stick my ear to the door. 'Astrid?' I repeat.

I hear a gentle moan from inside. She's trying to communicate, but seems to be struggling. I glance over my shoulder, down the long staircase to make sure there's no sign of Isaac, and then I try the door. It's locked. I try again, but it's definitely locked.

'Astrid, I can't get in. Can you open the door?'

The moaning gets louder, and I just make out the word 'no'. She can't open the door.

'Shall I get Isaac?' I'm so worried now that she might be really ill, that it seems an obvious question despite my suspicions.

Somehow, Astrid manages a loud '*NO.*'

I'm right. Isaac is keeping her locked in.

'Don't worry, Astrid. I'll get you out. You might have to wait till tomorrow, until Isaac leaves for work. Will that be okay?' I bite my lip, close my eyes and say a little prayer.

'Okay.' I think that's all she's going to say, until I hear a muffled, 'Thank you, Marta.'

I leave the tray by the door and scoot back downstairs, out to the patio.

'Did you leave the tray outside the door?' It's the first question Isaac asks when I reappear.

'Yes, sir. I rapped gently, but there was no answer.'

I stare at him. He's wiping his lips as usual. The plate is so clean, it could have come out of the dishwasher. There's not a scrap of anything left. He's managed to move the fish bones on to his side plate without any hint of mess. Hopefully, next time, he'll choke on a bone.

'She'll be asleep. I think she must have caught a bug when travelling. But she's strong. She'll be up and about in a couple of days.'

Why is he smiling? Does he know that it's unlikely she'll be up at all?

I'm already imagining the worst.

I clear away the empties, wipe down the table and tidy up in the kitchen. It looks as if I've no alternative but to wait until tomorrow to rescue Astrid.

* * *

As usual in the mornings, Isaac leaves early. He texted Pablo shortly before 6 a.m., asking to be driven to Marbella, and requesting that Pablo wait around until his meetings are finished.

Pablo is being commandeered more and more as a personal chauffeur. While he is frustrated at being taken away from the pool construction, he loves driving the Merc. Also, sitting in an air-conditioned luxury car has advantages over working outside in the scorching heat.

Once Pablo and Isaac leave, around seven, I rush up into the villa and I'm about to head upstairs when I see Astrid slumped on one of the cream sofas at the far end of the lounge.

'Astrid.' Thank goodness. She's alive. At least my worst nightmares haven't come true. 'Are you okay? I've been really worried.'

'I'm fine.' She coughs, looking far from fine. Her face is shrunken in on itself, and she has lost so much weight. It's been less than two weeks since they got married, and already she looks skeletal.

'Can I get you anything? A hot drink? Fruit? Anything at all?'

'I want you to order me a taxi. In thirty minutes' time to take me down to the port.'

'To the port? Are you strong enough?'

'Please, Marta. Just do as I say.'

Astrid struggles to get up, and when she does, she hobbles unsteadily towards the stairs. She's dressed in a long, soiled, once-white nightshirt that hangs below her knees. She clings to the banister as she hauls herself up, inch by inch.

I get out my mobile and google local taxi firms. The first one I try says they can be here in fifteen minutes. I tell them that's fine, as it's better if they're early. I know Astrid will pay them whatever the bill is.

Ten minutes later, Astrid reappears with a large handbag, and wearing very brightly coloured clothes. The yellow blouse and purple shawl clash, but she's so determined to get going, I doubt she's too worried about her appearance. Her lanky hair seems to be falling out; I spot a small tangle of strands stuck to one shoulder.

I open the front door for her, and she pauses for a few seconds. She seems to be trying to calm her breathing. She closes her eyes.

'Marta. Come here,' she says. She widens her arms and weakly pulls me towards her. 'This might be the last you see of me, but thank you. Be careful around Isaac. He's a very dangerous man.'

'Shouldn't we go to the police?' My eyes are wide and pleading.

'It's too late for that. Goodbye, Marta, and remember: be careful.'

With that, Astrid is gone.

56

After she's left, time stands still. I feel I'm waiting my turn on death row.

I can't get any work done, I'm so freaked by everything that's going on. I'm petrified what might happen when Isaac learns that I've been instrumental in Astrid's departure.

I sit rigid on a hard chair for the next two hours. I check my watch every few minutes, as well as my phone. I've texted Pablo half a dozen times, but he hasn't even read the messages. Taking calls while on duty is taboo. Another thing Isaac doesn't tolerate.

I jump out of the chair when I hear more than one set of footsteps coming up from the garage. At least Pablo must be with Isaac, which gives me a small measure of comfort, but I'm scared to death. It's as if I've masterminded a Colditz escape, and am about to be interrogated by a Nazi commandant.

When the pair finally appear, I'm up and dusting over spotless surfaces with a brand-new cloth.

'Where's Astrid?' Isaac snaps, looking all around him. He heads towards the terrace, pauses by the glass doors and turns his stony stare my way. 'Marta? Didn't you hear me? Where is Astrid? Is she still in the bedroom?'

I can hardly speak, my mouth is so dry. I need to be honest, as far as I can, without telling him where she's gone.

'She's gone out.'

'What?' he screeches. 'Where has she gone?'

He comes back, until he's so close to me, I can smell his sour breath. His tone is an ominous rumble.

'I've no idea. She called for a taxi.' I'm trembling so badly, that I lean against the table.

'You let her go out in the state she's in? You've got to be kidding me.'

'She insisted she was fine. I didn't think it was up to me to tell her where she could go.'

Pablo is hanging back, but he gives me daggers. He knows when I'm in a corner that my Latino temperament can get the better of me.

'Perhaps you should have used a bit of common sense. Where did she phone from?'

'She borrowed my phone.'

It suddenly dawns on me that Isaac might have confiscated Astrid's mobile.

'You lent it to her? Give it to me,' he orders, holding out a palm.

I walk very slowly towards the kitchen. I know my phone is there. Isaac will be able to track the taxi company Astrid used, perhaps also find out where it dropped her off. But at least she's long gone. If she's planning an escape, hopefully she'll be miles away.

I reluctantly hand over my phone, and watch as Isaac frantically scrolls through my recent calls. He connects to the last number dialled.

'Is that Marbella Taxis? I need information about where you dropped off my wife. The name is Marston. Mrs Astrid Marston. It's urgent.'

Five minutes later, Isaac orders Pablo back to the Merc.

'And Marta. I'll deal with you later.' He points a bony finger at my forehead. I think gun and trigger.

As they head off for the second time, I know mine and Pablo's time is up. We need to get away from this villa, and as far away from Isaac as possible.

If only I hadn't left Los Molinos.

* * *

The next two hours are torture. I wander inside and out, up and down stairs. When I do sit, I crunch down on my nails which are bitten to the quick. Despite cups of camomile tea, my stomach is churning.

Pablo and Isaac return some two hours later. When they appear, neither one is talking. Both men have their hands stuffed in their pockets. They look like conspiratorial brothers who have been up to no good.

'Did you find Astrid?' My voice is shaky.

'No. We didn't,' Isaac says. His whole body looks stiff, rigid, and his jaw seems to have locked, while a vein pulses in his neck.

'Oh.' I look at Pablo, and he shrugs. 'I'm sure she'll be back soon,' I say.

I'm not expecting Isaac to be thrilled by the prospect, but his answer is cryptic.

'I doubt it. I think she's gone.'

'Gone? Gone where?'

'Wouldn't we like to know?' Isaac manufactures a sarcastic laugh. He looks deranged. 'Now, Marta, rather than bother yourself with things that don't concern you, I'd like an early supper.'

'Of course. I can have it ready in half an hour, sir.'

'Perfect. On the terrace again, please. And I'd like white wine tonight. A cold Chablis perhaps.'

Why do I get the feeling that he's celebrating something? It's as if he's discovered, for certain, that Astrid has flown to the Arctic Circle, never to be seen again.

When I finally clock off for the evening, I rush home to find Pablo, but he's fast asleep on the sofa. It's a comforting sight, because if anything had gone seriously wrong this afternoon, he'd surely be waiting up for me.

But I'll never be able to sleep, not until I find out what happened when Pablo and Isaac went to look for Astrid.

57

'Pablo. Pablo. Wake up.' I have to screech in his ear, he's in such a deep sleep.

His body jerks, but I shake him violently to get his attention.

'Bloody hell. What's up?'

He stretches out and yawns. He is not worried at all.

'Did you find Astrid at the port?' I haul at his arm. 'Pablo. Wake up. This is serious.'

He sits up, rubs his eyes and looks at me, still no hint of concern.

'No, we didn't. But she'd been there. Why? What's the problem?'

'What's the problem? You've got to be kidding me.' I circle the sofa, wringing my hands. 'I helped Astrid get away. I called for the taxi. She was in a really bad way. She's lost a shedload of weight and looks really ill.'

I've got his attention, at last, but he's more concerned at the words 'I helped' than 'looks really ill'.

'I told you not to get involved.' He pulls himself up and hangs his head in his hands, as if the world is about to end. I want to say, it's not up to him to tell me when to get involved. It's bad enough listening to Isaac telling me what to do.

'Pablo. Astrid was scared for her life. She was in a dreadful state. How do you know she'd been at the port?'

'Isaac asked around, and apparently she hired out a small speedboat. She's done it before. Isaac seemed to know the guy who dealt with her.'

'A speedboat? Why the hell would she want to go out in a speedboat? In her state?'

Perhaps...

I have a ghastly premonition of what might have happened. I clasp my hands together, look to the heavens, and pray that I've got it wrong.

* * *

It's around 9 p.m. when there's a ring on the front bell. I've crept back into the kitchen to do a final clean and tidy up before the morning. I peek out through the gap between the frame and the door.

Isaac comes strolling in from the terrace, glass of wine in hand, and looks up at the security camera. He peers at the screen, then speaks into the pad.

'Yes. How can I help you?' he asks.

'It's the Policía, señor.'

I'm hiding in the kitchen, back in eavesdropping position, tucked behind the huge American fridge-freezer.

'Yes. What can I do for you?'

'We'd like to come in. Would you open up, please?'

Isaac must be keying in the code for the main gates, as everything goes silent for a moment, until a car pulls up to the side of the villa.

I feel I'm going to be sick. I'm shaking from head to toe, as if the police are here to arrest me. My head is spinning with possibilities, and deep down I'm guessing it's to do with Astrid.

I stay where I am, knowing that if I appear, Isaac will send me away, but I need to hear what's being said.

I peek through the gap again and watch as two stocky uniformed policemen appear, hats tucked under their arms. They block my view of Isaac, but I see one of the officers holding out something for him.

'Do you recognise this?' The officer is gripping something purple.

There's a few seconds' silence.

'I'm not certain, but it could belong to my wife.'

No. No. No. Astrid was wearing a purple shawl over her yellow blouse. It looks like the one the policeman is holding up.

'Where did you find it?' Isaac asks.

'Señor. We found it floating in the ocean, near an abandoned speed-boat, a few miles round the coast. On the speedboat we also found a handbag which we believe is the property of Astrid Marston. Your wife.'

My knees give way, and I slither to the floor.

'Can you excuse me one moment, Officer.'

I hear Isaac heading towards the kitchen, and he pushes the door so violently, it bangs against my body which is slumped on the floor.

'Marta. What are you doing? Get up and go to your quarters.' He glowers at me and shakes a balled fist.

It takes an almighty effort to get up, as the door has smashed into my right leg, and the pain is searing through my body. Dragging my injured limb, I somehow manage to make it along the corridor, and on down through to the basement.

When I get home, I'm shaking from head to toe. Pablo is watching TV, but at least he's awake.

'Pablo. Pablo.' I lunge at him, sobbing hysterically, and collapse along-side him.

'What's up? What's happened?' He takes my shoulders, holding tightly, and looks into my eyes. I must look demented because Pablo's brow has furrowed and he looks really worried.

'What's happened to your leg? It's bleeding, and it's starting to bruise.' He licks a finger, rubs it across the constant trickle of blood.

'Oh, that's nothing. Isaac smashed the kitchen door against it.'

'What?' He jumps up and heads for the door. 'Isaac did this delib-erately?'

Pablo is ready to punch his boss's lights out. When he sees red, his temper is even worse than mine.

'No. No. Forget that. Pablo, it's Astrid. I think she's fallen overboard.' I have to shout, to make him listen.

He stops in his tracks. 'Whoa, slow down. What's going on?'

'The police are here. They found Astrid's clothing floating in the ocean and her handbag and belongings abandoned on the boat she hired.'

'What are you saying?' Pablo is now towering over me, gripping my shoulders. Things are starting to register.

'Pablo. Pablo.' I can't stop crying, large choking gulps, as my palms cover my face. 'I think Astrid might have killed herself.'

58

After the police visit, I can't concentrate on anything. I'm in a constant state of anxiety, worrying about what has happened to Astrid. It's been exactly two weeks since she went missing.

Other than a vague Spanish mañana-style investigation, nothing is getting done in a hurry, and no one seems to care. There's no one batting for Astrid, and without a body washed up on shore, it's possible we'll never know what happened. Pablo says it could take years to have her declared dead.

Although everything is carrying on as usual, I'm a mess inside. It's worse because no one else seems to care.

Yet, surprise, surprise, Isaac is coping really well. It makes me mad to see him smiling for the first time in weeks, as he lazes round the villa keeping an eye on the pool construction. Not unlike Astrid, Isaac seems to be a complete loner. No family. No friends. Nobody to comfort him over his missing wife. I'm scared by my level of loathing for him. I'm not sure which is greater: my sadness at losing Astrid, or my fury at Isaac. The way I'm feeling today, the latter is nudging well ahead.

When I try to let off steam, using Pablo as a verbal punchbag, he tries to calm me down, but his responses make it even worse.

'It's sad for Isaac too,' he says. 'He has no one to sympathise with him.'

'You mean, he's no one to celebrate with,' I hiss.

It's not Pablo's fault, but he's concentrating more on his work than worrying over what has happened to Astrid. Also, he's still in awe of Isaac, treating him like a celebrity. What I can't forgive, is that Isaac has come between me and Pablo.

This morning I take a break and pop outside to catch up with Pablo. As ever, he's slaving over the new pool construction.

He's tireless in trying to please his boss. Apparently, if he finishes on time, there'll be a bonus. I told him not to count his chickens, as it's more likely a dangled carrot to keep him on his toes.

'What are those coloured tiles?' I ask.

'The light blue and yellow tiles? I'm designing a dolphin for the bottom of the pool. Apparently, Astrid once swam with dolphins and Isaac wants to keep her memory alive. The light blue tiles are for the body and the yellow for the fins.'

'You're not serious? *El es un bastardo*,' I snap. Isaac is relishing in Astrid's suicide, but why can't Pablo see it?

But Pablo is too busy to argue, and rather than rise to the bait, he carries on arranging the coloured tiles in a pattern.

I wander back inside, and mosey around, upstairs and down, dusting and wiping spotless surfaces. There's less and less to do. With Astrid gone, the villa is spotless and the time drags until bedtime.

I change Isaac's bedding every second day, and I asked him this morning what he wants me to do with Astrid's clothing.

'We'll give it a month. If my wife doesn't come home, you can pack it all away.' He's about to walk off, but adds, 'To be honest, Marta, I am prepared for the worst. I don't think Astrid is coming back.'

'Oh, I hope you're wrong. Do you really think she killed herself?'

I can't help myself. I stare stony-faced, unable to hide my feelings.

'Not that it's any of your concern, Marta, but yes, I do. She suffered serious depression issues, which you probably weren't aware of.'

Without waiting for a response, he strides off. He's certainly mastered the art of cutting a person dead when he doesn't want to connect. The subject of his missing wife is at the top of taboo subjects not to be discussed.

I need to bat for Astrid, and find a way to punish Isaac. He's the one who should be at the bottom of the ocean.

59

As well as battling my hatred of Isaac, Pablo and I are now at loggerheads about what to do once the pool work is finished.

Pablo thinks I'm overreacting, and that my fears are unfounded. To make matters worse, Isaac keeps tasking him with future projects. He's already instructed Pablo to landscape either side of the pool once the water is in. Isaac enjoys coming between Pablo and me, and I've caught his smug expression more than once when he thinks we're arguing.

But I've made up my mind. As soon as the pool is finished, we'll move on. I feel really mean for Pablo, but he'll have no choice if I put my foot down. Pablo is worried that Isaac won't pay him if he thinks we're moving on, and Pablo is determined to get what's his due.

I'm also paranoid that when we do finally pack up Isaac won't make it easy for us to leave. I'm starting to dread what he might do as he's used to getting what he wants. All I do know is that if we stay here much longer, I'll go crazy. Pablo is exhausted at the end of every day, and although I have no one else to talk to, I can't keep on at him. He's working so hard. And it's all for us.

Around midday, I tell Pablo I'm off to the supermarket for supplies and more fresh fish. At least I can't go wrong with Isaac's meals as he eats the same things every day. I've made suggestions for more adventurous recipes, but the answer is always the same.

'No, thank you, Marta. You know what I like. If I want anything else, I'll let you know.'

I'd be tempted to poison him if I could get away with it.

I've just got into my car in the garage and turned the engine on when Isaac appears and raps on the window. *Mierda*. I nearly have a heart attack, as I never see him in the garage.

'Open up,' he mouths, flapping his hand, until I roll down the window.

'Sir. You gave me a fright.'

'Where are you going, Marta? Haven't you work to do in the villa?'

He must have followed me down here. Why? I often go to the supermarket. But then he's not usually at home so much.

'To the supermarket. I'm off to buy your fresh fish, and pick up some supplies.' My mouth is so parched, it's hard to get the words out. He stands tight up to the car, clamps his hand on the roof. I grip the steering wheel, and feel the menace in his proximity.

It might be my imagination, but since Astrid has gone, he's constantly watching me, and in subtle ways warning me to behave. I thought his control issues were because he paid my wages, but now I'm not so sure. There's something else. Something darker.

'Well, don't be long. Shall we say you get back by two?' He lifts his hand off the car roof, and points at his watch.

'I'll be as quick as I can, but I planned on going for a walk along the beach.'

'Perhaps that can wait until your day off?' He smiles with pursed lips and wide unblinking eyes. He looks more than a little crazy.

I've told Pablo more than once that I would have been certain, if he hadn't been out with Isaac at the time Astrid went missing, that Isaac had killed his wife.

'Don't be ridiculous,' Pablo says. 'Isaac is an okay guy. A bit weird, but a murderer? Marta. You can't be serious.'

Pablo doesn't mean to wind me up, he's just so trusting. It drives me crazy that he can't see what Isaac is really like. If Pablo had seen Isaac push Astrid overboard, he'd still think they were only playing a game.

But I know Isaac is evil. My mission is to find out how he got rid of Astrid. If he didn't do it himself, he must have had someone else kill her. Money can buy you most things, even a Mafia-style hitman.

'When is my day off this week?' I ask Isaac.

'Why don't we say tomorrow? But I'd like to know where you're going in case I need to get hold of you. In an emergency,' he adds.

What sort of emergency? It's none of his nosy business what I do on my day off. And why is he so concerned to know where I'm going all of a sudden, and what time I'll be back?

'Of course. I'll not be going far.' I smile. 'Is that all, sir?'

He steps away from the car, patting the roof with his hand, and waves me off.

Bastardo. I'll not be telling him where I go when I'm not working. It's none of his business.

As the car slides out on to the motorway, I start to wonder if Isaac might have put a tracking device on my car.

Could that have been the reason he was lurking in the garage?

60

I get back, two and a half hours later. My heart's in my mouth, dreading having to face Isaac again. No doubt he'll grill me on what I was doing in the extra half-hour.

I amble up from the garage, struggle as always to open the fire door and lug the heavy shopping bags along the corridor to the main villa. I slow down though when I hear voices and laughter. It's not Pablo and Isaac. Isaac is talking to someone else. It's a woman. Astrid must be home.

A huge wave of relief washes over me. I've got it all wrong. Pablo has been right all along.

I make a greater effort to speed up, my heart fluttering, but my cheeks are flushed with joy. Astrid is okay. I realise, as I round the corner, that I've really missed her. She's scatty, messy, but usually full-on fun. In another life, another time, we could have become good friends.

A couple of the bags suddenly slip out of my grasp when I see who Isaac is talking to.

It is *not* Astrid.

'Hello, Marta. I thought I heard you.' Isaac takes a step towards me.

'Sorry I'm a bit late. The supermarket was really busy,' I lie. I'm certainly not going to tell him I was in and out in half an hour, and walked along the beach for a lazy coffee, and then stared out to sea for over an hour.

'That's no problem. Here, can I help you?'

You've got to be kidding me. I quickly pick up the bags.

'No, sir. I can manage, thanks.'

'Have you forgotten you can call me Isaac?' He gives a lazy smile and stretches out a hand, physically forcing one of the shopping bags from my grasp. 'These are really heavy. What have you been buying? All my favourites, I hope.'

He heads towards the kitchen, and I slope along behind, scared to look at who he was talking to. Who he was laughing with. It is not Astrid. It's a lookalike. She could be a twin. Lanky blonde hair, a generous waist-line, although her ankles are even more generous than Astrid's. But she's younger. I'd guess in her early forties, but still a lot older than the sort of woman I'd imagine Isaac to fancy. Maybe it's a mother-fixation thing. Who knows?

When he's helped me deposit the shopping bags, he holds the door open for me, which is a first, and propels me towards the guest.

'Marta. I'd like to introduce you to Emmeline,' he says. He smiles from me to Emmeline and back again. It's a big smile, but one with a big warning attached when it lands my way.

'Hello, Emmeline.' What do I say? That you need to get out of here quickly, and never come back?

'Hi, Marta.' Emmeline looks at me, and I look at her. Why is she so familiar? Then it dawns. I've met her before.

'I think you stayed at Los Molinos last year. I used to work there,' I say.

Isaac is clucking his tongue, a sign for me to get moving. The clucking speeds up and gets louder.

'Nice to meet you,' I say quickly. 'I need to get back to work.'

With that, I turn tail and hurry back to the kitchen. But before the door closes behind me, Isaac appears in the opening.

'Marta. I would like to have a word with you. I want to make it clear that you are not to become friends with Emmeline. She is *my* guest. You will look after her when she's staying here, but remember, I am your employer. Have you got that?'

'Yes, Isaac.'

'And you are not to engage in conversation with her when I'm not around. Do you understand me?'

Loud and clear. I simply nod, too scared of what I might say. I am beyond furious, but this is the last straw.

'Oh, and I was only joking about calling me Isaac.' He laughs, a sarcastic burst of venom.

'Yes, sir.' Somehow I manage to bite down on my tongue.

'Good. I hope I've made myself clear.'

I nod, knowing better than to answer back.

With that, he leaves me to unpack the groceries. I have the most violent urge to throw everything over the floor and yell for him to come back. When he slips on the stinking fish, I'll smash his skull in with one of the copper pans.

I've no idea how I'm going to keep a lid on the fury. All I do know is that I need to come up with a plan to pay him back for what he did to Astrid. He's definitely responsible for her death, one way or another.

I can't share any more with Pablo. This will be the first time in our marriage that I'll have to keep a secret from him. Isaac needs punishing for that too.

For now, I need to keep an eye out for Emmeline while I hatch my revenge.

I need to warn her to get out. Before it's too late for her as well.

61

Pablo is soon acting more than a little smug, as in 'I told you so', because Isaac is being delightful with Emmeline, spoiling her, wining and dining her, and not a bad word has passed his lips.

'Yet,' I hiss back at Pablo.

Since Emmeline arrived, I've been holding my breath. I know it's only a matter of time until Isaac puts a foot wrong, and I'm desperate for Pablo to see his true colours. It's torture waiting, as I'm petrified of what might happen next.

It's been a few days since Emmeline was first at the villa, and she's already officially moved in. She's sharing the master bedroom with Isaac, and I was ordered this morning to clear the wardrobes of Astrid's belongings and put them in storage.

I didn't like to ask what Isaac meant by 'storage', so decided to hang up all of Astrid's clothes in various wardrobes in the upstairs bedrooms, piling the shoeboxes underneath.

Isaac is unlikely to find them as he never ventures far from the master bedroom. He likes all the upstairs rooms to have their doors kept closed, presumably through a fear of dust mites creeping in.

But every time I touch Astrid's things, I start to well up. I smell her Dior perfume on every item. The only things I can't find are her paintings. They're nowhere to be found. I've looked high and low, and the thought that Isaac has thrown them out makes my blood boil... even more, if that's possible.

There's a big plus though. Isaac is back at work, wherever work is. Even Pablo has no idea. He drops him off at various locations, and picks him up a few hours later, but is never told where his boss goes in-between times. We joke that maybe he spends the day drinking coffee or wine.

Emmeline lolls around the villa all day. Waiting. The way Astrid used to do once she had finished with her painting. Unlike Astrid, Emmeline likes to exercise; she walks round the gardens in sturdy shoes no less than four times a day, and her spare time doesn't consist entirely of snacking and drinking. She reads a lot and is always on her iPad. The pool isn't filled yet, but Emmeline has told Pablo that she's really looking forward to a swim very soon.

She keeps trying to engage me in pleasantries. The weather. The views. The beaches. She tells me she is from Germany, from a small town called Cochem in the Rheinland, asking if I've ever been. I shake my head, not daring to speak, hoping she'll think I don't speak English.

She tested me with a few words in German, but gave up, assuming I didn't speak her native language either. I'd love to tell her that Isaac has ordered me not to speak to her, but he'd go ballistic if he thought I'd told her.

It makes me feel even more lonely having her here, not being able to engage. She seems nice, and again, starry-eyed over Isaac's charm. And good looks. Not to mention his money.

Tonight is the first time that she does something wrong. And yes. It's again to do with mess. When I say she does something wrong, I mean something wrong in Isaac's eyes.

They've barely started supper when Emmeline commits the sin.

'Emmeline. Please be careful with your food. Even the smallest crumbs can attract vermin,' he says. She's breaking open one of the crusty rolls I've set out, and bits are flying everywhere. Isaac is sitting stiffly, leaning across the table as he talks to her.

Here we go.

'Oops. Sorry.' She looks at the ground, at the scattered crumbs.

I scoot to the larder, dig out the dustpan and brush (again!) and get to work.

'Thank you, Marta. Hopefully, we'll not need you again this evening.'

'*Bueno*. Okay, sir.' My hand is shaking, and Emmeline is looking at me with concern. Little does she know.

62

The couple get into a routine of sorts, and Emmeline oscillates from singing highs, to silent, sullen lows. It's obvious that Isaac is chipping away at her, with his chiselled words and caustic putdowns.

It's then I overhear something I know I'm not supposed to. This time, I'm behind the barbecue kitchen at the end of the terrace, sweeping up, when the pair walk by, hand in hand. Isaac seems to be on the charm offensive again. My first thought is that Emmeline might want to leave and has had enough of him, and that he's trying to win her back.

I'm so naive. Of course she doesn't want to leave him. Why did I even think this?

I'm scared that Isaac might realise I'm within earshot, so I push my back up against the barbecue, and try to keep out of sight. I'm shaking like a leaf, my knees knocking, but my ears are on high alert.

'As you know, my wife, Astrid, has gone.' I'm sure I hear Isaac suck in a huge theatrical gulp of air.

'I know. I'm so sorry.'

I imagine Emmeline looking up at him with her doe eyes. All gooey and wistful.

'Although I'm prepared for the worst, that she took her own life, I won't be able to find closure for some time. The law in Spain works very slowly indeed.'

What is he trying to say? He can't want to marry her, can he? He's not even divorced from Astrid.

'It must be awful for you,' Emmeline says.

They're sitting on a couple of chairs taken from the stack of outdoor dining furniture. Pablo and I sometimes do the same when Isaac isn't around. I have to yell at Pablo to remind him to put the chairs back when we're done.

How am I going to creep away without being heard? I'm so scared, my body has gone rigid.

'The problem is, I have a few bills to pay. Well, bills that Astrid used to pay from her personal account, and I'll be unable to liquidate more funds until the end of next month.'

My hand flies to my mouth. He's after her money too.

No. No. No. *Emmeline, please do not lend him money.*

'How much are you short?'

'Just shy of 150,000 euros. We have plenty of money. Sorry, I mean, Astrid and I had plenty of money. I still do, but we used joint signatures on most things, and not knowing what has happened to Astrid... well, it's going to take time to sort things out.'

I imagine Isaac is likely now looking at the ground, wringing moisture from his eyes, squeezing his lids tightly together. I can't listen. I want to jump out and scream, tell Emmeline to run for her life.

When Emmeline doesn't immediately respond, Isaac carries on.

'Sorry. I shouldn't have brought it up. It was really bad form. Let's walk round the garden. And I don't think you've been on the roof terrace yet? Perhaps I'll ask Marta to bring us up a jug of sangria before supper?'

Go on, Emmeline. Tell him 'no'. Please.

But Emmeline says nothing. I hear the metal chairs being scraped back, footsteps moving off and the sound of the couple picking their way past the olive trees, back towards the villa. I need to somehow cut them off, and get back inside first. Isaac must not know that I overheard.

Or he'll kill me.

63

Today, there's a sudden break in the couple's pattern. Isaac, regular as clockwork, normally gets home shortly before seven.

However, today, I'm on my way back to the annex, heading down the corridor towards the basement, when I hear voices. Isaac must have got home early, as it's only three o'clock.

Instead of going through the fire door, and on down the stairs towards the garage, I lean my back against the wall and listen. When I hear Isaac's angry voice, I freeze. Even though it's Emmeline in the firing line, I get the most dreadful sense of panic.

'Emmeline. I told you I don't like mess. You've dumped stuff everywhere. I DO NOT LIVE like this.' He emphasises his words as if she's deaf.

'What are you talking about?'

'Your clothes are scattered all over the bedroom. You've left an empty glass on the patio. Wet towels are dripping in the bathroom. Do I need to go on?'

I can imagine Isaac hissing in her face. He's off-the-scale angry, I can hear it in his slow, clipped tone. I heard the same tone with Astrid when he spoke in dangerously low levels.

'I'll tidy up now. I'm sorry, I didn't realise.'

'Emmeline.'

Oh no. How do I guess what he's going to say?

I'm waiting for her to respond, but there's nothing. Isaac carries on.

'Listen, Emmeline. I'm afraid this isn't working out.'

'What do you mean?'

'I'd like you to move out. I'm sorry.'

At least he's said sorry, but I can feel, even from where I'm lurking, that Emmeline is in shock. I certainly am.

'What? I thought you loved me.' Emmeline 's voice is whiny, and suddenly everything goes quiet.

What's going on? I'm scared to move in case they hear me.

'I'm very fond of you, Emmeline. You know that, but...'

'But what?'

Come on, Emmeline. Fight. Tell him he's an arrogant prick, and you'll be happy to leave, only too glad to see the back of him.

'Until I know what happened to Astrid,' Isaac says, 'I'm not ready to make a commitment. I thought I was.'

No, you didn't. You lying bastardo.

'I understand. I can wait. I'll be tidier, I promise. Isaac, I love you.'

He's walking away from her. Noooo. I can hear her lighter footsteps follow behind.

'Emmeline. Don't do this. Have some pride, please.' Isaac speaks slowly, emphasising the syllables as if to a child.

What is she doing?

Then I hear huge blubbering sobs, before she screams at him.

'What about my money? The money I lent you?'

'Don't worry. I'll pay you back. Give me another week.'

I can hear the patio door close. He's gone outside and shut her in.

I can't bear the noise, as Emmeline is now wailing like a banshee. I push open the fire door, race downstairs to find Pablo.

Wait till I tell him. I was right all along. At least the pool is nearly finished and will be filled up with water in a few days. We need to get away from here, and this crazy man.

* * *

Pablo looks horrified, and nearly as stunned as I expect Emmeline feels.

'You're joking me,' he says. He's glugging on a long glass of iced water and throws the dregs over his head to cool himself down.

'She's demanding her money back.' I can't get my words out quickly enough. 'She must have lent him the 150,000 euros after all.'

'Seriously?' Pablo swipes the back of his hand across his brow. I can tell he's shocked because he seems to be having trouble taking it all in.

'I think he was only seeing Emmeline because of her money,' I add.

Pablo ambles round the room. His feet are covered in dirt, and he's depositing dust everywhere. Isaac would have him shot if he were a woman. But I don't say anything. He's my Pablo, and he can leave mess wherever he wants.

'Do you really think so?' He's now scratching his head.

'Yes. And I'm certain that's why he married Astrid. For her money. Listen, Pablo, we need to get out of here. Isaac is dangerous. I think he threatened Astrid, and that's why she killed herself.'

'Another couple of weeks, the pool work should be finished. The water is going in tomorrow, and the landscaping shouldn't take too long. Let's see then, shall we?'

I slump on the sofa, hang my head. I have such a migraine from all the stress.

'I've got to take Isaac to the airport tomorrow. Remember I told you?' Pablo says.

'I'd forgotten. Where's he going? Did he tell you?'

'He's flying to London – Luton airport, I think he said – and coming back the following day.'

'Oh. Well, at least we'll have a bit of peace and quiet.'

The thought that he'll be gone, even if only for twenty-four hours, is like a soothing balm. Perhaps I can help Emmeline pack, and tell her, when Isaac is out of earshot, what a total bastard he is. And that she's safer far away from here.

64

This morning, there's a creepy silence about the villa.

Pablo and Isaac left early. Pablo was to drop Isaac off at the port, pick him up later, and from there take him directly to the airport.

I'm already starting to unwind, knowing that I'll not have to face Isaac until tomorrow evening at the earliest.

I make my way to the kitchen, and spot Emmeline's suitcases by the front door before I see her. She's out on the terrace, staring off into the distance. She doesn't look round when I appear and doesn't try to make conversation. I suspect she's given up trying, as I've never engaged before.

'Emmeline. I'm sorry. I hear you're leaving,' I say.

She looks round and nods. Her eyes are bloodshot, circled by puffy red swelling. She looks as if she's been crying all night.

'I know you must be upset,' I say. Understatement of all time. 'But you'll be safer away from Isaac.' I'm putting my own life in my hands here, but I can't bear to see her so upset. I reckon if she knows Isaac is a really nasty piece of work, she won't feel so bad.

'I can't believe I made such a mistake. He threatened me, saying if I didn't get out today, he'd call the police.'

'No. You're joking.' I'm not sure what else to say to comfort her. How dare he threaten her like this?

'I realised last night that he's really crazy. I thought he was "the one".' She makes inverted commas with her fingers. 'I'll be okay. I've been on my own long enough. But...'

'Yes?'

'It's the money. I lent him 150,000 euros and I need to get it back. He says he'll pay me next week, but I no longer trust anything he says. It was my life's savings.'

'Oh, I'm really sorry. Where will you go?'

'I have a friend with a little flat in Calahonda. I'll stay there before going back to Germany. But I need to get my money from Isaac first.'

I don't like to tell her that she's unlikely to see a euro. She handed the money over willingly. Isaac has committed no crime. Taking advantage of wealthy women, or women with savings, is looking like his modus operandi. You can't be sent to prison for conning people out of money, not if they give it voluntarily. Pablo and I have been googling, and telling lies is not a federal offence.

I want to tell her to forget the money, put it down to experience and get the hell as far away from Isaac as possible.

Instead, I give as encouraging a smile as I can muster.

'Marta, would you order me a taxi please? I'd be really grateful. I'm ready to go.'

'Of course. I'll do it now.'

'I didn't realise you spoke English so well. I actually thought you didn't speak it at all.' She gives me a quizzical look.

'I'm not allowed to engage with guests. A rule of the villa.' I roll my eyes.

Emmeline understands. No need to say any more.

When I wave her off, I feel a weird sense of relief. While she was staying at the villa, I had a constant sense of doom. Maybe it was because of what happened to Astrid, but I really felt Emmeline's life might have been in danger.

Hopefully, she's learnt her lesson and will keep well away from Isaac. Now I need to start planning our own escape.

65

I haven't seen Isaac since he got back from his trip to England. Although I know he got back late last night because when I get to the villa this morning, there are empty glasses on the breakfast bar. In fact, there are two empty champagne flutes, alongside an empty Moët & Chandon bottle.

My first thought is that he's made up with Emmeline, although there's no sign of him anywhere. When I get to clearing up, Pablo pokes his head round the patio doors and calls me over.

'Marta. Marta.'

'Coming. What's up?'

Why do I feel like there's something up? It's in Pablo's voice, as if he's about to tell me something that he really doesn't want to.

'I forgot to tell you. Well, you were asleep when I got back from the airport, and I didn't like to wake you. But Isaac brought a young girl back here last night.' He grits his teeth and watches me.

'What?' My jaw drops, and my eyes gawp in horror.

'Apparently, she collapsed getting off the plane. Isaac helped her, brought her back here to sleep it off.'

'Sleep what off? Where is she now?'

'She was out cold in the car, but Isaac didn't seem concerned. She's probably upstairs asleep. Listen, I need to get back to work. Isaac asked me to ask you if you'd make her coffee and breakfast when she gets up.'

With that, Pablo is gone. He's not going to get trapped by the new mountain of questions I want to ask.

I lift away the dirty glasses and empty bottle, and take them into the kitchen. Emmeline has only just gone, and Isaac is already on the prowl for his next victim. No matter what Pablo thinks, his lady friends are definitely victims. Whoever this woman is, I'll not be getting involved. At all. I've learnt my lesson, and I'll not be saying a word.

Anyway, Pablo and I have already started the countdown until we are out of here. The pool has been successfully filled up, and the rest of the work should be completed in no more than two weeks. Pablo has finally agreed we'll leave once we've both been paid.

I dig out a couple of less-than-fresh croissants and set them on a plate, before putting the dirty glasses in the dishwasher. I'm moseying around the kitchen when I pick up the sound of footsteps coming down the stairs. I put the coffee on, wait a couple of minutes and carry out the croissants and hot drink to set on the breakfast bar.

When the woman tries to strike up a conversation, I keep my eyes averted, nod and disappear as quickly as I can back to the kitchen. I won't be making even a hint of eye contact with whoever the latest guest turns out to be. The Queen of Timbuktu for all I care.

The woman looks much younger than either Astrid or Emmeline – and so much prettier. She's slim, nicely dressed, with clear skin and healthy-looking hair. Perhaps her sudden appearance is down to a rare act of compassion from Isaac, but why am I not convinced?

Something else is now bothering me. Pablo has just popped his head back round and motioned for me to come outside. It could be because his feet are dirty, but also likely because he doesn't want the guest to hear.

He tells me that he has instructions to give the latest guest a lift to Los Molinos later. Her name is Jade, apparently.

It now seems more than a coincidence that Isaac met Astrid and Emmeline both at the hotel where I was working. And now, Jade appears to be staying there as well. The hairs stand up on the back of my neck, the thought crossing my mind that there's something more going on than a series of chance encounters.

'And Marta,' Pablo says, clasping his hands in prayer mode. 'Please don't get involved with this Jade.'

'Do you think I'm crazy? Isaac has forbidden me to talk to guests.' I can't help the snap in my voice. It's not Pablo's fault, but he doesn't need to warn me. Not this time.

Pablo grins, drops his hands, and gives me a peck on the cheek.

'Must get to work. Love you.'

When he disappears down the garden, I feel a rising panic. At least Pablo is coming round to my way of thinking, and although he doesn't like to admit it, he's now wary of Isaac. He's finally agreed that we'll leave the villa the second the landscaping is finished, and we've both been paid in full.

But even another few days feels like a lifetime, and I have such a sense of foreboding. I've no idea what might happen, but I can't imagine it'll be anything good.

Jade must have gone up to the guest room to collect her stuff. When I've almost finished tidying up, I hear her come back down and go outside. Probably to find Pablo and arrange her lift to the hotel. I keep under the radar until I hear Pablo head down to the garage to get the Merc.

I pick up the bunch of keys, and when I know Jade is waiting by the front door, I appear and open up as quickly as possible. I don't even look at her. I must seem so rude, but I'm beyond caring. I breathe a sigh of relief when she's gone, hoping it's the last I'll see of her.

Even if she never comes back to the villa, it'll not stop me working on a plan of revenge. Isaac won't know what's hit him. I feel mean keeping my thoughts from Pablo (he'd kill me if he knew what I was up to), but I can only tell him everything when the time is right. I can't risk him letting slip any secrets.

At least for me, it's a relief to no longer be working on my own.

66

As soon as Pablo and Jade have left, I set off in my Fiat 500. I feel bad not telling Pablo exactly where I'm going, but I can't risk him telling Isaac.

I drive into Marbella, park in a tight spot up a shady side street and head for what has become a regular coffee shop haunt. The cortado coffees hit the spot – I have at least four every time I come. It's dark inside the café, but cool, and it feels safer to sit in a dark corner than out in the open.

The heat outside is building, and there'll soon be red alerts. Stay indoors will be the advice, at least between eleven and five. Poor Pablo. Isaac doesn't let him stop until the end of the day. No siestas allowed. Pablo laughed for the first time in ages yesterday when I suggested we drown Isaac in the new swimming pool. He soon stopped laughing when I said I wasn't joking.

Pablo couldn't imagine I'd come to this sort of backstreet café, and it's best he never finds out. I've been a couple of times this week, as well as to a similar one in Malaga twice last week. Pablo knows I like to get out, do some shopping and people watch, but he has no idea why I really come here. If he saw the dingy cafés, he'd think I'd gone mad, or perhaps turned to drug dealing.

I love Pablo to heaven and back, but he doesn't always know when to hold his tongue.

Isaac would lock me up if he knew what I was up to. He'd definitely go more than a little bit crazy. I shiver. If he hasn't already murdered someone, I think my secrets would tip him over the edge.

After the four cortados, and not a little scheming, I leave the café and set off to wander round the shops. Feeling more upbeat than I have for ages, I treat myself to a nice pair of sandals. Spending makes me feel better. I can't remember the last time I treated myself or Pablo to new clothes, or anything new, for that matter. It was certainly long before we moved into the villa.

I pick up a couple of colourful T-shirts for Pablo, one of which has a dolphin on the front. He'll laugh at that. It'll remind us of the swimming pool project long after we've left.

An hour later I head back to the villa. When I get there, Pablo is slaving away under the baking sun again, wearing a wide-brimmed straw hat to protect his head. The sight makes my heart ache. I wave out at him before I set to preparing Isaac's regular meal.

Five minutes go by when Pablo suddenly appears in the kitchen. I nearly hit the ceiling.

'Don't creep up, Pablo. Please.'

'Sorry. I did try to make a noise.' He's a really bad liar, and grins from ear to ear.

'What's up?'

'I forgot to say. Don't worry about Isaac for supper. He's got other plans, and said we could use the fish ourselves.'

'Oh. Where's he going?'

'I hate to tell you, but I think he's taking the young lady who stayed here out to dinner.' Pablo clenches his jaw, worried the information will set me off again.

'Who? Jade?'

'Yep. I've got to drive him over to Los Molinos later.'

'You've got to be kidding me.'

When Pablo goes back to work, I start mulling over the plan. I may need to act much sooner than anticipated, as my gut tells me Jade might be the next woman Isaac asks back to the villa. If he does invite her to stay, I intend to make sure it'll not be for long.

I need to get Isaac to kick her out. Now I know what he can't stand, and what will tip him over the edge, it shouldn't be too difficult. My aim is that he'll have had enough of his new guest, before he can manage to rip her off, steal all her money – or do something much worse. The dread of what he's capable of makes me quake, but makes me doubly determined.

Implementing this first part of my plan won't be easy. But it'll be a lot easier than the second part. I know I mustn't think that far ahead in case I bottle out completely.

As I take the fish and fresh vegetables out of the fridge for mine and Pablo's supper, it crosses my mind that someone at Los Molinos might be tipping Isaac off. Someone is telling him when wealthy, single women arrive alone at the hotel. There's definitely a pattern to what's happening. On the surface, Jade seems to have been a random encounter, but I'm not so sure. Did someone at the hotel know she was catching that particular flight to Malaga? I might be overly suspicious, but I think I've sussed what Isaac's game is.

It's likely he's done this before, possibly at who knows how many other locations around the world. And from where I'm standing, he's got it down to a fine art. Also, knowing he doesn't use his real name of George Stubbs, as shown on his passport, makes me almost certain that he could be an international con artist, money his only goal.

He may have got away with it up till now, but the game will soon be up.

67

As the days pass, I start to have serious moments of doubt.

Perhaps I've got it all wrong, and this will be a new more peaceful chapter at the villa. I try to kid myself, but the paranoia gnaws away.

The villa is like a morgue. I wander round like a robot, cleaning and dusting already sparkling surfaces. I have such a sense of doom, as if waiting for a monster to appear.

It's exactly one week since Jade crashed out at the villa, and I've dared hope that maybe my worst fears will amount to nothing. Perhaps I'll never see her again.

How wrong could I be?

Pablo announced last night that Isaac has asked Jade to come and stay. As soon as he told me I had to sit down. I guessed this would happen, but I've been praying I might be wrong. Apparently, her time at the hotel has come to an end.

No sooner has Pablo set off for Los Molinos to collect the guest, than Isaac phones and orders me to prepare the guest bedroom. When I don't talk into the handset, he asks if I can hear him. My stomach lurches at the sound of his voice, and I feel so queasy I'm not sure how I'll get anything done.

I stay well out of the way when Jade and Pablo get back. Isaac then phones me for a second time (from wherever he's working) to tell me about the arrangements for supper. I'm to prepare the table outside on the terrace. When I think he's finished, he adds:

'And Marta. You are not, at any time, to engage in conversation with my guest. Do I make myself clear?'

'Yes, sir. Very clear.'

He doesn't need to worry this time at all. I'll be keeping a glacial distance from Jade, and not getting sucked into even the slightest pleasantries or small talk. Never again. I have only one goal: to get Jade away from here and back to safety before it's too late. I can't believe what I'm going to do, and the countdown is about to begin.

I keep a distance from Jade during the day, and am standing to attention by the kitchen door when Isaac finally arrives home. He doesn't formally introduce me to Jade, and within five minutes, he resorts to clicking his fingers to get my attention rather than communicating like a normal person.

This suits me fine. Hopefully, he'll even stop talking to me.

As I'm preparing the food, I don't hear Isaac creep into the kitchen. When the door suddenly slams, I swing round, and freeze when I see him watching me.

Before I say anything, he moves towards me, and with a bony finger, stabs me in the chest.

'Just to remind you, Marta. Under no circumstances are you to converse with my new guest. Okay?' He gives me one of his wide phoney smiles.

I simply nod, and watch as he marches back out, slamming the door off its hinges for a second time. I only manage to calm down when I start serving up.

It's the first time that I get a really good look at Jade. She's totally different from Emmeline and Astrid. A lot younger for one. She can't be much over thirty. Also, she's coming across as feisty, spirited. It's in the cocky way she flirts with Isaac.

I'd love to talk to her, get to know her the way I did Astrid. She looks bubbly, lots of fun.

Pablo is petrified that I won't be able to help myself, and I'll land myself in deep water with Isaac. Last night, he also gave me a stern talk-ing-to. I couldn't resist winding him up, telling him I might ask her just a few questions. He went ballistic, shouting and yelling that I must be mad, until I finally surrendered and told him I was only joking.

'Please. Don't even look at her, and no talking at all.' Pablo held my shoulders in his strong fingers, and stared deep into my eyes. I hadn't realised until that moment how worried he really is. It's definitely no longer all about the money. He's finally picking up the danger vibes.

'I'll behave. You mustn't worry.' I kissed and hugged him tight.

Poor Pablo. He has no idea what's coming next.

68

Pablo is now so wound up that he's taken to smoking again in the evenings, around the back of our plot. And occasionally he indulges in a beer mid-afternoon. He thinks I don't know about the smoking, chucking the stubs away before he thinks I've seen. I've so far cleared away at least twenty from around the grounds. No idea why Isaac hasn't picked up on the mess, as he notices everything, but I suspect it's because he's a misogynist.

Underneath all the charm and schmooze, Isaac hates women. I think he's overly respectful of Pablo in order to drive a wedge between Pablo and me. This has been one of Isaac's biggest mistakes. No one gets between me and my man.

Pablo visibly relaxed when I promised not to engage with Jade. When he'd mellowed, I used the moment to bring up what I'm about to do. Pablo needs to be prepared.

'Pablo. You need to keep your eyes and ears open. Listen into their conversations.'

'Why, in heaven's name?'

'I've got a plan.'

'A plan? Marta, please tell me you're not going to do anything stupid.'

Pablo stared at me. He instantly got uptight all over again. '*You said you wouldn't get involved.*' He stressed each syllable.

'I won't. I promise, but hear me out.'

He slumped onto the small wall at the front of our finca, dared pull out a cigarette in front of me (the first time in ten years), and flicked a lighter.

'I'm all ears.' He dragged in the smoke, and convulsed from coughing.

'You know Isaac doesn't like mess?'

'Yes...' Pablo didn't want to hear what I had to say, but he reads me like a book. I think he might have already guessed what my plan might be. Well, my immediate course of action. I know even Pablo won't guess the endgame, and I can't tell him. Not until it's over. Keeping a secret from him will be one of the hardest things I've ever done.

'I'm going to leave mess around the villa, and patio, for Isaac to find. He'll assume it's Jade's mess because he knows I wouldn't dare. Even after he tells her off, I'll carry on.'

'And? What then?' Pablo's voice rocketed a few decibels.

'Don't you see? Isaac hates mess so much, he'll throw her out. Like he did Emmeline. I'm not convinced even the pull of Jade's money can calm him down if I really go for it. He's got a real phobia. What do you think?'

Pablo dragged so hard on the cigarette, he struggled breathing. He smacked a hand against his chest.

'Why do you want him to throw her out?'

I hopped off the wall and eyeballed him. Pablo needs to be onside.

'Pablo. Isaac is dangerous. You must see that. He uses women, cons them out of their money, and then throws them out on the street. Or, worse still...' I take a deep breath.

'What do you mean, "or worse still"?'

'Astrid either killed herself, or someone was hired to murder her.' I gnawed the inside of my cheek and held his gaze. 'Either way, Isaac was responsible.'

'You really think if Jade stays here that her life will be in danger?'

Pablo always errs on the side of trust. It's his way. He likes to see the best in people, even when faced with rotten evidence. But this time, I can

see it in his eyes, the doubts are there. Although he'll not admit it, I think
he's smoking again because he's more than worried.

'Yes, I do think she'll be in danger. So I'm going to start tomorrow.
Either Isaac will get so angry that he'll throw her out, or she'll get so mad
with him that she'll walk away.'

Pablo let out an enormous sigh of surrender.

'Before she's handed over her life savings,' I added.

'I certainly wouldn't want to get on your bad side.' Pablo managed a
wry smile, stubbed out his flickering butt, and pulled me down onto
his lap.

'Pablo, I love you. Once you've finished the work, and we've got our
money, we'll start over. It's not safe to stay here. Things will work out fine,
I promise.'

I've no idea why I said things will work out fine. For all I know, I could
be the one who ends up dead.

69

It doesn't take long for things to get frosty between the couple. Quicker than I could have hoped.

Isaac has already screamed at Jade for a mud trail which appeared on the stairs, and for a dreadfully messy bathroom. I'm torn between guilt at being the one to pull the blinkers off Jade's eyes, and relief that my plan might be working.

Isaac is rising to the bait faster than I expected, and even though his anger is directed at Jade, I'm petrified that, somehow, he'll link the trails back to me. I daren't think about where it all might end.

A few more slovenly displays, and I think Isaac will snap, and hopefully fling Jade out on the street before he persuades her to hand over serious amounts of money. Pablo has heard through the grapevine, from a maintenance worker friend at Los Molinos, that this woman is seriously rich. Multi-millionaire rich, like Astrid was.

As always, when I get back to our finca after supper, I'm desperate to catch up with Pablo. He has become increasingly adept at eavesdropping. But when he hits me with a curve ball, my heart races. Isaac has already begun trying to extort money from his guest.

He tells me that Jade has agreed to pay Isaac's boat charter fees, as Mario is refusing to take Isaac out again until they're paid. I suspect not being able to get his hands as yet on Astrid's legacy has left Isaac short of cash. She used to pay for everything. I dread to think what he's done with Emmeline's money.

My first thought is that he's testing the waters with Jade. See how willing she might be to hand over even small amounts in order to hold on to her new, handsome, single, millionaire boyfriend.

'How much?' I snap at Pablo, as if it's his fault.

'How much what?'

Pablo has stripped down to his boxer shorts and flip-flops, and is soaking himself with the emergency garden hose. It's after nine, yet the heat is still unbearable. I'm tempted to join him, as I need desperately to cool down. Physically and mentally.

'How much were the fees?' I get an uneasy knot in my stomach when I ask the question.

'Five thousand euros, I think.'

'So has she paid them?'

'I think so.' Pablo sighs, not able to hide how fed up he is with all the domestic drama. He shakes his shaggy wet hair from side to side like a sodden sheepdog, and heads inside.

'At least it's not more. I wonder how quickly he'll pay her back.' I shout to try and hold his attention.

I follow him, but he's gone quiet, and locked himself in the bathroom. He hopes I'll let it rest, as he's too exhausted to hear any more.

I go to the fridge, lift out a half-drunk bottle of Viña Sol and pour myself a long glass. I take it outside and collapse on to a garden chair. Ten minutes in, Pablo's snore rumbles through our little finca. I'm jealous he's able to sleep because I'll be tossing and turning all night.

My mind is spinning, and my insides are in turmoil, with thoughts of what I plan to do. Messy bathrooms, spilt coffee, and trails of crumbling croissants are only the beginning. I'll not rest now until it's all over.

I take out my phone, and take a moment to come up with a text.

Tomorrow, usual time and place. Malaga, 11 a.m. New developments to report…

When a thumbs-up instantly bounces back, I turn my phone off.

The dark, seedy bar in Malaga is even more depressing than the one in Marbella, but needs must. It has to be somewhere no one would come looking for me. Even Pablo would never frequent these types of places. He'd forbid me to go, especially if he thought I was going on my own, and likely even if he knew I had company.

As the time draws closer to the final part of the plan, I need as much help and advice as I can get. I'm petrified at the thought of what I've agreed to do, but I'm at the point of no return. The question is, when will be the right time to carry through?

Only time will tell, because, who knows what the next few days will bring?

70

Santa mierda. Things are going even more topsy-turvy.

I certainly couldn't have predicted what happened while I was in Malaga, in the dark, seedy corner of the backstreet bar. Jade and Isaac were viewing a very expensive penthouse apartment at Puerto Banus.

I've popped back to the finca to freshen up before getting Isaac's supper. I'm beyond exhausted and desperate to collapse into bed. I'm so wrung out by the heat, and anxiety, that I could fall into a deep sleep. But when Pablo comes home for a much-needed cooling bath, he tells me what's been going on today. I'm soon wide awake again.

'What do you mean, Isaac lent Jade money? You must have got it wrong.'

I'm now seriously sweating. The conversation isn't helping tone down the temperature. My whole body is bathed in perspiration, my frizzy hair stuck in clumps to my damp forehead, and my vision is blurry from all the moisture.

'No. I listened in the car on the way back. They definitely went to see an apartment, and Jade fell in love with it.'

'Why did Isaac have to lend her money?' I wring my hands together, my palms squelching.

'Unless they paid a full 25 per cent deposit today, she would lose the place. Someone else had already made an offer.'

Pablo yawns as he strips off his maroon and pink speckled T-shirt. Even the thick matting of hairs on his chest are sodden. The heat is creeping through every chink in our stone cottage, and it feels as if we're in the cauldron of an active volcano which is about to explode.

'Why didn't Jade pay? She must have money. He surely can't be *treating* her?' My eyes are saucer wide. For a split second, I doubt everything again. Maybe Isaac isn't only after her money. What if I've got it wrong? Got Isaac wrong?

'She can't get such a large amount out all at once. I think she needs two days. She's going to pay him back so there shouldn't be a problem,' Pablo says in a flat monotone.

He wanders into the bathroom and pulls the door to. He's totally fed up with the same old conversations. At least he's ready to leave this place and for us to live again as a normal couple. A couple in love. He's started talking up a holiday for us in Portugal. Lisbon. Barcelona. As soon as the pool landscaping work is done, he's agreed we'll get away. He's also agreed that if it's what will make me happy, we'll never return.

I sit outside the bathroom and try to bite back the fifty millionth question: why did Isaac lend Jade the money so readily? Could he really care for her? She is different, younger than Astrid and Emmeline. Perhaps he'd like to have children?

I can't believe I'm having these thoughts. I'm desperate to believe they're true, but who am I kidding? He's probably used Emmeline's money to fund the deposit.

'Oh, I nearly forgot,' Pablo yells over the sound of water filling the bath. 'Jade is going to buy Mario's yacht for Isaac, to say thank you.'

Hairs stand up on the back of my neck. Of course I wasn't wrong. There had to be a catch.

I push open the bathroom door.

'That's why he lent her the money,' I say. 'The yacht must be worth at least fifty thousand euros. Once she's paid him back the deposit, he'll have got meaty interest on his investment.'

I clap my hands together, but Pablo isn't looking. Instead, he slips under the cool bath water and blows bubbles to the surface, waving at me with one hand and clipping his nose closed with the other.

* * *

I'll now have to go back into Marbella tomorrow, to a new café. I've become paranoid that Isaac might be having me trailed, but I've no choice. I need to report what I've just heard. I've got an uneasy premonition that Jade might be trying to play Isaac. It's a female intuition thing. Pablo says I'm like a witch, but I usually sense correctly what's going on before I'm told.

If Jade has got Isaac's money and doesn't pay him back, I dread to think what might happen. If Isaac is pushed hard enough, heaven knows what he'll do.

If she's got the measure of Isaac, and is not as smitten as Astrid and Emmeline, she could be in serious danger. She might not realise what Isaac is capable of.

I overheard Jade on the phone, telling her mother that she was flying back at the weekend. But unless Isaac has got his money back, he's unlikely to let her go. And I'm not sure even then, if he'll let her.

I get out my mobile and send another panicky text.

We have a problem! Tomorrow. Marbella. Bar Quattro. 11.00 a.m.

Instantly, another thumbs-up, followed by a smiley face. Really?

71

If I thought things were bad, they are getting worse, minute by minute. Isaac has now locked Jade in the villa. With me.

He summoned me late last night, and demanded, in no uncertain terms, that I wasn't to let Jade leave, and I wasn't to go anywhere either.

'What if she asks me to let her out?'

Isaac glowered at me from a great height, until I was trembling from head to toe.

'You are not to talk to her. Keep out of matters that don't concern you. How often do I have to tell you?'

'But...'

'*There-is-no-but*. You've been told.' He narrowed his eyes, and seemed to grow another foot.

Rather than heading into Marbella as planned, I'm trapped in the villa.

I have to communicate everything by text, sending regular updates.

Help! What should I do?

It's small comfort when I get instructions back, because, however I look at it, I'm here on my own. It's all down to me, and it's likely now or never. The laughing emoji responses don't help in the slightest. I'm on such high alert, a war could be imminent.

I sidestep Jade all day. She's been combing the villa trying to find me, and I keep hiding behind doors when I hear her footsteps.

Last night, as Isaac and Jade ate supper, I was busy leaving a trail of dirt up the stairs to Jade's bedroom. It was a last futile attempt to push him over the edge, to get him to fling her out. Deep down, I know he won't, unless she's paid him back.

He screamed at Jade for over half an hour. Then a door slammed, and there was a deathly silence.

Today is Friday, and I now know Jade is booked to fly home tomorrow. Pablo heard Isaac and Jade talking, and she's already booked her flight for the evening. This wasn't the first time Pablo had listened in, as we already knew Jade was planning on going back at the end of the week. At least I now know exactly when.

Time has run out. I now have to complete the plan, sooner than anticipated, but I'm desperate to get it done before the maggots completely gnaw through my insides.

I'm in bits, having to lie to Pablo again, but this afternoon when I tell him I've had instructions from Isaac about a job that needs doing, he downs tools and follows me up onto the roof terrace.

'What does he want? The furniture moved out? Why?'

I move skittishly across the roof terrace. The gigantic walls have locked in the heat, and it's like being trapped in a sauna. Pablo has plonked the round concrete doorstop against the door to keep it open as we get to work. He doesn't notice that the door handle on the roof terrace side has been removed, so without the doorstop, we'd be locked in until someone came and let us out. Although, unless someone came looking, there'd be a problem, because the roof terrace is the only place in the whole villa without a mobile or Wi-Fi signal.

'Astrid, before she disappeared, had ordered new roof terrace furniture,' I tell Pablo. I feel awful pretending, but there's so little time left, I can't risk confrontation. 'A barbecue, new table and chairs, a couple of four-poster sun beds. Isaac wants to get rid of the old stuff before the new stuff arrives.'

'Can we keep all this? Looks pretty good to me.' He fingers the pristine loungers and the glass-topped outdoor dining table. He wanders over to the pile of parasols in the corner. 'We could use all of this in our own garden.'

His eyes are puppy-dog excited.

'I wouldn't dare ask,' I say. 'Isaac hasn't been in too good a mood. We'll store it in the garage for now and maybe ask once the new stuff arrives. But...'

'But what?'

'We'll not be here much longer. Remember?' I give him a stony stare.

He doesn't rise to the bait; rather, he looks confused. He's not quite sure what's going on, but that's good enough. He doesn't need to know. He's not overly inquisitive by nature, preferring an easy life. And I can cope with confused.

But he suddenly lobs a question out of nowhere.

'What's really going on?' he asks as he hoists up a couple of chairs.

'Nothing. What are you on about?' I throw my hands out in front of me. 'We just need to get rid of everything up here. Come on. Let's get started.'

He tuts and sighs heavily before he starts to negotiate the narrow staircase.

The chairs and parasols are relatively easy to get down, and the table, luckily, isn't as heavy as it looks. We manage to manoeuvre it to safety, working well as a team.

It's only when I tell Pablo that the fridge – loaded with champagne, bottled waters, soft drinks and smoothies – also needs to go, that he plonks his hands on his hips.

'Really? You are kidding me. Why would he want the fridge taken down?'

'He's ordered a new one. A top-of-the range American monster.' I laugh, roll my eyes. 'Typical Isaac.'

'Okay. But it's bloody heavy.'

Together, we unload the fridge and set all the contents to one side.

'I'll have one of those beers when we're finished,' Pablo says, tapping the top of one of the bottles.

'Let's get this thing down first.'

Pablo leads the way, taking the bulk of the weight, but when he stumbles on the last step, I scream. There is an almighty bang, and the fridge crashes downwards, smacking against Pablo's leg on the way.

'Shit. Shit. Shit.' Pablo screams in pain, and rubs his ankle. 'I hope we haven't broken the damn thing.'

I couldn't care less if we've broken the damn thing. Pablo is all I care about.

'Are you okay? Don't worry about the bloody fridge. Can you put weight on your leg? Will you be able to carry it on to the garage?'

'I'll try.' He struggles up, and I notice the edge of the fridge has clipped the side of his face.

'Oh, Pablo. You'll have a nasty bruise on your face tomorrow. I can already see a small bump on your head. Are you okay?' I stare in horror.

Pablo runs a finger along his cheek, licks off a smattering of blood.

'I'll live. Now let's get this blasted stuff into the garage.'

It's then I freeze. I pick up sounds of Jade moving around. She'll likely have heard the noise.

'Shhh.' I put a finger to my lips and shoot Pablo a warning look.

'What?' he mouths. I can tell he's in pain, because he's grimacing, and breathing heavily.

'Jade. She mustn't know what we're doing.'

'Why, for heaven's sake?' He gives a look that could turn me to stone. 'Marta. What are you up to?'

'Please, Pablo. For once, stop asking questions. You need to trust me, and help get this stuff away. You'll know soon enough.'

Pablo is in no fit state to argue. We work in silence, and manage eventually to get everything through to the garage. I then order Pablo back to the finca to rest up and ice his ankle, which has swollen like a melon. At least he hasn't broken anything. I look at him, and somehow hold back the tears.

'I'll have to clean up your face. You look as if you've been in a fight,' I say, fingering his swollen cheek. I pull him in for a hug, and cling tightly. I try to squeeze out the guilt I feel for having caused his pain. I make a promise to myself, that once things are over, I'll make it up to him. And I'll never again keep secrets from my man.

Pablo needs to be okay, because the way things look, tomorrow is likely to be Armageddon.

And there'll be no going back.

72

Sleep is impossible, and I toss and turn all night long.

At first light, I creep out of bed, and leave Pablo snoring, as I head up to the villa.

I've never been as scared in my whole life, but I need to appear calm, even if my insides are in turmoil. Saturday is finally here. It's now or never.

I manage to avoid Jade with the covert skills of a ninja, leaving her out a ridiculously flaky croissant and a milky coffee for breakfast before I slip out of sight.

Isaac isn't due back until mid-afternoon, but when I hear the front door open shortly after eleven, I freeze. He's back much too early. My heart starts to race, and I come over hot and dizzy.

Jade must have gone outside. I left the patio doors slightly ajar at one end, even though Isaac instructed me to keep the doors closed. He would rather have her wandering around inside than in the gardens.

It's not as if she could escape, but he's determined to keep her locked in. I'll be in serious trouble for disobeying his orders. But for now, Jade is going to be the one in the firing line.

My hands shoot over my ears when I hear Isaac holler. He's by the breakfast bar.

'Jade? Jade?'

I'm hiding in the kitchen, scared to breathe. I'm clinging on to the edge of the sink.

I listen to Isaac stomp around downstairs before he goes outside. When he yells Jade's name several more times, she eventually responds.

They're both now back inside.

'What the hell is this?' Isaac couldn't yell much louder. I picture his face, puce from anger, his trademark throb pulsing in his neck.

'What? That's nothing to do with me.' Jade's voice is shaky, but she's in battle mode. She's no pussycat, thank goodness. She's feisty, unlike her predecessors. I'm depending on her to play ball when I tell her.

I feel really bad for having made such a mess when she finished breakfast. I crumbled the leftover flakes onto the floor and spilled some extra milk over the marble tiles. The place is in a right state.

'What the hell do you mean, it's nothing to do with you? It's obvious it's your bloody mess. Listen, Jade,' Isaac hisses, 'you need to pack your bags and get out of here. First though, you're going to pay me back my money. Every penny, before you go.'

Then I hear a slap. My hands fly over my mouth. It sounds as if he's hit her. My legs almost give way, but then I realise it's the other way round. What? Jade's the one who has done the hitting. He'll kill her before I get a chance to take him out.

The kitchen seems to be spinning. Suddenly, there's a crack, as if someone has banged their head against a hard surface, and then everything goes quiet.

No. No. No. Please don't let it be Jade.

The seconds feel like hours, but I let out all the pent-up air when I hear Jade speak. Her voice is shaky, but she's okay. Thank God.

But the relief is short lived. She's now telling Isaac that her phone battery is dead and that she couldn't charge it because he'd taken the plug adaptor back. Although her voice is unsteady, she's fighting. She's determined not to let the bastard beat her. She couldn't ring the bank, or anyone for that matter, she says. She needs to talk to them, as she hasn't got her log-in details to hand. I'm not sure if she's lying about this, but she's also insisting, because it's Saturday, it won't be easy to speak to anyone at the bank.

The next thing I hear is Jade walking away, towards the stairs.

Isaac screams after her, 'You've got thirty minutes, tops, to sort out my money. *Do you hear me?*'

Another eerie silence follows. I cling to the kitchen worktop and pray.

I nearly throw up when Isaac bashes his fist on the kitchen door.

'Marta? Are you in there? Can you come out and tidy up this mess?'

He might only be guessing I'm in the kitchen, but I've no choice. I need to face the music.

I somehow manage to reach the door and slink out. My cheeks are flushed, and I can't find my voice. Isaac knows I've heard everything, but he's in such a state, beyond angry with Jade, that he doesn't take me to task. He doesn't even look at me, but I can see, even from a few feet away, that his eyes are glazed over, and his mind is miles away.

If ever there was ever a moment when I should back out of my plan, it's now. I should tidy up and creep away. Let Jade face the music on her own. But I can't. There's too much at stake, and judging by Isaac's demeanour, he has murder on his mind. I think I might be the only person who can save Jade's life.

While I start to tidy up, Isaac goes outside on to the patio and lights a cigarette. I've never seen him smoke before and he's prowling back and forth like a caged lion.

Jade has slammed her bedroom door. I dread to imagine how she must be feeling.

73

I watch as Isaac wanders away from the villa in the direction of the pool.

This could be my one chance. I need to act fast. I scoot back into the kitchen, and lift out the small plastic container hidden under the sink. I prick my ears, hover for a couple of seconds, and creep back out when I'm sure the coast is clear.

I hurry past the main staircase, and on down the corridor until I reach the foot of the stairs that lead up on to the roof terrace. My hand is shaking so badly, I struggle to prise the lid off the tub. Finally, it flicks off and I start to scatter wet, muddy, dirty sand all the way up the stairs and out on to the terrace.

It doesn't take more than a minute to empty the contents, and I'm soon on my way back down. I nearly break my neck trying to sidestep the slippery mess, but once I'm at the bottom, I head straight for the down-stairs cloakroom and lock myself in. It's only twenty paces from here to the bottom of the stairs up to the roof. I try to calm my breathing, close my eyes, and start counting down from one hundred. This is it, there's no going back.

With my senses on high alert, I hear Isaac's footsteps. They get louder with each step, and I wonder if Jade can hear them too. If she's not already terrified, she will be in a few seconds. She needs to stay in her bedroom or all will be lost.

It's then Isaac must see it. The trail of mud.

'What the fuck?' His voice is threateningly low, but even from behind the cloakroom door, I hear the venomous growl.

Timing is now key. If I get it wrong, it's all over. For Jade, and for me.

A deep breath, three Hail Marys, and I slide back the bolt. Isaac turns when I appear.

'What's up, sir?'

He swats his hand for me to follow him.

'Oh my goodness,' I say, putting a hand over my mouth when he points to the trail of dirt. I pretend I'm seeing the mess for the first time.

'Marta. Where is Jade? Get her. NOW!'

I'm not sure how I manage to form the words, but somehow they tumble out.

'She's up on the roof terrace, sir. I saw her go up a minute ago,' I whisper. The last thing I need is Jade to hear, and come downstairs. I'm struggling to keep my voice steady, and my throat's so dry the words barely come out. I offer up a silent plea. *Please God. Let him follow the trail.*

It seems my prayers are answered, as he storms up the staircase towards the roof. It seems to take him forever to reach the top. The heavy doorstop is holding the door open, but I've been practising. With a quick swipe of my left hand, I can lift it away, get it down one step, and with my right hand, I can slam the door closed.

Isaac steps over the top riser onto the terrace. I'm a couple of paces behind, but he's not looking my way. He's scouring the terrace for Jade, murder on his mind.

When I finally slam the door shut, I collapse onto the stairs and swallow back the nausea.

It's done. Isaac won't be able to get out. Not until the cavalry arrive. When I text the deed is done, they'll be here within the hour. With the temperature at almost forty degrees, and without shade or water, Isaac will be beyond scared. It's the least he deserves.

By the time he does get out, Pablo and I will be long gone.

I slither down the stairs from the roof and scoot round to the bottom of the large staircase. Now it's my turn to yell.

'Jade. Jade. It's Marta. Come down now. You're safe.'

Although I can't hear any noise from the roof, I keep looking over my shoulder. In my nightmares, I see Isaac appear behind me.

A few minutes pass. Although the thick fire door leading on to the terrace blocks out most sound, I can hear the faintest rapping coming from the other side. It's persistent. I wonder how long Isaac will keep it up.

'Jade. Jade.' I scurry to the bottom of the main staircase and scream even louder.

There's no sign of her anywhere. Why isn't she coming out? Perhaps she's gone outside.

My heart is hammering so fast, that I'm scared I might pass out. I need to hold it together. I take my phone out of my pocket, and call Pablo. I'm sweating so badly that I have difficulty gripping the handset.

'Pablo. You need to take Jade to the airport.' I'm so breathless that my words tumble out. 'Please, Pablo. Get the Merc ready in the garage.'

I have to hold the phone away from my ear as Pablo rants down the line. He wants to know if Isaac has given the instruction.

'Pablo. Pablo. Pablo. Stop asking questions. Please, just do as I say for once. I'll explain everything when you get back.'

I can hear Pablo's mind work in the silence. He doesn't say anything, but doesn't hang up either, until I scream through the handset.

'Pablo. NOW. Go. Go. Go. It's urgent. Jade's life in in danger.'

More than Jade's life will be in danger if Isaac does somehow get out, so Pablo needs to move fast.

I know he's far from happy. He's confused, anxious, but finally agrees to down tools and get the car ready. If he wonders where Isaac is, he doesn't ask. My Pablo knows when further discussion is futile, and this is certainly one of those times.

I do a quick scan outside, round the patio, and down by the pool but there's no sign of Jade anywhere. When I come back into the villa, I spot her suitcase under the stairs. She must be nearby.

I frantically check all around downstairs, and then head for the cloakroom.

'Jade. Are you in there?' I yell.

Although I'm the one looking for Jade, I'm on such high alert that I'll jump out of my skin if she does appear, or even answers me.

I turn the handle, fling the door wide, but she's not in here either. I don't waste time, as I need to find her. And fast. We all need to be away from here in the next hour.

I scoot along the corridor which leads to the garage, but still no sign. Then I hear footsteps on the stairs. She's gone up to her bedroom. Maybe she forgot to bring something down.

As I head up the staircase, she suddenly appears above me.

'Jade. Come with me.' I stretch out my arm, letting out a huge sigh of relief, and encourage her to take my hand.

I hesitate for just a second, glance over my shoulder, when I think I hear a noise behind me. Isaac. It can't be. He couldn't have got out, could he?

Then all of a sudden, Jade swipes past me, knocking me off my feet and clobbering me with her shoulder bag. I scream, and tumble back down the stairs. The last thing I remember is Jade feeling in my neck for a pulse, and then shoving past me, and racing along the corridor. For some reason she heads for the garage. I didn't tell her Pablo would be waiting, so why is she heading that way?

I give in to the pain, close my eyes, and the last thing I remember before I lose consciousness is saying a prayer to save us all.

74

When I finally come round again, the first thing I do is check my watch. I've been out cold for at least half an hour. Thank heavens it hasn't been longer.

I manage to struggle upright, and sitting on the bottom stair, I get out my phone. Luckily it's still intact after my tumble.

Before I phone Pablo, I need to send an urgent text. Isaac will have been on the roof terrace now for about forty-five minutes. Time is ticking.

It's done. Pablo and I will be gone in an hour.

I press *send*, and stare at the screen. Please God, let them respond. Isaac doesn't have long.

I needn't have worried. Less than a minute later, a thumbs-up emoji appears on the screen, along with birthday streamers, and a champagne bottle.

Next, with damp, shaky fingers, I call Pablo. He picks up straight away.

'Pablo. Pablo. Pablo.' I can hardly get the words out. 'Are you on the way back?'

He tells me he's dropped Jade off, and he'll be at the villa in half an hour, tops.

'Thank you. Thank you. I love you. And, Pablo...'

I hold my breath. He'll freak out when he hears what I'm about to tell him, but I can't put it off any longer. There's an ominous silence as I speak.

I tell him I'm packing up all our essential belongings, and as soon as he gets back, we'll be heading off in the Fiat. We'll be leaving the villa for good. The plan is to make our way up through Spain, and across into Portugal, and I'll tell him everything on the way.

I try to calm him down by telling him not to worry. But it's hopeless. He repeats my name, over and over. Marta. Marta. Marta, and asking what I've done.

'Pablo. The only important thing to know is that I love you. Now hurry.'

With that, I disconnect, and head as quickly as my trembling, achy body will allow. When I pass the stairs that lead to the roof terrace, I know better than to look up.

There's no time for delay. I need to get back to the finca, and start packing.

And get the hell out of here.

PART III
JADE

PART III

JADE

75

I don't know which is worse: the fear that Isaac, or Marta, or both of them are coming after me, or the fear that I'm going to die on the road to Malaga airport.

Pablo is in the worst maniac-driving mode ever. He seems to have gone crazy. As for fear of flying, it's currently at the back of my mind. At the moment, I'm more concerned that I won't arrive at the airport in one piece, and also, I think I might cope better with a mid-air collision than having to face Isaac and Marta again.

As usual, Pablo is reluctant to talk, and the traffic seems to be taking up all of his concentration as he weaves in and out. We could be part of a high-speed cop chase. When the speedometer hits 150 kilometres per hour, I grip the overhead handle with white knuckles.

Pablo screeches to a halt at the airport, and before I have time to dig him out a healthy tip, he's already roared off. If he doesn't crash, he'll need plenty of spare cash for speeding tickets.

It's nearly two o'clock, and although my flight doesn't take off until shortly after five, I head straight for Departures. The sooner I'm through to the other side, the safer I'll feel. No idea why, as I suspect Isaac could pay airport staff to bring me back out. I haven't forgotten his familiarity with the passport personnel on the way in.

I wonder how long it will take him to work out I've gone. For all I know, Marta might have already finished him off with a meat cleaver. He suddenly seemed to disappear. But, as soon as I'm airborne, I need to put the whole horror show behind me.

Once through Departures, I make a beeline for the bar. I pick a corner seat, but one that affords me a good view of the security gates. As the minutes tick by, and there's no sign of Isaac, my fear of take-off is coming back with a vengeance. I make light work of a half-bottle of white wine in an attempt to calm my nerves.

Having only had a few flakes of croissant earlier, my stomach is growling. I head back up to the counter, pick up a ham and cheese panini, and another half-bottle of wine which, if I haven't finished before take-off, I'll decant into my empty Evian water bottle.

I slowly start to unwind, although it doesn't stop me checking the security gates every few minutes for any sign of Isaac. I can't imagine Marta having the same sway with officials, so I'm not expecting to see her. But who knows? I seem to be a seriously bad judge of character.

I get out my phone and start to text. I tell Mum I'll pop round tomorrow so I can tell her all about my holiday. I'll tell her nothing, of course, other than Spain was hot and sunny, the sea was blue and the paella to die for.

When the flight for Luton finally comes up on the departure board, I knock back the last of the wine (surprise, surprise – nothing left to decant) and set off for the gates. I start to hum, realising that my worst fears have come to nothing, and I'll soon be back in England.

Once Isaac catches up with me, I'll pay him back the money. No point in being a hypocrite. I may be daring, but certainly not daring enough to rip him off, the way he did Emmeline. I'd love to take revenge for his obscene behaviour, but who am I kidding? Peace of mind is worth much more than money in the bank. I doubt I'll ever forget the hatred and anger in his eyes. I really thought he was going to kill me.

As I walk across the tarmac, I think of Marta. The wild glazed look in her eye, and I feel doubly lucky to be alive.

Soon, I'm climbing the rickety steps up to the plane. The queue behind me likely snakes forever but I don't look back properly, because when I see so many people, the panic escalates. At least this time, I haven't got any diazepam tablets to knock me unconscious. I packed them in my suitcase, which is still at the villa. I certainly wasn't intending to ever make the same mistake again of mixing tranquillisers with alcohol.

Anyway, a whole bottle of wine down, and I'm feeling relaxed, soporific almost. After all the drama, I might even manage forty winks when we're up in the air. It's a tall ask, but just maybe.

When I reach the top of the steps, I close my eyes, count to ten and step inside the cabin.

Before I squeeze along row 2 to take my seat by the window, I dare a glance over my shoulder. The plane is already heaving further back, people cheek by jowl as they fight for overhead baggage space. My heart skips a beat, and I remind myself to keep my eyes looking forward. Sometimes I imagine the luxury of being in a private plane, with a maximum capacity of twelve passengers. It's all an illusion as I know a private plane is every bit as likely to crash as a jumbo.

I slip into my seat by the window: 2A. The seat is so familiar, it could have my name on it. I drop my belongings on to seat 2B and buckle my seat belt. I'm still peeved that someone got to seat 2C before me, but it's a small price to pay for knowing that I'll soon be back in England, a world away from Isaac.

As the plane begins to fill, I start to get excited at the idea the person in 2C mightn't be coming after all. Perhaps they've missed the flight.

As one of the cabin crew is about to close the front door of the plane, there's an announcement from the captain.

Ladies and gentlemen. Sorry for the delay. We're waiting for one more passenger, and we believe they're on their way. Thank you for your patience.

I pull myself up, and my stomach churns in panic.

Could Isaac have held the plane up? I'm not a fan of coincidence, but why am I so convinced the delay is somehow connected to me?

It crosses my mind that if Isaac is the late arrival, perhaps I should come up with a story so that I can get off the plane before take-off. Perhaps I can feign a heart attack.

76

I squeeze my face up to the porthole and watch the late arrival crossing the tarmac. I let out a huge sigh of relief when I see it's a woman, and not Isaac. Also, she's nothing like Marta.

But I'm soon freaking out, not because I recognise her, but because she's so overweight. She's waddling like a duck towards the plane.

Connor tells me I'm a nasty person, I'm so judgemental. He calls me fatphobic. But he's wrong. I've nothing against people who battle their weight, it can't be easy, but I'm so claustrophobic when I'm forced to sit beside a large person on a plane. I really struggle.

At least I've got the middle seat free, but a large person on the aisle is going to make me feel blocked in. It's like the fear of being stuck in a lift.

Shit. Shit. Shit.

A security guard accompanies the lady towards the front of the plane, and is carrying her small flight bag. I wonder if she's paid him for his services. He's now carrying the expensive-looking shiny black bag, leather if I'm not mistaken, up the steps. The lady is puffing heavily, and it hits me that she might be disabled. Either that or so obscenely rich that she can manipulate budget airlines.

Yes. Of course. Just my bloody luck. She's the person who has booked seat 2C.

I'm going to need a few mini bottles of fizz to get me through and help forget she's there.

She's soon trying to hoist her bag up into the overhead locker, completely blocking my view across the aisle. There's no room in the locker, of course, and a member of the cabin crew jumps to attention, telling her not to worry, they'll find space for it.

As the front door of the plane closes, the lady finally settles into her seat. I'm relieved when her full hips manage to squeeze into the confined space. She is so not sharing my paid-for extra seat.

As the plane begins to taxi, I shove in my EarPods and start a ritualistic chant. It's a prayer of sorts, and the steady hum, along with a heavy music beat, helps to block out the roar of engines. I swivel my eyes right, and the lady on the end is smiling. She's pretending to look past me through the porthole, but I sense she's looking my way. God help her if she's laughing at me.

Anyway, we're soon climbing, over the ocean, away from Malaga, away from Marbella, and away from Spain. The coastline slowly disappears, and I breathe more easily.

When we're fully in the air, I take out my EarPods, pop them in my handbag and make a very hasty decision. To recline my seat, and risk the appearance of relaxation.

'Don't you like flying?'

What? It takes me a second to work out that the lady is talking to me.

'No. Not a fan.'

I so do not want to get into conversation. Talking makes me more anxious – and scared I'll forget to stay alert.

'This is my first time going to England,' the lady says, smiling broadly. She makes me envious, she's so at ease.

'Oh. Really?'

'I'm so excited. So many places to see.'

I can't place her accent, but she soon fills me in.

'I'm from Norway. You?'

'I'm from London. From a place called Crouch End.'

'Would you like a drink? My shout.' She's already flicking her fingers at the cabin crew. Why do I think of Isaac? Her sense of entitlement reminds me of him.

'Yes. Why not?'

'You look like a Prosecco sort of woman. Am I right?'

'How did you guess?'

'Prosecco it is then.'

You know what? This lady is growing on me. When she orders four small bottles of fizz, two each, I think maybe we'll hit it off. Perhaps I'll forget for a while, my fear of flying.

Soon I'm unwinding, and we make small talk, covering all sorts of topics, until about half an hour into the journey, she asks my name.

'Jade. And you?'

'Astrid.' She smiles at me, as if I should know who she is. With the same intent as if she'd said Beyoncé. Or Rihanna. Or Cher. Perhaps she's a celebrity I've never heard of. The name is familiar, but the drink isn't helping. It's making my mind more and more mushy.

'Hi, Astrid,' I say. 'Should I know you?'

I look sheepish, like a fan who has just come face to face with Adele.

'Yes, Jade. You should. Why don't I fill you in?'

She doesn't need to. It suddenly twigs.

77

You've got to be kidding me. It's Astrid, Isaac's wife. Of course. Hearing her name has put me back on the panic track. I haul myself into mega-alert upright position, feet plonked squarely on the floor.

'I think you know my husband,' she says. Her full lips, plump rather than Botoxed, latch on to the rim of her plastic tumbler.

It suddenly dawns on me. Casa De Astrid. The name of the villa. Astrid was Isaac's wife who died. She did die, didn't she?

'Oh. Who is your husband?'

She suddenly laughs, an explosion of mirth that causes spurts of Prosecco to jettison against the seat in front.

'Come on now. You tell me.'

'Isaac?' My voice comes out as a squeak. I empty the last of my first bottle of fizz into my plastic container and take a slug.

'You've got it in one. I hear he's been looking after you.'

'What? Looking after me? He's a nutcase.'

Through the haze of alcohol, something tells me to be careful what I say, even though Astrid doesn't seem like a threat. I could be wrong, but who knows? My judgement hasn't been the sharpest recently.

'You could say that again. Cheers.' She thrusts her wobbly cup my way and knocks it against mine, sending more Prosecco over the rims. What a waste. If Astrid doesn't need her drink, I certainly do.

'I'm sorry, Astrid. But I thought you'd died.'

It sounds the most ridiculous thing to say, but it sort of pops out.

'I know. Everyone thinks I'm dead. Well, almost everyone. The most important thing is that Isaac believed I was.'

'Oh.' My eyes widen of their own free will. Now she's really got my attention.

The cabin crew are making their second trip through the cabin. Astrid clicks her fingers, again, and orders two small boxes of Pringles.

'I know I shouldn't,' she says, 'but I'm in a celebratory mood.'

I don't dare ask what she's celebrating, and watch mesmerised as she tugs at the lids on the Pringle containers. Soon, she's thrusting the cheesy-flavoured ones my way.

'Who can drink without a nibble?' She giggles this time and flicks a floppy fringe off her eyes.

I momentarily forget that Astrid is blocking me in, as I'm desperate to hear the rest of her story.

'What happened? Why do you want Isaac to think you're dead?'

'He tried to kill me, and he very nearly succeeded. He wouldn't let me eat, and locked me in the villa. Can you imagine?'

Astrid narrows her eyes, and turns right round to look at me. She wants me to believe her. I don't yet share that Isaac did the same to me, as I'm desperate for her to carry on.

'You weren't married that long,' I say. 'He said you drowned shortly after your honeymoon. He hinted you might have taken your own life.'

'It was only on honeymoon that I realised what a bastard he is.' Now she starts to really laugh out loud, so loud that passengers across the aisle give us dirty looks. 'Should I say, was.'

'Pardon?'

'Was. What a bastard he was.'

'He still is. Believe me. He locked me in the villa, and I thought he was going to kill me too.' I certainly don't want her thinking he's changed. He's still an evil bastard.

'You shouldn't have taken his money. It was feisty, but if you didn't pay him back, with interest, he would never let you rest. He would most likely have made you disappear. Or drowned you in my lovely new infinity pool.'

Another crazy-sounding laugh from Astrid makes me shiver.

Holy shit. How does she know I took his money? Has she been in touch with Isaac? They can't be working together, can they? To con me out of my fictitious millions?

Suddenly the seat belt sign lights up, and the plane buffets up and down.

Ladies and gentlemen. The captain has switched on the seat belt signs. Please return to your seats, and the toilets are currently out of use.

My insides turn to liquid, and I have an urgent need to use the loo. I feel like I might throw up. I'm not sure what is making me feel worse, the slight turbulence (although to me it's supercell tornado) or the conversation with Astrid. The latter is definitely nudging ahead, as Astrid's story is seriously freaky. And why do I feel she's a long way from the punchline?

But until the plane steadies, I need to close my eyes and straighten my seat. I have to concentrate on staying alive.

I tug the seat belt several times to make sure it's done up. Meanwhile, Astrid's belt is undone, lying loosely across her lap. She's relaxed like a cat in the midday sun.

I can almost hear her purr.

78

It takes about ten minutes after the plane has steadied, and the seat belt signs have gone off again, to collect myself. Enough to carry on the conversation.

'Shall I tell you about Isaac?' Astrid asks, keeping her eyes locked on the seat in front. Crumbly Pringles flakes dot her blouse, and she licks a further few away from her lips. When a member of the cabin crew shuffles past, Astrid wiggles her empty Pringles tub, and asks for another. 'Jade? One for you too?'

'No, thanks.' I am so not interested in any more Pringles, but I'm desperate to hear what she's going to tell me about Isaac.

'Well, I met Isaac at Los Molinos. I think you stayed there?'

'Yes, I did.' I don't expand, willing her to get a move on.

'Anyway. He swept me off my feet. I was so smitten. It was love at first sight. Or so I thought.' She chomps on the new Pringles and slurps the Prosecco to wash them down. 'When he asked me to marry him, I thought I'd died and gone to heaven.'

She closes her eyes a second.

'What happened next?'

'He changed overnight. As soon as we set off for honeymoon, he turned into a monster.'

'Oh.' I manage my surprised look, but it's all an act. I'm anything but shocked.

'He locked me in the car when we stopped at the first service station we came to, told me he wouldn't be long. The bastard went inside, waved at me through a window and sat down and ate a huge plate of fish and chips.'

The hairs stand up on the back of my neck. I know Isaac is a bastard, but I dread what's coming next.

'He finally came back to the car, bringing me a bowl of soggy salad and a cup of black coffee. Then he drove off without another word.'

Astrid carries on talking. I don't interrupt, like a therapist urging a patient to get it all off their chest.

'By the time we reached the hotel in France where we were to marry, I was starting to question everything.'

'Why did you go through with it?'

'Oh, Jade. Haven't you ever been in love?' Astrid stares at me, aghast that I might not understand. 'I couldn't just give him up. I'd never been in love before.'

'So you went ahead and got married?'

'Yes. But on our wedding night, he disappeared, and left me for two whole days on my own at the hotel. I was distraught. You see, I thought something bad had happened to him.'

'Where had he gone?'

'I still have no idea. He never told me, just warned me to mind my own business. And that was the start of our married life.'

Astrid then tells me how Isaac wouldn't let her eat anything. He controlled her diet, what she wore, and if she made the slightest mess anywhere, he would go ballistic. He then cut short the honeymoon, telling her he'd had enough, and they headed back to the villa.

'You know, I lost fifteen kilograms in the two weeks after we got married. I looked like a super-model.' Astrid laughs, a default reaction, but it feels more like a cover-up for pain. 'I suppose, how do you say? Every cloud has a silver lining. I always dreamt of being that thin.'

I look at her now and suspect the overindulgence and weight gain came back as soon as she was shot of Isaac. Who could blame her?

'But I was so weak. If I'd stayed, I think Isaac might have starved me to death.' A single tear appears in the corner of her eye.

'Really?' I lean across the middle seat and pat her gently on the shoulder. 'I'm sorry. It sounds dreadful.'

'It was. It really was.'

'But I do understand. I think I had a lucky escape. If I hadn't managed to leave the villa, I'd probably be dead myself.'

'Here's to Marta.' Astrid hauls herself up, out of her slouched position, and offers up her plastic cup to bang against mine again.

'Marta?' My stomach does a double flip.

'Marta. She saved my life. And I suspect she saved yours too. Cheers,' she says, and knocks back the contents of her glass. 'To Marta.'

I swivel right round to face her.

'What do you mean Marta saved my life? She tried to kill me.'

'Ha. Ha. Ha. Marta never tried to kill you, Jade. But she did kill Isaac. She's one smart, as you say in English... *one smart cookie*.'

Marta killed Isaac? WTF.

I can't get my head around what Astrid is saying. The fact her voice has dropped to a whisper makes me think she could be telling the truth. But murder? Really?

'How did Marta kill Isaac?' This time my eyes are wide as saucers. I can't hear any other noise around the cabin, as all my focus is now on Astrid. But she's in no hurry, and is relishing the attention.

'Haven't you guessed?' Astrid does a furtive look across the aisle, and pretends to look behind her although she can't see over the headrest.

'No.' I'm trying to work it out. Come to think of it, as I tried to escape from Marta there was no sign of Isaac. He'd gone ominously quiet, and I assumed he must be outside.

'Well, Marta left a final trail of mess, with your name on it, leading up to the roof terrace. And, lo and behold, he followed it. He was coming to find you, and probably lock *you* up there.' She emphasises the word 'you'.

Again, Astrid thinks this is very funny. I'm not sure why she's so gleeful.

'So, did Marta lock him up there? How?'

'When he followed the trail to find you, Marta followed. Then whoosh! She slammed the door behind him, and locked him out there.'

'Is he still there?' I look at my watch. It's at least five hours since I fled the villa.

'Yep. He is indeed. There's no shade at all up there during the day. Marta and Pablo moved all the furniture down into the garage, along with the drinks. Isaac will be dead in a day or two.'

This woman is crazy. And what's worse, she could be telling the truth. The noises I heard yesterday were coming from the roof terrace. That must have been Pablo and Marta moving the furniture. Holy shit. Marta has really killed Isaac.

'Why did Marta kill him? She could surely have left at any time.'

'Come on. Think, Jade. Why does anyone do anything? You should know.' She rubs her thumb back and forth against her fingers. 'Money, what else?'

I'm tempted to tell her I don't have any money, and that's not the only thing that makes people tick. But who am I kidding? I've been lording it up all round Marbella, waving my fictitious millions in the air.

'If it was for money, who paid her?'

OMG. That's it. Astrid paid Marta to trap Isaac on the roof terrace. I start to sweat, and fiddle furiously with the air-vent button above my head. I lean across seat 2B and open that vent as well.

I flap the menu card up and down in front of my face, which must be puce from drink, heat and shock. I'm sitting alongside a premeditating murderer.

'Don't look so shocked. Pleeeeeaaaseee.' She rolls her eyes. 'You're not whiter than white yourself, are you?'

'What?'

'Well, you did con Isaac out of nearly £150,000.'

'I didn't murder him though.'

'Weren't you ever tempted? Even a little bit?' She snips her thumb and forefinger together to show what a little bit looks like. As if I didn't know.

It takes a minute for things to sink in, although I doubt they'll sink in completely for a long time. Possibly never.

'How do you know Isaac lent me money?' I avoid using the word 'con', as I've always intended on paying him back.

'Marta kept me posted. I got in touch with her after everyone thought

I was dead, and we'd meet up and make plans. It's all come together rather neatly, don't you think?'

'Marta told you Isaac lent me money?'

It's like a horror story.

'Yes, good old Marta. She has no idea that Isaac is dead. She's on her way to Barcelona now.'

'Didn't she mean to kill him?' Although I was scared shitless of Marta before I left, did I really think her capable of murder?

'No. She's a bit naïve... how do you say? Green, I think it is.'

Astrid unbuttons her floaty blouse, releasing a fulsome white cleavage. The storytelling must be getting her hot too.

'But before I tell you about how I tricked Marta, don't you want to hear how I faked my suicide? It would make a great movie. A Netflix spectacular.'

I don't want to hear any more, but Astrid is only warming up.

'And Jade, you need to let me know how you got Isaac to hand over all that money your way. You're quite a little con artist yourself, aren't you?'

She leans across and pats me on the thigh.

I need to get off this plane, but there's another forty minutes of hell to get through.

80

I tell Astrid about how I worked with Carlos to get Isaac to pay me across the deposit for the flat.

Astrid is all ears.

'Clever,' she says, licking her wet lips. 'You're not just a pretty face.'

I own up that Isaac's doubts were soon quashed when I told him I'd buy him Mario's yacht, as an interest payment.

Telling the story makes me cringe. It sounds as if I'm a first-rate gangster.

Astrid leans across the middle seat, cups a hand over her mouth.

'You should be pleased that Isaac is dead. Or going to be soon. You'll now be able to hold on to all that money he lent you. No trace back to you.'

My insides somersault. She's making me sound like an accomplice. I had nothing to do with what has, or might have, happened to Isaac.

'I don't want the bloody money. I have every intention of paying him back.'

She sits back in her seat, and speaks in a theatrically loud voice.

'Oh, let's not be holier than thou. Enjoy the money. It's yours.' She pauses for breath. 'But I'm not sure you'll need it. It's a drop in the ocean,

I think, compared to your windfall. Although it'll still be nice to see a little extra in the bank. Don't you think?'

'How do you know I had a windfall?' This time I'm the one to whisper across seat 2B.

'Oh that was Logan. The guy at Los Molinos. He's been a spy for Isaac. In return for handsome payments, Logan kept Isaac posted about wealthy women who booked in at the hotel. Not sure what Logan will do now. He earns a pittance at the hotel. But who cares? All water under the bridge.'

Outside the porthole, there's nothing but blue sky stretching heavenwards as far as the eye can see. Below, through a break in the clouds, the green fields of England are coming into view. Half an hour and we'll be down. I don't think I've ever been more eager to get home.

'Last question. How did you persuade Marta to go through with it? Trapping Isaac on the roof terrace, knowing that he'd die quickly in the heat? Did she do it just for money?'

Could Marta have really been evil all along? Was Pablo involved? He drove me to the airport, so perhaps he knew nothing about it. Or perhaps he knew everything about it, and thought it best I got well away.

'Oh, to get people to do what you want, needs more than a little cunning. And a lot of money, of course.' Astrid's chest puffs out, until her breasts are resting on the small pull-out table.

'So you paid her?'

'Yep. She's on her way to Barcelona with Pablo. They'll not be back. I gave her enough money to set them up in style. Marta has a lot of apartments to view with Pablo.'

'All about the money.' I make a scoffing sound, mortified that my life has become all about money overnight.

'Okay. I'll come clean. I told Marta...' Astrid reinstates the whispering, and re-covers her mouth with a podgy hand, '...my bodyguards, two big hunks of muscle, would arrive an hour after she texted telling me Isaac was trapped. They'd let him out, rough him up, and tell him to get the hell out of my villa. And my life. They would make sure he never bothered me again.'

A huge wave of relief floods over me. There's been no murder involved. Isaac should be free. Why though, did Astrid tell me earlier that he was already dead?

'So did your guys go and free Isaac?'

'Jade. Don't be so naive. Of course not.'

She throws back her head and laughs, the noise rebounding all around the cabin.

81

I need to disengage from this crazy lunatic. Shock doesn't describe how I feel. It's as if I'm in a nightmare that I'll never wake up from.

Despite the fact Astrid has just owned up to getting away with planning her husband's murder, she seems hysterically happy. She's even started to whistle.

I need to get off this plane, and as far away from her as possible. I don't care how she masterminded her apparent suicide, but no doubt it involved paying crazy sums of money to buy off the local Mafia.

She's going to tell me anyway. It's the last revelation she has to share with me, and I've no choice but to listen. When I book my next flight, anywhere in the world, I'll be booking the whole row of six seats. 2A to 2F. No matter the cost.

'You know Mario, the handsome skipper with the yacht? For a price, he helped me stage the suicide. I hired a speedboat, and Mario followed me round the coastline. A couple of hours later, he telephoned the coastguard, alerting them of the abandoned vessel.'

'How did you get back to shore?'

'With Mario, of course. I stayed on his boat until dark, and then a taxi took me inland.'

She claps her hands in the telling. She's the one-woman audience for her own brilliance.

I simply nod.

Having finished her story, Astrid turns her attention across the aisle and is about to engage in pleasantries with a young man sitting in seat 2D.

The seat belt signs suddenly ping on. My hands are shaking so badly that I can hardly get my EarPods back in. I tug at my belt, and start the countdown to landing. As the plane starts its rocky descent, Astrid concentrates her attention on the young man. He must be all of thirty, and she's old enough to be his mother.

I wonder how long it will take her to tell him she is Norwegian royalty. Perhaps that's all made up too.

As the plane banks towards the runway, my thoughts for once aren't on the possibility of crashing on to the tarmac, but on everything Astrid has just told me.

Before we hit the runway, I glance round, and wonder if it is a coincidence that Astrid is sitting beside me on 2C. I seriously doubt it, but who cares? I just want to get home.

Astrid and I don't talk again until we're inside the airport. I follow slowly behind her as we head towards the terminal building. She is trying to keep up with the guy who was sitting across the aisle, but he's likely trying to shake her off as he strides ahead. It looks like a wise move. Perhaps she never got a chance to tell him that she's of royal descent, or perhaps he doesn't care. Not everyone is motivated by money.

Although I've no suitcase in the hold, I have to walk past the baggage-reclaim carousel on my way out.

Astrid is sitting on a bench waiting for the luggage to appear. She's bright red in the face, and is patting her chest with a stubby hand as she tries to catch her breath.

I wander over.

'Astrid. One thing is bothering me,' I say.

'Hit me,' she puffs.

'I met Isaac on the plane going out to Malaga. Was that a coincidence?'

She laughs between wheezing. 'You know there is no such thing as coincidence.'

I raise a questioning eyebrow.

'Logan told him you'd be on it,' she rasps.

I try not to look surprised, but I've trouble swallowing back the shock. Astrid is watching me, agog with excitement that she's fed me another horror titbit.

'Anyway, I must be off. Nice to meet you, Astrid,' I lie. What I really mean is, *nice to see the back of you*, but what's the point?

'Oh. Don't you have any luggage in the hold? A suitcase or two?' she asks.

'No. I left the villa so quickly, that...' OMG. My case is at the scene of the crime. WTF.

'Your suitcase is still in the villa? Oh my goodness. Now that is a turn up for the books.' Astrid's crazy smiles returns.

I stare at this murderous villain in panic. If Marta and Pablo have gone, my case will be where I left it. It'll be evidence that I was there at the time of Isaac's death.

'Don't stand there gawping, Jade. It was indeed nice to meet you.'

With a dismissive wave of her hand, Astrid heaves herself back on to her feet, and ambles towards the carousel where the young man from seat 2D is offering to help lift her cases down.

'Stephen,' she says, touching his arm. 'It's the four Gucci cases. The ones with the gold embossing and leather trims.'

Stephen blushes, willing to oblige. I wonder how long it will take her to tell him she's a millionairess, with a villa in Marbella. I imagine by the time they reach the taxi rank if she hasn't already told him.

82

ONE MONTH LATER

It's been a month since I got back, and I've been marooned in my dingy bedsit, scared to venture outside. I can't stop the nightmare visions of a gargoyle version of Isaac in my sleep.

A small part of me dares to hope that Astrid made the whole thing up, and that Isaac might still be alive, and thousands of miles away in Spain.

But as the days pass, I start to wonder if even Astrid was a hallucinatory figment of my drunken, paranoid imagination.

My biggest fear now is that if Isaac has been murdered, my suitcase was at the scene of the crime. It proves I was one of the last people to see him alive. If Pablo and Marta did flee, I might be the only link to his death. If Astrid needs to point a finger, I wouldn't put it past her to point it in my direction. Any direction away from her.

I've been googling incessantly for info on Isaac Marston, but so far I haven't found anything. All I can find on social media is information on an Isaac Marston, a jurist and politician, from the nineteenth century. I've trawled images, but no lookalike pictures come up.

This morning, I spread out *The Telegraph* on the coffee table, and scan the day's main stories. For a change, I'm not even looking for news on Isaac, until something catches my eye.

There's a small article, several pages in, bottom right-hand corner, with a very blurred head-and-shoulders shot of a person who looks like Isaac. I peer at the picture, lifting the paper up close to my face, and sure enough, it's him.

Bloody hell. It looks as if Isaac wasn't his real name.

British Conman Found Dead on Marbella Roof Terrace

British man, George Stubbs, aged 38, from Peckham, South London, has been found dead on a roof terrace in Marbella.

Recently married to a Norwegian millionairess, Astrid Olsen, Stubbs got locked on their villa roof terrace in 40-degree heat and wasn't able to get out. According to police, he would have died through dehydration within twenty-four hours of being trapped.

Ms Olsen and Mr Stubbs had split up several months before, and while it was believed at the time that Ms Olsen may have committed suicide, it has been revealed that at the time of her estranged husband's death she was travelling around England. Ms Olsen states that she walked out on Mr Stubbs claiming he was a violent and abusive husband.

Ms Olsen made the grim discovery when she got back to Spain, some three weeks after her husband's death. His body was so badly burnt, an autopsy wasn't carried out.

It appears to have been a tragic accident, with no suspicious circumstances. Ms Olsen confirmed that the handle on the fire door leading from the terrace back into the villa had needed replacing for some time. Sources believe that the heavy fire door slammed shut, locking Mr Stubbs outside. Unfortunately, there was no mobile phone signal on the roof.

Since the report of his death, several women have come forward, with claims that Mr Stubbs conned them out of their life savings. However, as the women seem to have handed the money across to Mr Stubbs willingly, no legal action can be taken, and the money is unlikely to be returned to the victims. Ms Olsen has so far refused to comment further on this matter.

Holy shit. Isaac, George, or whatever his name is, really is dead. I wonder if Marta knows that she accidently killed him. She's unlikely to come forward, that's for sure.

At least I've got the money in my bank account. *If money is handed over willingly, then no legal action can be taken.* That's what it says.

I get up and dance around the bedsit. I'm richer by 145,000 euros. Even if the money is traced back to Isaac, I won't have to pay it back.

But then it hits me. My suitcase. I'd almost forgotten, Astrid has still got it as proof that I was at the villa around the time of Isaac's death. If she hasn't shown it to the police, maybe she's keeping hold of it to use against me at a later date. No. No. No.

Astrid has masterminded the whole thing. She got Marta to trap Isaac on the roof, and got her villa and life back in the process.

Astrid is a cold-blooded assassin.

83

I've no idea how to get on with my life.

It's been two days since I read the article about Isaac's death, and I'm still unable to get out of bed. I doubt I'll ever function like a normal human being again.

When there's a knock at the door, I'm tempted to ignore it. But when there's a persistent hammering, I drag myself up.

'Jade. Are you in there?' It's Maggie from next door. 'There's a package for you. I'll leave it here.'

'I'm coming.'

I look through the peephole, and wait until she's gone.

And there it is. My pink suitcase with an envelope attached to the outside. The case is mighty battered, but if Brad Pitt was standing on the doorstep, I couldn't be more excited. There's all sorts of sticky labels plastered over the sturdy framework. It seems to have come via Portugal.

I glance up and down the street, hoist the case into the flat, and wheel it across the floor. I yank off the envelope, my hands shaking so badly that it takes a few seconds to rip it open. I'm scared to hope Astrid might be letting me off the hook.

But the note inside isn't from Astrid. It's from Marta.

Hi Jade

I think this belongs to you. When we left the villa for good, I took your case with us. I've been meaning to send it on sooner, but have been so busy setting up home in Barcelona.

Sorry, I had to open your case to see if I could find an address for you. When I lifted up your book, How to Live Like a Millionaire, *a receipt from Los Molinos dropped out and it had your name and address on it.*

I hope you're well, and without saying too much... I'm sorry about leaving all the mess around the villa. I guess you might have worked out why I did it.

Forgive me.

Best wishes

Marta

* * *

Over the next few days, I start making plans. I might not have won millions on the lottery, but the extra 145,000 euros in my bank account is a dream come true. It really is mine.

For the first time in days, I boot up my laptop, and start firing off emails which I've saved in draft form. Just in case.

One of these is a reply to Carlos.

Hi Carlos

I have heard the dreadful news about Isaac. Very sad.

The good news is, I'd love to come and join you in selling properties in Marbella. I am quite the salesperson, as you know, and I'd be thrilled if you could arrange a little apartment for me to rent down at the port. One bed is fine.

In good time, I'll find my perfect villa, with pool, lots of space and bedrooms... but no need for a roof terrace! We can discuss when I get there.

I look forward to hearing from you.

Best regards

Jade

I've decided not to tell anyone (ever) I didn't win big on the lottery. I like the kudos that goes with money. I like *living like a millionaire*, and am already rereading my life-saving manual. If I work hard enough in Marbella, I'll definitely put down a deposit on a small apartment. If Carlos wonders why I don't splash out on an obscenely priced villa, I'll tell him I've decided on an international portfolio of small bolt-holes.

I'm learning the spiel. Any why would he doubt me? I'm a great actress.

I dither before I log off. Should I or shouldn't I?

I take a deep breath, and begin to type.

Hi Astrid

It was nice to hear from you after meeting on the plane. I'm not sure how you got my email address, but what a pleasant surprise.

Thanks for the offer to come and stay for a few days, but I think I'll pass. You understand.

However, I am coming back to Marbella. I've been offered a job by Carlos down at the port, selling properties, and I'm very excited.

Would love to meet up for a drink, especially as you tell me you're selling Casa De Astrid.

Perhaps you'd let me act on your behalf? I've told Carlos that we're in touch, and I'd be thrilled if your villa might be my first sale!

Oh, and how is it going with Stephen?

Best

Jade

I take at least ten attempts to get the email right. I keep my professional hat in place. If I can be in charge of selling Casa De Astrid, I'll get two per cent commission. Two per cent of five million euros will do nicely. If I can make the sale, I'll then cut Astrid completely from my life. But why look a gift horse in the mouth?

Also, they say, *keep your friends close, and your enemies closer*. That's how I feel about Astrid. Would I have replied if she hadn't told me she was selling up? Unlikely.

Once she's moved away, then I can really get on with my new life.

Maybe one day soon, I'll be a real, live millionaire. In the meantime, I'll carry on living the dream.

ACKNOWLEDGEMENTS

As always, thank you to readers everywhere, who pick up each new book in anticipation of getting lost inside the intrigue of someone else's story. Readers, you are an author's greatest prize.

I usually have a long list of people to thank when a book finally gets into print: special early readers; friends and family members who encourage me along the way. As ever, I am grateful to you all, and trust by now you know who you are. Thank you.

But with *The Girl in Seat 2A*, I have one stand-out person to thank. Emily Yau, my most amazing editor. When she read the final first draft, she picked out in such amazing detail how the book could be improved. Her suggestions always make sense, but this time I feel they have made the content so much richer, and atmospheric. She has an uncanny knack of spotting what needs to be done. Thanks, Emily.

Boldwood Books are the most amazing publishers. I feel more than blessed to be in their fold. I would like to thank each and every member of the team for their tireless and professional efforts in getting authors' books out into the world.

Finally, the biggest thanks, as always, goes to Neil, my long-suffering husband who encourages me all the way. And to James: still the most wonderful son in the world.

ABOUT THE AUTHOR

Diana Wilkinson writes bestselling psychological thrillers, including her debut novel *4 Riverside Close* published by Bloodhound. Formerly an international professional tennis player, she hails from Belfast, but now lives in Hertfordshire.

Sign up to Diana Wilkinson's mailing list here for news, competitions and updates on future books.

Follow Diana on social media:

x.com/DiWilkinson2020

facebook.com/DiKennett

instagram.com/dianakennett37

ALSO BY DIANA WILKINSON

One Down

Right Behind You

The Woman in My Home

You Are Mine

The Missing Guest

The Girl in Seat 2A

THE
Murder
LIST

THE MURDER LIST IS A NEWSLETTER DEDICATED TO SPINE-CHILLING FICTION AND GRIPPING PAGE-TURNERS!

SIGN UP TO MAKE SURE YOU'RE ON OUR HIT LIST FOR EXCLUSIVE DEALS, AUTHOR CONTENT, AND COMPETITIONS.

SIGN UP TO OUR NEWSLETTER

BIT.LY/THEMURDERLISTNEWS

Boldwood

Boldwood Books is an award-winning fiction publishing company seeking out the best stories from around the world.

Find out more at www.boldwoodbooks.com

Join our reader community for brilliant books, competitions and offers!

Follow us
@BoldwoodBooks
@TheBoldBookClub

Sign up to our weekly deals newsletter

https://bit.ly/BoldwoodBNewsletter